Behind
The
Lies

Behind

The

Lies

Fictional Crime Thrillers

Mark R Beckner

Mark R Beckner Publishing

First Edition: April 2021

ISBN: 978-1-7369607-0-7 (paperback)

This book is dedicated to my wife Sally, daughter Kimberlee, and son Chad, who have supported me throughout my sometimes difficult career. It is also dedicated to all the law enforcement officers who have given their lives to save others.

I would like to thank my copy reviewers and editors who helped guide me through this effort.

    Sally Beckner - review and editing

    Kimberlee Hipsher – review and editing

    Dan Davidson – review

    Roxy – who kept me company late into the many evenings

Preface

After 36 years of policing in Boulder, Colorado, some teaching, and consulting, I decided it was time to put my experience and knowledge of crime and the criminal justice system to good use. My law enforcement experience, from patrol to detectives to management to Chief of Police, provides the canvas from which I draw my ideas for creating crime thrillers. Additionally, I remain interested in and follow other crimes from around the country.

Being an activist community and college town (University of Colorado), Boulder provided the opportunity to experience many interesting and strange events that seemed to occur regularly. It was a great proving ground for officers, supervisors, and management alike. From dealing with the old hippy culture, Halloween Mall Crawls, drugs, naked bike rides, out-of-control parties, protests, and student riots, officers had to navigate the issues while trying to keep the politicians and activists happy. On top of it all, officers and investigators had to investigate serious crimes, including homicides. Two of the most notorious I was involved in was the hunt for escaped convict Michael Bell, who killed four people, and then of course there was the JonBenet Ramsey case.

In writing these stories, I am doing something I find enjoyable that allows me to utilize my knowledge and writing skills to hopefully provide entertainment to those who enjoy a good fictional crime drama. I've tried to create intrigue, suspense, drama, and mystery in these stories, while also creating a sense of realism. I hope you enjoy finding out what is "Behind the Lies."

Table of Contents

The Candy Man Killer

I t is the day after the long Labor Day holiday weekend and Chicago Police Detective Juan Garcia is reporting to his new assignment in Area 4, which consists of the neighborhoods generally referred to as the west side of Chicago. Before his transfer, he had been working homicides in Area 5, the northwest section of Chicago. However, due to a staffing shortage and a recent spike in violent crime on the west side, Garcia and five other detectives have been reassigned to assist the Homicide Unit in Area 4. Garcia's new partner will be Detective Mike Ricci, a 34 year veteran of the Chicago PD and a seasoned homicide detective of 13 years.

Area 4 is considered one of the roughest, most dangerous areas to work. It usually rivals Chicago's south side as having the highest violent crime rates. Much of the crime in these areas is driven by poverty, unemployment, and drug trafficking. Three of the most violent neighborhoods of Chicago; West Garfield Park, East Garfield Park, and North Lawndale are in Area 4. The presence of local gangs, usually involved in the selling of drugs for Mexican drug cartels, results in an over-abundance of shootings. The number of homicides in Area 4 keeps detectives much busier than they want to be.

Garcia is not particularly pleased with his reassignment, but he understands Area 4 needs assistance. On the positive side, Garcia will have a shorter commute to work, as he and his family live in the lower west side of Chicago in the historic Pilsen neighborhood, which borders the Chicago River. He and his wife, Rosa, had purchased a nice three-bedroom two-story brick home several years earlier. The Pilsen neighborhood is a mixed ethnic community, primarily Hispanic, with a rich Latino culture. However, there are also a good number of African Americans and whites who have recently moved into the area. The Garcia's like the diversity of their neighborhood, believing it will be a good place to raise their three children: 11-year-old Jose, 8-year-old Maria, and 6-year-old Julio.

With redevelopment, the eastern part of Pilsen now attracts artists, galleries, and boutique shops, transforming Pilsen into a desirable cultural arts center. Expansion of the nearby University of Illinois Chicago is a draw to more middle and upper-class Latinos and whites. Younger families, like the Garcia's, are moving in, attracted by the still reasonable housing prices. The Garcia's early faith in the neighborhood is paying off, as they have seen a nice appreciation in the value of their home.

Area 4, Garcia's new assignment, is located just a bit north of the Pilsen Neighborhood and south of Area 5, the northwest section of Chicago. Unless the workload in Area 4 results in longer hours, he anticipates being able to get home sooner in the evening to spend more time with his family.

Juan Garcia had grown up in Chicago, not far from the Pilsen Neighborhood he now lives in. His maternal grandparents immigrated from Mexico and settled in Chicago, where his grandfather found work in the steel industry. On his paternal side, the family tree traces back to immigrants coming to America sometime in the early 1800s. Eventually, both families settled in Chicago. Garcia met his wife Rosa while attending Northern Illinois University. After graduation, Garcia applied to be a police officer with the Chicago PD, something he was always attracted to. His desire grew from watching police drama shows while growing up. His three favorites were NYPD Blues, Law and Order, and CSI: Crime Scene Investigation. Given his education and clean background, Garcia was hired on his first attempt as a 23-year-old rookie officer.

After six years in patrol, he was promoted to the rank of Detective and assigned to the robbery division in Area 5. Garcia proved to be an excellent investigator with a keen sense of people and a knack for knowing when they were lying or hiding something. He seemed to be a natural. His success as a robbery detective led to his assignment to the homicide unit only three years after being promoted to Detective. Now, with two years of homicide experience, he is being sent to one of the toughest areas of Chicago.

Garcia wears one of his finest dark brown suits for his first day, accompanied by a white dress shirt and light brown tie. His first task is to meet with Detective Commander John Marshall, a three-year veteran of Homicide Area 4. Commander Marshall is 47 years old, barrel-chested, wavy brown hair, wire-rimmed

3

glasses with a look of all business. He is wearing a well-tailored grey suit with red striped tie.

"Welcome to Area 4 Juan," greets Marshall. "We've been looking forward to getting some help around here and you come with an outstanding reputation."

"Thank you sir," responds Garcia.

"I've got just a few rules, and if you follow 'em you will do fine. First, don't take any shortcuts. Your cases need to be solid. We have a great conviction rate in this division, and I expect it to remain so."

Garcia nods.

"Second, no drinking on the job, got that?"

"Of course not sir," says Garcia with a surprised look.

"Third, it's dangerous out there, you need to always have your partner's back. And carry a backup weapon, you never know when you might need it. You might want to carry a blade as well. Finally, do what Ricci tells you to do. He's a seasoned detective and knows these neighborhoods better than anyone. Got that?"

"Yes sir, no problem."

"VICKIE!" yells Marshall as he looks out his office door.

"Yes sir, what do you need?" responds Vickie, the Commander's administrative assistant, as she hurries into the office.

"Take Garcia here and introduce him to his new partner."

"Will do," Vickie answers. "Juan, if you follow me I will take you to your new desk and introduce the two of you."

Garcia follows Vickie through the maze of desks, room dividers, and filing cabinets that fill the homicide investigative office.

"Mike," says Vickie as she approaches Mike Ricci sitting at his desk reading a report. "This is Juan Garcia, your new partner."

Ricci looks up, "Thank you Vickie. Juan, have a seat," as he motions Garcia to sit at the desk opposite of him. "Welcome to the fourth."

Detective Mike Ricci is 58 years old, and his rugged facial features look all of that. However, His physique looks more like he could be 48. Ricci keeps himself in excellent shape by regularly working out three days a week. He is also rather large at 6'3" and 220 lbs, most of which appears to be muscle. Ricci comes from an Italian family and Garcia notices Ricci has the characteristic look of someone who is Italian. His hair is wavy black with plenty of gray mixed in. Garcia is no slouch, but at 5'10" and 180 lbs, Garcia wouldn't want to tangle with Ricci.

Ricci is dressed in beige dress pants, light blue button-down long sleeve dress shirt, unbuttoned at the top, and a dark blue patterned tie hangs loosely around his neck. A large half-consumed cup of Dunkin' Donuts coffee sits among the many papers on Ricci's desk.

"You come with quite a reputation," states Ricci with a sly grin.

"I just do the job the best I can, sir."

"Well, the first thing you can do is knock off the sir stuff. You call me Mike and I'll call you Dickhead, how's that?"

Garcia stares back at Ricci with his mouth slightly open, not sure how to respond.

Ricci then breaks out with a big laugh, "I'm just messin' with ya! I'll call you Juan, how's that?"

Garcia laughs back, "You had me there for a minute."

"Have you been briefed at all?" asks Ricci.

"Yes, I've been told you recently had a homicide that matches a pattern of homicides from a couple years ago. Drug dealers being stabbed to death."

"That's pretty much it."

"And what makes you think this new case is related to those from two years ago?" asks Garcia.

"The weapon. Two years ago we had a string of drug dealers getting stabbed with a kitchen knife right through the gut, then left to bleed out. What made it unique was that each time, the perp left the murder weapon at the scene, usually right on top of the victim. Our most recent victim was a drug dealer stabbed with the same type of knife, and the knife was left at the scene."

"Really?" replies Garcia. "I've never heard of anything like that before."

"Nope, quite unusual."

"Haven't you been able to get prints or DNA off the knives?" asks Garcia.

"Nothing. The knives have always come back clean. No prints, DNA, nothing."

"Hmmm, do we have anything to go on?"

"Not really," answers Ricci. "My guess it has something to do with the drug wars over territory. We did get a report of a suspicious person near the scene of one of the homicides two years ago, but nothing panned out. Someone saw a male wearing a dark windbreaker, dark pants, full black beard, and dark-rimmed glasses. Oh, and he was supposedly wearing a flat beret style hat and walked with a limp."

"Well, that's something to go on. What race?"

"In this area? Most likely black, but the witness couldn't tell in the darkness," says Ricci. "Besides, we have no idea whether this unknown person has anything to do with this case."

"What about fingerprints?"

"Nope, nothing. Scene is always clean, with the exception of the murder weapon being left behind."

"What was the brand of knife, how long, type of handle?"

"A Cardet seven-inch kitchen utility knife with black handle. I'll tell you what, instead of all the questions, why don't you first read the case files. Here's a stack of all seven, the six from two years ago and the most recent. Start reading and when you're done, we can discuss any questions you have."

Garcia takes the stack of seven case files from Ricci, gets as comfortable as he can in his desk chair, and opens the first file. It will take him several days to get through all the reports. He also plans to get up to speed on the drug and gang activity within Area 4.

Later that evening, Ricci is on his drive home thinking about Garcia and what he brings to the table. Ricci's initial impression is Garcia has the potential to make a good homicide detective, but still has a lot to learn about how things work in Area 4.

Ricci's drive home is quite a bit longer than Garcia's. Ricci lives in Forest Glen, a neighborhood in northwest Chicago. It's an upscale neighborhood of upper-middle-class, and while there is some diversity, most residents are white. Ricci's home is a well-maintained two-story brick home with three bedrooms, three baths, and a two-car garage on a tree-lined street. He has converted half of his garage into a woodworking shop. His yard, like most in the neighborhood, is neatly trimmed and well maintained.

Ricci has lived in the home alone for the past five years following the death of his wife Ella from a brain aneurysm. He has a son, Chris, who is a 28-year-old attorney living in Naperville, a city approximately 33 miles west of Chicago. His oldest child, a daughter by the name of Lisa, died unexpectedly in Los Angeles six years ago. Ricci believes the stress of his daughter's untimely death contributed to his wife's aneurysm. He has struggled to recover from both his daughter's and then his wife's death. He often helps himself get to sleep by having one or two Bud Lights in the evenings.

When not working, Ricci spends most of his free time maintaining the house, working in his makeshift woodshop, and exercising to maintain his strength and fitness. One of his wood-working favorites is making beautiful birdhouses. He sells most of them at a local craft store and gives others away as gifts.

Ricci has worked at the Chicago PD for thirty-four years. His interest in law enforcement was honed while serving in the Air Force Military Police for four years after high school. Upon leaving the Air Force, Ricci worked security at a plastics fabricating plant for six months until he was hired by the Chicago Police Department. He could have retired at age 55, but after the death of Ella, he couldn't see the point in retiring. What else would he do? Besides, he still had things he wanted to accomplish as a detective.

Three Days Later

It is now Friday, and Garcia believes he has garnered enough information from the case files to have a more intelligent discussion on the facts with Ricci. Garcia agrees the most recent homicide fits the circumstances of the previous six attacks from two years ago. In the latest attack, the victim was a black male just 19 years old. He had been found in an alley three doors from the home he lived in with his mom and two siblings. He had also been a known dealer of cocaine, often selling to local high school students. If this was indeed the work of the same person, this was his seventh victim.

Unfortunately, Garcia is not able to talk to Ricci today, as Ricci called in sick. Instead, Garcia decides to talk with one of the narcotics detectives, Trevon Jackson. Jackson has been assigned to coordinate any intelligence with Ricci and Garcia. Given the presence of the drug cartels in Area 4, it is not unreasonable to believe the dealer killings are related to the drug business. In fact, the unknown assailant in the serial killings of drug dealers from two years ago had been nicknamed the "Candy Man Killer." Candy Man is a name sometimes used when referring to a dealer on the street.

Trevon Jackson is only 29 years old. He started with the police department when he was 21 and quickly discovered drugs and street gangs were responsible for much of the violence in Chicago. He now believes he can put his skills to better use in Narcotics by trying to stem the drug trafficking and violence associated with it. After being selected for Narcotics, it isn't long before he becomes a valued undercover detective known for his ability to elicit information from gang members and drug dealers. As an African American, he's able to relate and build trust with most of the blacks living in Area 4, an important skill in working drugs. However, Jackson has the knowledge and skill to get information from most, regardless of race. It is sometimes said he can get information from a turnip. Because of this, he has a wealth of knowledge on the drug trade in Chicago, especially in Area 4. He can speak the language and is trusted by many of his developed sources.

Jackson's last assignment had been with the Chicago High Intensity Drug Trafficking Area Task Force (HIDTA). He was part of the latest months-long operation that led to the recent arrests of 27 individuals on various narcotics and firearms violations out of the west side of Chicago. The drugs being peddled were primarily cocaine and Fentanyl. It was soon after this operation when Jackson was tabbed to assist homicide detectives with the investigation of what appeared to be another attack by the "Candy Man Killer."

Jackson gives Garcia a quick lesson on the drug and gang activity in the area. Some of the neighborhoods in Area 4 are notorious for such activity. It is not unusual to find heroin, cocaine or Fentanyl being sold on the streets of Chicago. A good quantity of drugs are pipelined to Chicago from Mexico by Mexican Drug Cartels. Drugs are transported across the country using intermediaries with various methods, such as by car, airplane, trucks, and even shipped to Chicago.

After the drugs arrive in Chicago, other intermediaries distribute the drugs to local dealers, many of whom are gang members selling on the streets of Chicago. Some sell from street corners, some from businesses, and others from their homes. There are many street gangs in Chicago. Some of the better-known ones are Gangster Disciples, Black Disciples, Gaylords, Vice Lords, and Latin Kings. Some estimate there may be over 100,000 active gang members in the Chicago metropolitan area. This provides a lot of opportunity for drug distribution.

As a result of competition, sometimes turf wars break out among the gangs which can result in violence, including killings. Given that the Candy Man Killer targets drug dealers, Jackson believes it is a real possibility there is a turf war going on. However, he does not yet have evidence of that. Jackson has worked his sources and thus far, everyone has denied knowing about any turf wars.

"What would explain the two-year absence of any similar killings?" asks Garcia.

"Well," says Jackson, "It's quite possible that whatever was driving the killings two years ago stopped. Maybe the dispute was settled. Maybe the killer has been in jail. Maybe this recent murder has nothing to do with those from two years ago. It could be a copycat type of thing. Really hard to say right now. The strange quirk is the leaving of the knife at the scene."

"Yeah, that's interesting," agrees Garcia. "And it's a very specific knife. In this case and all six cases two years ago, the knife used was…. let me check my notes. Here it is, a Cardet kitchen knife with a seven-inch blade and black handle. Uses the same knife each time."

"Yep," replies Jackson, "strangest thing I've ever heard of. And then leaving the knife lying on the victim's chest. It's almost like someone is teasing us by giving us the weapon."

"I wonder if we could track down who is making multiple purchases of this knife," questions Garcia. "I'll get Ricci's thoughts on this next week. I have no idea how common this knife is or how many places sell it. Hey, thanks for the help Trevon."

"No problem. I'll keep checking my sources and keep my ear to the ground. I'll be sure to pass along anything I find."

"Great, thanks again."

From the autopsy reports on each victim, Garcia finds in each of the now seven cases, the victim was stabbed from directly in front. The knife was thrust into the center chest cavity just below the breastbone. The knife was then pushed up into the area behind the breastbone toward the heart and probably twisted as well. This action caused severe damage to one or more of the thoracic aorta or vena cava veins. The thoracic aorta carries blood from the heart while the vena cava vein carries blood to the heart. In a few cases, the blade of the knife was shoved far enough into the chest cavity that the heart itself was cut. Victims with such damage bleed out and die quickly. Based on this, Garcia does not believe a female would have the strength to overcome each victim and cause such damage. *The attacker is a male,* thinks Garcia.

Garcia discovers all the cases occurred in the early morning hours, sometime between 2:00 and 4:00 am, a time when not many people would be out and about. Every victim has been a young black male involved in drug dealing. Each victim either lived alone or had been alone at the time of the attack. Two years ago, three of the victims had been killed just inside their residence, while three others were killed in the back alley in the rear of their home or apartment building.

In the most recent case from two weeks ago, the attack took place in the West Garfield neighborhood. The victim lived in the bottom flat of a two-story, brownstone multi-unit house. The victim, a 19-year-old black male was found lying approximately 10 feet inside the front door. There was no sign of forced entry, so it appeared as though the assailant was allowed entry into the residence. This was similar to the other three previous cases in which the victim was found inside his home.

On Monday, Garcia is at work early, as he has been going over the facts in his head all weekend and wants to discuss the cases with Ricci. Ricci walks into the office at 8:05 am with his usual large cup of Dunkin Donuts coffee.

"How are you feeling today?" asks Garcia.

"Oh, I'm fine, just a touch of nausea last Friday," replies Ricci. "How is the review going?"

"I think I'm up to speed on everything. Would like to discuss your thoughts on a couple things."

"Sure, what's on your mind?"

"Are you aware of any other serial killers who used different weapons each time and then left the weapon at the scene?"

"Not that I can ever recall."

"Why do you think someone, assuming it is the same person, uses a different knife each time and then leaves it behind?" asks Garcia.

"Because he's smart," answers Ricci. "What's the one thing you don't want to have in your possession after killing someone?"

"Bloody knife" nods Garcia.

"Damn right. We've got our work cut out for us with this guy. He is incredibly careful about leaving any trace behind."

"I've checked on places that sell this Cardet kitchen utility knife and wouldn't you know it, you can buy it most places, including Amazon," sighs Garcia.

"Yeah, this guy knows what he's doing."

"Have we captured anything on security cameras?" inquires Garcia.

"No. Remember where these attacks occur. Not many people in the Garfield Park neighborhoods or Lawndale have security cameras."

Garcia then suggests they re-interview the person who reported the suspicious male in dark clothing who walked with a limp.

"We can, but do you really think there's some handicapped dude carrying out these attacks?"

"Probably not, but it can't hurt. I like to be thorough," reasons Garcia.

"You're right. Go ahead and set it up."

By Wednesday afternoon, Garcia has set up an appointment to visit 64-year-old Mrs. Elaine Henderson, the woman who reported seeing a suspicious person in the neighborhood the night of the third attack by the Candy Man Killer. Garcia and Ricci knock on her door at 2:00 in the afternoon. Mrs. Henderson invites both detectives in and offers them some sweet iced tea. Both politely decline.

"Mrs. Henderson, I would like to review your statement from two years ago about the suspicious person you observed in the neighborhood," advises Garcia. "Can you please tell us what you thought was suspicious about him?"

"Well, it's been some time ago now, but I remember I couldn't sleep due to the heat that night. I got up and went to sit a bit on my front porch to get some, you know, fresh air and cool off."

"Sure, go ahead," encourages Garcia.

"As I was sitting there, I see this man come walking from around the corner, right down that way," as she points east. "He then crosses the street and walks west to the corner of Edison, then heads north and out of sight."

"What was suspicious about that?"

"It was just a feeling really. It was early morning and not many people are out at that time of day. He was dressed in dark clothing and just seemed a bit out of place."

"Two years ago you said he walked with a limp."

"Yes, yes he did. If I remember correctly, it appeared as though he was favoring his right leg."

"And you said he had a beard?"

"Yes, it was a full beard, and he had a dark beret-type hat on."

"Could you tell what race he was?"

"No. It was dark and with his beard and hat, I couldn't tell. He never looked my way."

"Okay, thank you Mrs. Henderson," replies Garcia. "Do you also remember him wearing glasses?"

"Oh yes, it looked to me like dark-rimmed glasses, but I could not be sure. Again, it was very dark."

"Anything else you can remember about him?"

"Only that he was a tall man, probably over six feet tall."

"Do you remember what time it was?"

"I knew two years ago. I think it was sometime between two and three in the morning. Like I said, he just didn't seem to belong in the neighborhood."

"Mrs. Henderson, we appreciate your time," thanks Garcia. "Here is my card. Please don't hesitate to call if you remember anything else."

As they are heading back to the station, Ricci asks Garcia if he learned anything from the interview.

"Sure, after two years of thinking about this, she still finds his presence suspicious. I'm not saying he is a suspect, but he was only three blocks from the scene at about the time we believe the attack occurred. You can't just dismiss it."

"Nope, you can't dismiss it," agrees Ricci.

For the next several days Ricci and Garcia continue to review the case files while also assisting with other homicide investigations. Being assigned a case did not relieve detectives from simultaneously working on other cases or in helping other detectives with interviews and follow-ups. It has been a busy week, with the Area 4 Division experiencing two more homicides. One, a domestic argument over an alleged affair by the husband led to the wife shooting him dead with a 9mm Smith and Wesson semi-automatic handgun. The second one being a shooting between two gang members, resulting in the death of a 17-year-old African American male over a theft of "happy dust," a slang term for cocaine.

On the following Friday, Detective Jackson advises Ricci he has some information from the street. According to Jackson, there is new fear among street dealers that the Candy Man Killer may be back. Dealers are being more cautious over who they sell to. Some members of the Black Disciples are concerned someone is trying to start a new drug war, and if the police can't handle the issue, they will take matters into their own hands. After Garcia returns from assisting on some interviews in the investigation of the gang shooting, Ricci fills him in on the new information.

"This can't be good," says Garcia.

"Oh, I don't know Juan, there could be some value there," muses Ricci.

"Like what?"

"Drug wars, so long as they are only killing each other helps us clean up the neighborhood a bit, don't you think?"

Garcia pauses, "I suppose you could see it that way, but we really don't want people shooting each other on our streets. Innocents will get killed as well."

"I said only if they are killing each other. I don't want anyone innocent getting hurt. But think about it, fewer drug dealers would mean fewer crackheads, fewer addictions, fewer drug overdoses. You do know these assholes prey on innocent people, right?"

"Sure I do, I grew up in this town. Drug dealers need to be taken off our streets, but not murdered," challenges Garcia.

"Their drug pushing harms a lot of young people. A few less wouldn't be a bad thing, that's all I'm saying. I see too many young kids' lives ruined by hard drugs."

Garcia lets it go, realizing Ricci has been dealing with the fall out of the drug trade much longer than he has. He knows Ricci has worked hundreds of drug overdoses, violent assaults, and homicides over the course of his long career. He surmises that Ricci probably has good reason to be a bit jaded.

Eighth Attack

The following Saturday it happens again; another apparent victim of the Candy Man Killer is found in a West Garfield Park neighborhood alley by a 13-year-old boy. Both Garcia and Ricci are called at 11:45 am to respond to the scene. Garcia arrives on the scene first and meets with Detective Sergeant Gloria Pennington. Patrol officers have already secured the scene and crime scene technicians are on their way to collect any evidence.

"Thanks for coming out Juan," greets Sgt. Pennington. "It looks like the same M.O. as the last one."

She leads Garcia past the crime scene tape to where the body is found lying behind some trash containers. Garcia has read the reports describing the previous crime scenes, but the sight of a young man gutted in an alley is still a bit shocking. The victim appears to be a young black male, probably early to mid-twenties, wearing black pants and white short-sleeve button-down shirt that is now saturated with blood. The victim is on his left side in a fetal position with a clear gash in the midsection of his chest. A large pool of blood has formed under and around his body. Lying next to the victim's body is a bloody kitchen knife.

"What do we know about him?" inquires Garcia.

"His name is Jimmy Johnson, but goes by JJ," replies Pennington. "He lived in the house right here and worked at the fast-food chicken joint three blocks from here. According to the manager there, our victim worked last night until closing. They stay open late on Fridays and Saturdays, closing at two am. He apparently walks to work, so our guess is he was attacked as he was returning home, sometime after two am."

About that time, Ricci arrives on the scene. "Hi Juan, hi Gloria."

"Hi Mike, thanks for coming," says Sgt. Pennington.

"Of course, what do we have?"

Pennington and Garcia fill Ricci in with what they know so far. Sgt. Pennington turns the scene over to Ricci and Garcia, then turns her attention to coordinating officers to conduct a neighborhood canvass looking for any possible witnesses.

Ricci crouches down close to the body and studies it for several minutes. He is careful not to step on any blood. He then stands up. "Do we know whether he was a drug dealer?"

"Not sure yet," answers Garcia. "I've got a call into Trevon to see if he knows this guy."

Ricci nods, "I'm going to start taking some photos of the scene and surrounding area while you try to find out if he was a dealer. We also need to look for anything that might be evidence within fifty feet."

Crime scene technicians arrive on the scene and begin their process of documenting and collecting any potential evidence, including the murder weapon.

Approximately 30 minutes later, Garcia receives the phone call he has been waiting for from Detective Trevon Jackson. As suspected, Jimmy Johnson, 24 years old, is known as a dealer who primarily sells heroin, referred to as brown sugar on the street, as well as Fentanyl, a powerful synthetic drug often called china girl. In the past, Johnson has been linked to an intermediary associated with the Beltran-Leyva Cartel out of Mexico. Johnson has a record of several drug arrests. Garcia then relays this information to Ricci.

"I would say we officially have a serial killer on our hands," says Ricci. "And it's probably the same perp from two years ago."

"I agree," concurs Garcia.

The following Monday, Ricci, Garcia, Jackson, Sgt. Pennington, and Commander Marshall meet to review the case.

"Alright, tell me what we know," directs Commander Marshall.

Ricci leads the discussion, explaining that Johnson, known by the street name JJ, had been a drug dealer. The M.O. in this case is virtually the same as in the previous seven homicides. The weapon of choice is a kitchen knife. In each case, the knife is specifically a Cardet kitchen utility knife with a seven-inch blade. All victims have been stabbed just below the breastplate. In each case, the murder weapon is left at the scene, usually resting on the chest of the victim. In this latest case, the knife was found lying on the ground next to the victim. Thus far, no forensic evidence of value has been found at any of the scenes.

In the recent attack, detectives believe the victim was either stalked as he walked home from work and attacked in the alley just as he was arriving home, or the killer was waiting for him in the alley. Either way, this suggests the killer had some knowledge of the victim and his habits.

"What about witnesses?" asks Commander Marshall.

"None," replies Sgt. Pennington. "We conducted a thorough canvass of the neighborhood and most likely route home and could not locate anyone who heard or saw anything. If they did, they are not willing to share."

"People are pretty frightened right now," interjects Jackson. "These killings are putting some real fear into the neighborhood, especially for those in the drug business. The only thing I have of value is that JJ may have been involved in some sort of dispute with another dealer a couple weeks ago by the name of Nathan Smith, nicknamed Snowman."

"At least that gives us a starting point," states Commander Marshall. "Mike, Juan, I'd like you to run this down as soon as possible. Get Snowman in here. We can't have another string of six homicides in this community. What about forensics?"

"Nothing yet," responds Ricci, "and I don't believe there will be. The lab will find nothing on that knife other than the victim's blood and DNA."

"We collected the usual trash, cigarette butts, and such from the alley," adds Sgt. Pennington. "But I doubt any of it will be of any use. Whoever the killer is, he is incredibly careful."

Commander Marshall then concludes the meeting. "Alright then, we've got work to do, let's get on it. I'm tired of this crap happening in our Area."

Back at their desks, Garcia asks Ricci why there hasn't been more media attention brought to the case.

"Because no one outside this slum gives a rat's ass about low-level asshole drug dealers," insists Ricci. "And how can you blame them?"

"You don't mean that Mike. All murders are bad."

"Well, some not as bad as others. If this were a string of Northwestern coeds in Evanston it would draw national media attention. All of Evanston and Chicago would be in fear. But drug dealers in bad neighborhoods, no big deal. You don't have to like it, but that's the way it is."

Garcia knows he has a point. "Maybe, but the people of these neighborhoods are concerned and frightened. We owe it to them to stop this."

"Yes, and that's what we're trying to do," insists Ricci. "But whoever this perp is, he is very selective and careful. It's not like someone is randomly shooting up the neighborhood. I just like to keep things in perspective."

On Wednesday, Ricci leaves work early, telling Garcia he has some personal business to take care of. On his way home, he stops at the Paganelli Oncology Center in northwest Chicago. Unbeknownst to his co-workers, Ricci's pancreatic cancer from two years ago has returned and is now in his liver.

During his first bout with cancer, Ricci had surgery, then took chemo and radiation treatments to knock down the cancer. The treatments, as well as the stress of the drug dealer killings, took their toll. He started to lose weight and strength. Shortly after the first string of killings stopped, Ricci was forced to take a five-month leave of absence to complete his treatments and recover.

Two months ago, during his regular cancer screening, he was told the cancer was back and was now in his liver. The prognosis was not good. With surgery, chemo, and radiation, doctors gave him only a 20% chance of beating the cancer. If the treatment did not work, doctors gave him twelve to eighteen months to live. With aggressive treatment, he was told he would probably be too weak and sick to continue working. After considering his options, Ricci chose to only undergo radiation treatment. He did not want to go through the sickness that comes with both radiation and chemo like he had two years ago, finally forcing him to take the leave of absence. He just wanted to feel as good as possible for as long as possible and would continue working for as long as he could. There was no sense sitting in that big house by himself just waiting to die.

Ricci has noticed in recent weeks that he has started to lose some weight again and is not as strong as he used to be. His thrice-weekly workouts have become more difficult and he's getting nauseous more often. But Ricci is at peace with his decision. The Candy Man Killer is back, no time to quit now.

Ninth Attack

It is the last Monday in September when Garcia shows up to work early to review the crime logs for the weekend. He likes to keep up on all the crime in the area, as you never know when something might indicate a connection to the Candy Man Killer. Being thorough in his investigations, Garcia looks for all possible angles.

Garcia also likes to check the arrest logs, as Nathan Smith, aka Snowman, has still not been located and he hopes Smith will show up on an arrest record sometime. The Snowman seems to be laying low right now, as even Detective Jackson has been unable to find him.

At about 8:20, Ricci walks in later than usual. Garcia notices Ricci looks particularly tired this Monday morning. "You doing okay Mike?"

"Huh? Oh yeah, I'm fine, just didn't sleep well last night is all. Anything on the crime log we have to be worried about?"

"A couple robberies, minor assaults, couple drug busts," responds Garcia. "At least no one got killed."

"Do we have a meeting scheduled today with Marshall?" asks Ricci.

"Yes, at ten-thirty."

Neither detective makes the meeting. At 9:45, notice of a ninth homicide in which a local dealer stabbed to death sometime over the weekend. Garcia grabs his small .38 caliber handgun and straps it into his right ankle holster. He started carrying a backup after his first-day talk with Commander Marshall. Both detectives then leave for the crime scene.

This time, the attack took place inside a home in the East Garfield neighborhood. The victim lived on the ground floor of a two-story multi-family brick home. The front door faces the street. The victim, a young black male, was found lying on his back approximately eight feet inside his front door. He has a large gaping hole in his midsection from which a large amount of blood has flowed, soaking his gray t-shirt. The blood around the body has already coagulated and much of it is already dried. The odor of decay has started to fill the room. The only other clothing worn by the victim is a pair of black running shorts. Placed neatly across his upper chest is a Cardet kitchen utility knife. Officers on the scene find identification from the victim's bedroom identifying him as 31-year-old William Logan.

Upon their arrival, Garcia takes in the crime scene. "Unbelievable. Again, no obvious forced entry. He must have known his assailant. I mean, why else would his victims just allow him to come into their home?"

"You're probably right Juan," agrees Ricci. "That's why I suspect it all ties back to the drug trade. Someone is not happy with these guys. And don't you find it curious Snowman has suddenly been invisible?"

"Oh yeah, it's definitely crossed my mind. But without any evidence, unless he confesses we have nothing to tie him to these murders."

Sergeant Pennington and Commander Marshall both arrive on-site in the same car, Pennington driving. They survey the scene. It all seems so familiar.

"My god, what do we have going on here?" exclaims Marshall.

"It's not good sir," says Garcia. "We need a break. A witness, piece of evidence, anything."

"It looks and smells like he's been dead for some time," says Marshall.

"Yeah," interjects Ricci, "I'd estimate Friday night or early Saturday morning."

"Who found him?"

"His cousin over there," says Ricci as he points to a young adult male being interviewed by officers. "He says he came over to check on our victim because he had not heard from him for two days. This is what he found."

Crime scene technicians arrive and begin the process of working the crime scene. They swab for foreign DNA, look for fibers, and dust for prints as they always do. But by now, the hope for finding forensic evidence left by the assailant is extremely low. Whoever it is, he is careful not to leave any trace of his existence.

Garcia and Ricci go to the upstairs flat above where the victim lived to see if the occupants heard or saw anything over the weekend. They meet a single mom of three kids by the name of Nancy Madison. Ricci explains the reason they are here.

"I heard," Madison tells them. "When I seen all the commotion this morning I went out to see what was goin' on."

"Ms. Madison," Ricci asks, "did you see or hear anything at all over the weekend? Anything you can tell us may be important."

24

"It's been unusually quiet down there the last two days. It's usually a busy place, with people coming and going. You do know he sells drugs, right?"

"Yes, we do. When was the last time you noticed or heard activity downstairs?"

"Oh, I'd say Friday night. I heard some shoutin', but not for long."

"Are you sure it was Friday night? Could it have been Saturday morning?"

"Let me think.....Yeah, probably early Saturday morning cause I remember it waking me up. But I couldn't tell you what time."

"What exactly did you hear?"

"It sounded more like a scream. A man screaming. Again, it was really short, and I didn't hear what was said."

"Thank you, Ms. Madison. If you think of anything else, please call us."

As they are walking away, Garcia asks, "What do you think?"

"I think our victim was killed early Saturday. Probably laid there for two days until cousin found him."

"Yeah, same as the last two. Seems the Candy Man likes to work weekends. Specifically early in the morning on Saturdays."

After a pause, Ricci responds, "It would seem that way, wouldn't it."

Back at the station, Commander Marshall calls everyone into his office for the missed meeting, including Detective Jackson.

"Okay," starts Marshall, "what do we know about our latest victim?"

"We know he lived alone in the lower flat and apparently dealt drugs from the same location," offers Ricci.

Jackson speaks up, "William Logan, thirty-one-year-old black male, goes by Billy, has been on our radar. He's been known to deal in all sorts of drugs, primarily selling from his house. We weren't able to get anyone on the inside to build a case on him, but we do believe he was the source of drugs for several overdoses in the area."

"No surprise," says Ricci angrily. "These unrighteous assholes are like tigers who prey on our youth."

"Okay Mike, tone it down a bit," admonishes the Commander.

"Well it's true," Mike continues, "do you know how many kids in these neighborhoods have had their lives ruined by drugs?"

"We all do Mike, but right now let's focus on finding our killer,"

"Alright," says a frustrated Ricci, "Clearly, the M.O. fits our Candy Man Killer to a T. Same type knife, placed squarely on victim's chest."

"Yes," adds Sgt. Pennington, "but at a couple of scenes, the knife was next to the body. Does it just fall off?"

There was a pause in the room before Ricci speaks up. "In all the attacks inside a home, the knives have been found on the chest. In only two attacks were the knives found on the ground, both of which were in alleys. My guess is whoever this Candy Man Killer is, he's not in such a hurry to get out of a house as he is to leave an alley. Much more dangerous to kill someone outside, even at three in the morning. Inside behind a closed door, he can take more time to be sure the victim is dead. Therefore, when he places the knife, the victim never moves again. Outside, the victim may not be completely dead when the suspect feels he needs to get out of there. So, in at least two cases, the victim probably moved, causing the knife to fall off his chest."

Impressive, thinks Garcia, *that is very insightful. I wouldn't have thought of that. It's almost as though he can get inside this guy's head. That's what experience teaches you.* He looks around the room and others seem to be nodding in agreement, probably just as impressed.

Garcia chimes in, "According to the condition of the body and autopsy, the Coroner believes the death occurred early Saturday, sometime between two and eight in the morning."

"Makes sense," adds Sgt. Pennington.

"Where is this Snowman character?" asks Marshall. "Weren't we supposed to pick him up for questioning?"

"Yes," replies Jackson, "but we haven't been able to find him. I think he got word we were looking for him and went into hiding. My sources aren't saying much. There is fear amongst the dealer networks."

"Try harder," demands Marshall. "We need to make an arrest. This has gotten the attention of the high brass and even the media is calling. I've hesitated doing a press conference because I didn't want to overly alarm the neighborhoods, but I think it's time. I'll have Jackie set it up for tomorrow. Oh, and we're going to start meeting twice a week. I expect some progress by this Thursday. Now, let's get to work."

Back at their desks, Garcia says to Ricci, "the Commander seemed a little pissed."

"Yeah, he's being pressured to get this thing resolved. He may be waiting a long time."

"Why do you say that?"

"Look at what we have, not much of anything. Unless this Snowman character pans out."

Garcia understands Ricci's negativity but is also getting tired of it. Garcia likes to keep a positive attitude, always believing the answers will come if they just keep at it. He figures as the pressure continues to build and with the community now more engaged, the Candy Man Killer is bound to make a mistake.

On Tuesday afternoon, the Commander and Sgt. Pennington hold a press conference about the Candy Man Killer. Marshall announces the existence of a serial killer targeting drug dealers in the west side neighborhoods. They reveal the method of killing, but do not identify the brand or type of knife used. They do not want whoever the killer is to change his type of weapon, as it is the only fact that clearly ties the crimes together. Community members are implored to help police by providing any information they may have or to pass along any suspicious activity. Unfortunately, they are unable to provide any description of a suspect. Marshall then opens it up to questions.

Reporter #1: "You say there have been nine murders going back over two years ago. Why have you not been able to make an arrest?"

"We simply do not have enough information to identify a clear suspect at this time."

Reporter #1: "Wouldn't this have gotten more attention and resources if the victims hadn't been black drug dealers?"

"No, we have as many resources on this case as we need. We are now asking for assistance from the public. Whoever this person is, he is very smart and careful."

Reporter #2: We've heard the unknown assailant is referred to as the Candy Man Killer. Is this true?"

"Yes, that is the name we've attached to an unknown suspect."

Reporter#3: "Isn't that somewhat disrespectful to the victims in these cases?"

"I don't think so, it's just a name we've attached to identify the particular case. We could call him the drug dealer killer. Would that be any better? The fact is, each victim has been a known dealer of drugs."

Reporter #4: "Is this a case of vigilante justice?"

"We don't know the motive at this time."

Reporter #2: "What have you done to protect this community?"

"As I said in my statement, we've increased our patrols of the neighborhoods, we have detectives working their sources for information, we have extra detectives assigned to assist our two lead investigators, and we are asking for help from the community. We are sharing what we know with you so that everyone is aware to be on the lookout for anyone or anything suspicious."

Reporter #3: "Why aren't you calling this what it is, a hate crime?"

"It could be, but we don't know the motive at this time. Once we make an arrest we will know more about what is driving this killer. With that, I'm going to end this press conference. Thank you for coming."

On the following morning, the headline in the Chicago paper screams, **CANDY MAN KILLER STRIKES AGAIN**.

"Nice," mutters Garcia sarcastically.

When Ricci walks into the office, Garcia notices he is not looking so well. Garcia thinks he looks thinner and a little pale. Ricci does not seem to be in a talkative mood. Maybe the case is getting to him.

"Are you okay Mike?"

"Yeah, I'm fine, just a little tired."

"Why don't you take the day off, I can handle things here today."

"No, just a little nauseous. My ulcer is acting up, that's all."

"Oh, I'm sorry, I didn't know you had an ulcer."

"It'll be alright. It comes and goes."

"I can handle the neighborhood canvass today if you'd like," volunteers Garcia.

"Why don't we split it up," says Ricci. "I'll take south of Logan's residence and you take the north. Maybe we can find someone who saw something."

Both Ricci and Garcia go door to door looking for anyone who may have some information or saw something over the weekend that could help them solve this case. A few neighbors offer vague information like seeing a nondescript car driving in the area, or hearing screams late at night, but nothing the detectives can say with any certainty has anything to do with the case.

Garcia does find one person who describes a dark-colored, mid-sized four-door sedan he had never seen before parked three blocks from the crime scene in the early morning hours of last Saturday. He cannot provide a make, model, or license plate, but it is more than they had gotten from anyone else. Maybe it is unrelated, or maybe not. It did strike Garcia as coincidental the described vehicle was seen three blocks away from the crime scene. In the third homicide from two years prior, Mrs. Henderson had described the person in black walking three blocks from the scene. *Is there any connection?*

On Thursday, the investigative team once again meets with the Commander. Ricci is not there. He again calls in sick for the day. Garcia is becoming more concerned over Ricci's health.

The conversation centers around the information obtained during the neighborhood canvass. Commander Marshall says he will put the information out to patrol and send out a press statement asking residents to be on the lookout for a dark-colored sedan not familiar to their neighborhoods.

"I know patrol will now get dozens of calls over the next couple of nights on every dark-colored car someone doesn't recognize," laments Commander Marshall. "But, we have to put it out there."

"I agree sir," adds Jackson, "the residents are genuinely concerned now, and I think this will at least give them something to do. It might also temper the tensions between some of our gangs. At least they will know the police are working the cases. I've had some of our people working the streets trying to keep a cap on things."

"Thanks Trevon," responds the Commander. "Anything else?"

"I've not been able to track down the purchases of the knives," announces Garcia. "There are just too many places to purchase them, and they sell thousands of them. I did check with some of the major online retailers, including Amazon, and no one could find multiple purchases by any individual."

When no one can provide anything further, the meeting is adjourned.

Tenth Attack

It's now the first Saturday in October when Garcia's phone rings at 4:00 am, waking him from a sound sleep.

"Hello? Oh, hi Sergeant. No, that's okay, what's up?"

"Our Candy Man Killer has struck again," advises Sgt. Pennington.

"Oh my god, not again," sighs Garcia.

"Yep, this time off South Cedar in the North Lawndale area. A neighbor discovered our victim about thirty minutes ago. Heard a commotion in the back alley, trash cans and such, and went out to investigate. Found the victim bleeding out behind the trash cans. He called 911, but it was too late. He bled out before the medics could save him."

"Alright, text me the address and I'll see you there."

"What is it Juan?" asks his wife Rosa.

"Another stabbing," groans Garcia, as he gets out of bed, stretches his back, then heads for the bathroom to shave and brush his teeth.

"I'm so sorry Juan."

"Yeah, me too. This is starting to happen much too frequently. We've got to stop this guy." Garcia quickly dresses, straps on his primary and backup handgun, grabs his brown leather portfolio, a dark blue windbreaker jacket, and heads out the door.

Within 45 minutes Garcia is on the scene. Ricci has not yet arrived.

"Good morning Juan," greets Pennington.

"Not really, but always good to see you Sarge."

In this case, the victim is not at the scene. He had been picked up by paramedics and rushed to the hospital while performing life-saving measures. Unfortunately, emergency efforts to revive the victim failed. He was pronounced dead at the hospital. Word of his death quickly reaches Garcia.

Damn, thinks Garcia. *If only he had lived we would have our first real witness. We just can't catch a break, and neither can our victims.*

The crime scene looks especially gruesome. It appears as though there had been a struggle before the victim succumbed to his injuries. Blood is splashed and spattered across a 12-foot area of the blacktop alley and concrete skirt of a garage adjacent to where the victim had been attacked. A bloody handprint is found on the light green garage door approximately 5 feet off the ground. Two trash cans have been knocked over, spewing trash and rotten food across the entrance to the garage. A dim yellow alley light off the peak of a nearby garage across the alley adds an eerie glow to the scene. The air carries the mixed scent of blood, vehicle exhaust, and rotting garbage. It will certainly take more effort to record and process this scene. Garcia is encouraged by the handprint. *Hopefully, we can get prints off that.*

The most significant difference from previous attacks is the location of the knife. It is not close to where the victim was discovered by the witness. It is found lying approximately 12 feet north from where the victim had fallen. It looks as though the attacker may have dropped or thrown the knife as he was leaving the scene.

Garcia observes the bloodstains and spatter emanating from the apparent point of attack. The resident garage with the bloody palm print is on the south side of the alley with the garage door facing north. Garcia notes a series of raindrop-shaped blood spatter approximately three to six feet from the victim. This indicates the blood had hit the ground at an angle, rather than falling straight from above. Examination of this blood spatter will help blood spatter analysts determine information such as the direction of attack and potentially whether the attacker was right or left-handed.

Patrol officers have quickly obtained victim identification from neighbors who have gathered after hearing the commotion and seeing all the flashing police lights through their windows. The victim is known as Miguel Gomez, a Hispanic male, age 27. Gomez lived in a multi-unit brownstone house about five houses away from the scene. Two neighbors admit to knowing Gomez was primarily a cocaine dealer who managed his drug trade over the telephone. It is said he would take orders over the phone and then deliver them to his customers. He did not want customers coming to his residence. He also preferred to make his deliveries under cover of darkness, primarily using the alleyways to make deliveries.

Detective Jackson, who arrived a short time earlier, tells Garcia that Gomez had been on the task force's radar, but they had been unable to make a case against him.

"He was careful about who he sold to," says Jackson. "Liked to make his deliveries on foot to scan the area for anyone who might be a cop. He figured it was easier to hide from a passing patrol car or run from an officer on foot than if he was in a car. I talked to Ricci about him last week."

"You talked to Ricci about Gomez last week?"

"Yeah, he wanted some names of known dealers to interview about these attacks, hoping to get some information on who might be doing this."

"Now that you mention it, I remember Ricci saying something about interviewing known dealers. We've just been so busy."

Garcia is anxious to interview the witness. *Just maybe he got a good look at our killer. What is taking Ricci so long to get here? I hope he is feeling okay.*

About 10 minutes later, Ricci pulls into the alley and walks toward Garcia and Jackson. "What have we got this time?"

Garcia gives him the rundown on what they know right now and allows Ricci some time to inspect the crime scene.

"This is a bloody mess," says Ricci.

"Looks like our victim had time to resist a bit," replies Jackson.

"Any witnesses?" asks Ricci.

"Yes," says Garcia, "a resident by the name of Jarvis Harden. He lives right here. This is his garage. He heard some banging noises and shouting at about three twenty this morning. He came running out his back door and found our victim stabbed and bleeding. Victim was still alive at the time, but the wounds were too severe. He died on the way to the hospital. Our witness is waiting to be interviewed."

"Right," responds Ricci. "Let's get him to the station and interview him there."

Jackson volunteers to take Harden to the station. "I'll meet you there."

"Good, thanks Trevon," says Garcia.

Back at the station, witness Jarvis Harden is placed in a small interview room where everything can be recorded. He is provided a cup of freshly brewed coffee and offered a cinnamon roll, to which he gladly accepts. Jarvis is a 34-year-old African American living with his girlfriend and her two children. He works at a local lumber yard and to the detective's knowledge, has no connection to the drug trade or to any gang. According to

Harden, he hates the drug issues plaguing the community he lives in.

"Please tell us what happened Jarvis," says Garcia.

"I was sleepin'when I heard some loud noises behind my house, you know, shoutin' and stuff. Then I hear some bangin', like trash cans being dumped on the ground. So, I get up and go out back to see what's happenin' and I see this dude on the ground moanin'. He has blood all over him and trash is spilled out everywhere."

Garcia continues with the questioning. "Did you see anyone else?"

"Yeah man, there was some guy runnin' away down the alley"

"What direction?"

"Uhhh, it would be east direction."

"Can you describe him for us?"

"He was a big dude. It was dark, so I couldn't see very well, but he had dark clothing."

"You said big. How tall do you think he was?"

"At least over six foot."

"Any hat or anything?"

"Uh, yeah, he had some type of hat on, black I think."

"Do you know what type of hat?"

"Looked like one of those fancy hats with the short brims."

"Like a beret?"

"Yeah, I think so."

"Do you know what race this person was?"

"It was pretty dark, but my impression was he was a white dude."

"What do you mean by impression? Did you see he was white?"

"Not really, but from the back, I just sees him as a white guy. His mannerisms and all, if that makes sense."

"Sure. What about facial hair or glasses?"

"I really didn't get a look at his face."

"When you first came out, was this man attacking the victim?"

"No, by the time I came out, I just saw this big dude runnin' away."

"Okay, is there anything else at all you can remember about this person? Anything can help."

Harden thinks for a moment. "Yes! I remember he kind of ran funny like."

"What do you mean?"

"Like he was favorin' one leg."

"Like limping?"

"Yeah, kind of like limpin' while he was runnin'."

"Where did he go?"

"Once he got to the corner he turned and was out of sight."

"What did you do when you saw all this?"

"Well, I checked on the stabbed dude and saw he was hurt really bad, so I ran back into the house to get my cell. I then dialed 911."

"Did you touch anything or move anything Jarvis?"

"No sir, well, maybe one of the trash cans to check on the guy, but nothin' else."

"Did you know the victim?"

"No."

"Thank you so much Jarvis, we appreciate your cooperation," Garcia tells him. "If you remember anything else at all, please call me.

"Sure will. I hope you get this guy. The whole neighborhood is upset this is happenin' on our streets."

After the interview concludes, Jackson drives Harden back home.

Garcia confers with Ricci, who sat in on the interview. "This is the second witness now who has seen a suspicious tall person in dark clothing, beret type hat, and a limp. I'd say we now have a real lead."

"I would agree," replies Ricci.

The following Monday, the detectives meet for their regularly scheduled meeting.

"Good morning everyone," starts Commander Marshall. "Not a good weekend, obviously, but at least we have a little more information than we had last week. Who wants to start?"

"I will," says Garcia. "The best news is that we now have a description of our likely killer. He has been described as a large person, over six feet tall, wears dark clothing, dark beret-type hat, and most importantly, walks with a limp. If he is the same person seen by Mrs. Henderson over two years ago, he may have a beard and wear dark-rimmed glasses. And, our witness thinks he may have been white, but he's not sure."

"If he is as large as described, it may explain why he can quickly overcome his victims," adds Jackson.

"It wasn't quite as easy for him this time," says Sgt. Pennington. "The blood evidence at the scene indicated a struggle. Then we have the bloody handprint on the garage, maybe to regain his balance, and of course, he was unable to leave the knife on top or near the victim. Our witness almost caught our killer in the act."

"Is our witness solid?" asks the Commander.

"Oh yes," responds Garcia. "He is a reliable witness. It's my belief that our killer heard Mr. Harden coming out of his house and that's when he took off running. Harden did not see the suspect attacking the victim, but did see him leaving the scene."

"I think that's a fair assumption," agrees the Commander. "Could this witness be our suspect and he's lying about this mystery person running away?"

"I don't believe so," replies Garcia. "He seemed perfectly legit and has no criminal history. He also had no blood on him, other than on the bottom of his slippers."

"What about forensics?" inquires the Commander.

"Not much," says Cindy Cross, one of the department's criminalists invited to the meeting. "The handprint had no ridge detail. In a blood print, it would be quite common to have some ridge patterns from fingers or the palm of the hand. Given that there were none, we believe the suspect was wearing gloves. We have not found any blood at the scene other than the victim's. However, in analyzing the blood spatter evidence our analyst believes the suspect is right-handed. The elliptical shape of the blood spatter provided directional information indicating the victim was facing east when stabbed, as we know the victim was stabbed multiple times from the front. The blood spatter then came from the point of attack in a northeast direction. Our analyst believes the most likely source of the spatter was from the suspect quickly pulling the knife out while stabbing the victim at least two times. This motion would have flung blood off the suspect's hand and knife. Another theory is the victim resisted by knocking the suspect's arm away as he was being stabbed. We also found a series of round blood drops six feet from the point of attack and toward the direction of the knife.

This blood likely dropped from the hand or knife as the suspect moved away."

Cross continues, "We also found some blood smears leading from the scene. We believe these were made from the suspect's shoes as he was leaving. Having no pattern possibly indicates smooth bottomed shoes, such as a leather dress shoe. It is likely a good amount of blood was on his shoes, and possibly some on his clothing. Find the owner of those shoes and I'll bet we can get the victim's DNA from them."

"Very good information Cindy, thank you," says an appreciative Commander.

Pennington adds, "We already have the description out to all officers across Chicago. A press release was distributed to the media Saturday night, also with the suspect's description."

"What race are we going with?" asks the Commander.

"We put it out as unknown, but possibly white, and to be on the lookout for any male of any race otherwise matching the description."

"Let's add right-handed to the description," directs the Commander.

Garcia then points out that Miguel Gomez was Hispanic and not African American like all the previous victims. "Maybe this isn't just about black drug dealers like we thought."

"Too soon to tell," interjects Jackson. "It's only one out of ten and our suspect may have thought Gomez was black."

"Maybe," answers Garcia.

Commander Marshall then thanks everyone for their hard work and dismisses the meeting.

Garcia noticed Ricci had not spoken up during the meeting. He hopes Ricci isn't suffering from his ulcer. Although, after this past weekend, it wouldn't surprise him if he was.

Back at their desks, Garcia expresses to Ricci how unfortunate it is to lose another person to this so-called Candy Man Killer. He has never been involved in a serial killer investigation, and each new victim makes him angrier. "We really need to catch this guy," laments Garcia.

"Yes we do," responds Ricci, "and eventually we will. Just don't forget the victims these assholes prey on all the time. For every dealer that gets killed, there are probably a dozen or more kids whose lives are ruined by drugs. And in some cases, they die. These dealers aren't the only victims here."

Once again, Garcia believes Ricci is being too cavalier over the murders of these men. "Remember, those who take drugs carry some responsibility as well," says Garcia. "There would be no dealers if there were no buyers."

"You don't have a clue Juan," responds Ricci, "kids get suckered in. They don't know what they're doing or know the dangers of these drugs. I'll do my job and help find this killer, but I wouldn't piss on these guys if they were on fire."

Garcia can feel Ricci's anger and knows some of what he says is true, but he doesn't believe it justifies Ricci's contempt or attitude. There are many cultural, economic, and environmental factors involved in the world of drug usage. It isn't all the fault of the dealers as Ricci seems to believe. Garcia decides to just drop the subject.

That afternoon, Sgt. Pennington calls Garcia into her office. "Juan, I need to ask you something."

"Sure, what is it Sarge?"

"Have you noticed any changes in Mike recently?"

"What do you mean?"

"Well, he just doesn't seem to be himself lately. His sick time usage is up, and he just hasn't looked well to me the last couple of weeks. It could just be the stress of the case, but he's always been a tough cookie in the past, so I'm concerned. I keep asking him how he's doing, and he always says fine, but I'm not sure. You work with him closely, so I wanted your opinion."

"I think the stress is getting to all of us," says Garcia. "I have trouble sleeping at night thinking about this case, so I imagine Mike does as well. The whole drug dealer thing has him worked up."

"What do you mean?"

"Oh, he just has a hatred for drug dealers and no sympathy when they get murdered. He actually believes it helps clean up the neighborhood each time one gets killed. Now, he still works hard and wants to find the killer, but I've found he has no sympathy for the victims."

"You can hardly blame the guy for that."

"What do you mean?" asks Garcia with a puzzled look.

"You know what happened to his daughter right?"

"He only told me she died six years ago in Los Angeles."

"Yes, from an overdose of Fentanyl she bought from a street dealer!"

Garcia is shocked. "Oh my god, are you serious?"

"Yes. She had moved out to LA a year after high school to start a career in acting, something she was good at. I don't know all the details, but she somehow got hooked on hard drugs until one day it took her life. They traced the drugs to one of the local street dealers there. Mike and his wife were absolutely devastated. He had to take a leave of absence to recover. I just assumed he would have told you."

Garcia feels sick to his stomach. "I wish I had known. I would have better understood his attitude."

"Two years later, his wife dies from an aneurism," continues Pennington, "which he blames on stress from his daughter's death. In his eyes, a drug dealer took the lives of both his daughter and his wife. I thought maybe this case was becoming too uncomfortable for Mike and may be affecting his health. That's why I wanted to talk to you. Mike always just says he is fine."

"He did tell me he has an ulcer that's been acting up. He hasn't felt well a few times recently, but he still seems very capable to do the job."

"Okay," says Pennington, "but if that changes, please let me know. I don't want this case to ruin his health."

"Yeah, I'll keep an eye on him. Thank you Sarge."

The next morning Garcia asks Ricci if he can talk with him privately in the interview room. Ricci agrees.

"I just want to apologize," says Garcia. "I just found out the whole story behind your daughter's death. I had no idea. I'm so sorry Mike. I have a better understanding of your position on dealers now."

Ricci says nothing for a couple of seconds. It appears to Garcia that Ricci's eyes are watering up.

"It was a very tough time Juan, and one I will never fully understand and never fully recover from. As you know, I lost my wife two years later. I'm sure it was the stress of losing our dear Lisa that caused her death."

"I'm very sorry Mike."

"Thank you Juan, I appreciate that," says Ricci softly. "I probably should have told you myself, but it's hard for me to talk about."

"I completely understand Mike. And I would understand if this case is too stressful and brings back painful memories for you."

"This case is too stressful for everyone," responds Ricci. "The entire community is stressed over it. I'll be fine, but thank you for your concern."

"Sure Mike, if you ever want to talk more about it, I'll be here for you."

Later that night, Garcia shares with Rosa the tragedy of Ricci's daughter, and the subsequent loss of his wife.

"Oh my goodness," says Rosa. "No wonder he is so angry at drug dealers. I'd probably shoot them myself if anything like that happened to one of our kids."

"Rosa, so long as some people want drugs, there will be drug dealers. Murdering drug dealers is not the answer. Finding ways to improve our communities, our education system, our economy; those are ways to reduce the drug usage in this country."

She knows Juan is right of course, but it still makes her sad and angry to hear about Mike's daughter.

On Wednesday, Ricci leaves work early for a doctor's appointment at the Paganelli Oncology Center. There will be no treatment this time. This appointment is to review Ricci's latest scans and test results. As Ricci walks into the center he notices the smell of fresh-cut flowers from a large, assorted flower bouquet that sits on a table in the corner. *Are these supposed to make people feel better?* thinks Ricci. He doesn't have to wait long before his doctor calls him in.

"Good afternoon Mike. How are you feeling today?" asks Dr. Baylor.

"About the same as last week. I don't seem to have as much strength or stamina as several months ago. What do my tests show?"

"I wish I had better news, Mike," says Dr. Baylor. "There has been some slowing of the growth, but the cancer still continues to spread. I still recommend we do the surgery and start you back on chemo. A three-prong approach is the best chance we have of beating this thing."

"Have my chances of recovery improved?"

"No, but your chances diminish the longer you put it off."

"I really don't want to go through all that again for only a twenty percent chance of recovery. At least now, I can continue to do the things I want to do for as long as I can."

"Mike, radiation alone will only slow the growth. The chance of it killing all the cancer is very slim."

"Thank you, but if you just do what you can to keep me feeling as well as possible, I will appreciate it."

"Okay Mike, we will do what we can. I will keep you on the Zofran for the nauseousness. Have you lost any more weight since your last treatment?"

"Just a few pounds. I'm drinking those protein shakes and they are helping a bit."

"Drink as much as you can tolerate. Let's make your next radiation appointment for Friday."

"Alright, thank you doc."

As he is driving home, Ricci drifts off into thinking of Ella and the wonderful life they had together until the tragic death of their beloved Lisa. Since then, life has not been the same. Ricci wants to remain well enough to work for as long as possible, but is content in his decision. He will soon be with his wife and daughter again. He does feel bad for his son, but Chris is strong and independent. His practice as a young attorney is growing. Ricci knows Chris will be saddened by his death, but Chris will survive just fine. Ricci has already explained to Chris his decision not to accept full treatment for his cancer. He wants to live the last months of his life doing what he wants and feeling as well as possible. In the meantime, part of his plan is to spend more time with Chris in the coming months.

Eleventh Attack

It is now late on the last Friday in October. There have been no more attacks by the Candy Man Killer since the death of Miguel Gomez and there have been no sightings or reports of the suspicious man in black.

Ricci is straightening up his cluttered desk and packing up his briefcase before heading home for the weekend.

Garcia has noticed Ricci seemed especially tired this past week. "Get some rest this weekend Mike, you look tired."

"I plan to take it easy," responds Ricci. "I'm going to be working on some projects in my woodshop and visit my son on Sunday for dinner."

"Oh, that sounds nice. Say hi to him for me."

"I will Juan. You have a nice weekend."

"Thanks, same to you. Hopefully, we'll get through another weekend."

Unfortunately, that will not be the case. On Saturday, it is a particularly warm and sunny afternoon for this time of year in Chicago. Garcia is at his neighborhood park having a picnic with his wife and three children when at 12:15 pm he receives the call he is dreading. The Candy Man Killer has struck again. This time, it is in the Hermosa neighborhood outside the three neighborhoods he has always attacked before. Hermosa is north and west of the West Garfield neighborhood. Unlike where the other killings have occurred, Hermosa is primarily a Hispanic community with approximately twelve percent of the population being white or of another ethnicity.

"Honey," Garcia softly says to his wife. "I'm so sorry, but I've got to go. We just had another attack."

"Oh no," she says. "Do you have to go?"

Garcia just gives her that look that says, *you know I have to go.*

"Oh alright, you go on, I'll call my sister to pick us up. I don't want to take the kids home yet. They're having too much fun."

"Thank you honey, I'll be home as soon as I can."

Rosa just rolls her eyes as she kisses him goodbye. "Be careful."

Garcia rushes home to change his clothes, grabs both his handguns and briefcase, then heads toward the address in Hermosa. Being further north, it takes longer than usual to get to the scene. It takes Garcia about 40 minutes of drive time to arrive on the scene, which happens to be the home of the victim.

Patrol officers and Detective Jackson are already on the scene and have it secured with yellow crime scene tape. This time, the victim was killed inside his house, a light brown, brick, 2-story bungalow in a residential area lined with similar-looking homes. The house is small, with only two bedrooms with a bath upstairs, and a living room, kitchen, bath, and laundry room on the first floor. Five concrete steps with a black wrought iron railing lead to the wooden front door. There are no signs of forced entry into the house.

"Hello Juan," says Jackson.

"Hi, Trevon. What have we got this time?"

"A friend came over to victim's home this morning around eleven-thirty, found the front door ajar, walked in, and found our victim dead in a pool of blood."

Garcia shakes his head, "Same M.O. as our others?"

"Pretty much the same. Our victim was a known drug dealer, got killed inside the living room, probably no more than 8 feet inside the house. One major difference though."

"Oh? what's that?"

"Our victim is white."

"So, this wasn't our Candy Man Killer?" Garcia asks.

"If not, it's a copycat. Same type knife left on victim's chest."

"Well, it's got to be the same guy then. That's just too distinctive and we never told the public the quirk about staging the knife."

"You may be right," nods Jackson. "But it could be a copycat. I mean, he is our first white male, and this neighborhood has never before been targeted."

"This case just keeps getting stranger. Last time a Hispanic and now a white victim. Maybe race has nothing to do with it," suggests Garcia.

"Let me walk you through the scene," says Jackson.

Garcia and Jackson put on their latex gloves and hospital-type booties before entering the scene. They enter through the back door and are careful not to step on any blood evidence or touch anything. It will be the task of the crime scene techs to document and process the evidence.

The victim, a white male, in his mid-thirties, with blond shoulder-length hair, is lying flat on his back on the living-room floor. His legs are splayed open, with his right leg bent at the knee and his right foot nearly touching his left knee. The victim is dressed in white boxer shorts and a worn gray bathrobe. The robe is opened, exposing his chest and upper abdomen. The trauma to his mid-chest area is obvious. He has been stabbed and gouged, creating an opening approximately two inches wide. The victim's robe and underwear are soaked in dark red blood, much of it already dried. A pool of blood has formed underneath the victim, with some of it running toward his head. The right side of his hair is stuck to the floor in dried blood. It looks to Garcia like he has been dead for at least several hours. Left on the victim's chest was a Cardet kitchen utility knife.

Garcia also notices the victim has what appears to be two large cuts on the inside of his left hand and a smaller one on the top of his left forearm. Garcia believes they are probably defensive wounds. In looking around closer, Garcia can see blood spatters on the dark wooden floor.

"It looks to me like our victim had some time to fight like our last one," suggests Garcia.

"I would say so," responds Jackson. "I also think our suspect may have been cut during the attack. Look at this"

Jackson leans over and points to some spotting on the floor leading back to the door. "Someone walked to the door while bleeding."

"If that's our suspect's blood," says Garcia as he looks at Jackson. He can tell Jackson is thinking the same thing he is.

"Let's go back around and check out the porch and walkway," suggests Garcia. "Maybe we will find some blood outside."

Sure enough, when they inspect the porch and walkway, there are more drops of blood. Most of the drops have a slightly elliptical shape, indicating whoever left the blood was moving quickly as he bled. The drops ended halfway to the sidewalk in front of the house.

"I'll bet he went across the grass somewhere in here," states Jackson.

Sgt. Pennington has now arrived on the scene. Garcia approaches her and gives her a quick update.

"So," says Garcia, "we need officers to tape off this walkway and entire front yard. We then need our techs to search this grass to see if they can find more blood drops. A direction of travel would be great to have."

"I'll assign some people on it right away," responds Pennington.

"By the way," asks Garcia, "didn't Ricci get called out?"

"Yes, but he can't make it. He got hurt real bad in his woodshop last night. Cut himself on a saw and had quite a few stitches. He might need surgery."

"Damn. I hope he'll be okay. I'll call him tonight. Thanks for telling me." *That's right, he said he had work to do in his shop yesterday,* remembers Garcia.

Crime scene techs finally arrive on the scene and start their work photographing, documenting, and processing the evidence. Given the nature of the scene, it will take them at least the remainder of the day to get everything completed.

Meanwhile, Garcia and Jackson are able to identify the victim as 35-year-old Dylan Rogers, the only resident of the house. He is a white male, 6'1" tall, and approximately 220 lbs. He has an extensive history of arrests for property crimes, possession of narcotics, and sale of narcotics.

Garcia, Jackson, and several patrol officers then begin the tedious task of doing a door-to-door neighborhood canvass in hopes of finding any witnesses. In one of the residences across the street, diagonally from the victim's home, an officer finds a 19-year-old Hispanic male who says he observed someone leaving the victim's home earlier in the morning. Garcia and Jackson immediately respond to interview the witness. After introductions, the detectives begin asking questions.

Jackson starts, "Okay then, what is your name?"

"Michael Hernandez, I go by Mike."

"Mike, do you live here?"

"Yes, with my parents and two brothers."

"And do you know Mr. Dylan Rogers from across the street?"

"Oh yeah, he's lived there awhile."

"Are you aware he was dealing drugs from his home?"

"Yes sir."

"And you won't be in trouble here, we just want all the facts. Did you ever buy drugs from Mr. Rogers?"

"No sir, but I see people going there to buy drugs. I've heard on the street he sells hard stuff, like heroin and Fentanyl."

"Tell us what you saw last night."

"I couldn't sleep so I got up to play some video games when I heard some noise across the street. Not loud, just some voices."

"Go on."

"I look out the window and I see a guy dressed in dark clothing go inside Mr. Roger's house."

"Did he force his way in?" asks Garcia.

"It didn't look like it. He was at the door for about 30 seconds talking to someone, I assume it was Mr. Rogers. Then, he just walked in. I was curious as to what was going on, as it was pretty late."

"What time was it?"

"It was about four in the morning."

"Keep going, just tell us what you saw," states Jackson.

"I guess it was about five minutes or so when the guy comes back out and leaves. He headed that way toward the

51

intersection," states Hernandez as he points in a south direction. "I lost sight of him at the corner."

"Can you describe him for us?"

"Sure, he was a white male, pretty tall, with dark jacket and pants, and a pullover hat."

Jackson continues, "How sure are you he was a white male?"

"Oh, I'm positive. I could see his face when he turned and walked toward me."

"Wasn't it dark?"

"Yes, but there was enough light to see."

"You said a pullover hat?"

"Yeah, just a knit pullover hat. I think it was black."

"What about facial hair?"

"He had a full beard."

"Glasses?"

"I don't remember seeing glasses."

"How about how he walked?"

"He was moving quickly, but I didn't notice anything unusual. Oh wait, he was holding his arm close to his body."

"Was he bleeding?"

"I don't know."

"Had you ever seen this person before?"

"No."

"Could you identify this person?"

"Maybe, I'm not sure though."

"Okay, thank you so much Mike. We will be in touch," concludes Jackson.

"Yes, thank you, you've been a big help," agrees Garcia.

Garcia can't believe their good fortune. "We finally have some evidence that will help us."

"Yes," says Jackson, "we now have a more conclusive description and if that blood checks out, he's likely to be in the system somewhere."

Garcia calls Ricci on Sunday morning to see how he is doing and wish him well. Ricci says he is recovering, but it will probably be a week before he can return to work. He tells Garcia he has suffered a serious cut on his left hand using a band saw. Some of his tendons are severed and he needed 22 stitches. Garcia shares the details of the latest attack and the fact they may have blood from the suspect, and even a better description of the suspect. Ricci agrees it is good news.

The Following Week

It is Monday morning and there is a new energy in the detective bureau. An updated description has been issued to the public. Calls on people matching the description are starting to filter into dispatch. Officers are being dispatched to check out each one.

"Who would have thought there were this many tall white males with full dark beards and walking with a limp?" muses Garcia.

"People will call in on anyone who is close," says Jackson. "I'm sure patrol will be overwhelmed."

Later that afternoon everyone shares the latest information during Commander Marshall's case review meeting. The big news comes from Criminalist Cindy Cross.

"I do have good news," announces Cross. "We had our lab technicians come in over the weekend to get this blood tested as quickly as possible. I'm happy to report we did find two separate blood specimens at the scene. There was a mixture of two contributors at the point of the attack. It is a good assumption that during the struggle, the suspect was somehow injured, probably cut, given the amount of secondary blood at the scene. The second contributor of blood inside the house is the same source of the blood collected on the porch, walkway, and some from the front yard. We were able to get a full DNA profile on our suspect. It has already been entered into our state database and will be entered into CODIS this afternoon."

(CODIS stands for Combined DNA Index System, maintained by the FBI.)

Garcia adds, "We're starting to do a database search of Illinois arrestees looking for people who match our suspect description."

"Excellent," replies the Commander. "Our goal is to get this guy before we have another death. Thank you, everyone. Now let's get back to work."

On Tuesday, Garcia calls Ricci to give him an update on the blood findings as well as to see how he is doing.

"How's the hand feeling?"

"Better than expected," replies Ricci. "Doctor says he can clear me for light duty on Thursday and I will start physical therapy next Monday."

"Excellent Mike, we miss you around here. We'll see you on Thursday then."

Later that afternoon, Garcia and Jackson are at their desks reviewing reports and statements over a lunch of burgers and fries when Garcia's phone rings.

"Detective Garcia. Uh-huh, yeah sure, we can head over there this afternoon. Alright, got it, thanks"

"What's ya got?" asks Jackson.

"Another potential witness. Isabella Santos lives around the corner from Dylan Rogers and believes she may have seen our suspect entering his car last Saturday."

Both Garcia and Jackson quickly finish up their lunch with Jackson gulping down the last half of his Pepsi. They then head to the residence of Isabella Santos.

Santos lives just around the corner at the end of the block where Rogers lived. Her home is in the direction Hernandez saw the suspect go. Santos is 42 and lives with her two teenage boys in a bungalow-style home similar to others in the neighborhood.

"Thank you for calling the police Mrs. Santos," starts Garcia. "I understand you might have some information for us."

"Yes," says Santos. "I saw the news last night before going to work and I might have seen the man you're looking for."

"When do you think you saw him?"

"Early in the morning last Saturday when I was getting home from work."

"Where do you work?"

"At the Donut Stop on Bell road. I work nights making fresh donuts for the following day."

"What time did you get off work last Saturday?"

"Around three-thirty in the morning. It takes me about fifteen minutes to get home."

"Okay, so when you got home, what did you see?"

"As I was pulling up, I see a man in dark clothing and dark hat walk up to a car parked across from my house. He looks like he's hurt, which I thought was strange. He then gets into the car and drives off."

"Why did you think he was hurt?"

"He was holding his left arm and appeared to be in pain."

"Can you give us any further description?"

"Yes, he was a white male, big man, with a dark beard. Like what you are looking for."

"What kind of hat?"

"Just what you are looking for, a knit pullover hat."

"Any glasses?"

"I don't remember him wearing glasses."

"Mrs. Santos, this is important," interjects Jackson. "Have you ever seen this person before last Saturday?"

"No, I don't recall ever seeing him before."

Jackson continues, "What about his car? Can you describe it?"

"I don't know cars very well, but it was definitely very dark-colored. I think it had four doors, not a real big car."

"Thank you Mrs. Santos, you've been a big help. Juan, you got anything else?"

"Yes. Did you notice if he walked with a limp?"

"I can't say, as he was kind of hunched over holding his left arm. He was in a hurry, I know that."

"Okay, thank you for your time. If you see or hear anything else, please give us a call." Garcia hands her his business card.

"We now know for sure our suspect is a large white male with a beard," confirms Jackson as they drive back to the station. "And he drives a dark-colored four-door sedan."

"Probably also has a limp," adds Garcia. "Not everyone would notice that."

"True," Jackson agrees.

Back in the office, Garcia is starting to feel confident they are close to identifying the Candy Man Killer. He expects at any time now they will get word on a DNA match for the suspect. He can hardly wait to put handcuffs on this brutal serial killer.

That evening at home, Garcia is sharing the update on the case with Rosa. Rosa can tell he is encouraged over developments in the case and that the Candy Man Killer will soon be identified. She is also concerned over Ricci's injury and thinks it is too bad he has not been able to participate in the latest developments.

"That's a shame Ricci has not been available this week," Rosa says with empathy. "Having been involved for all the murders from day one has to be hard on him."

"I thought of that too," answers Garcia. "But he will be back on Thursday for light duty. I'm sure he would like to be there for any arrest."

"What a coincidence," says Rosa, "he gets injured the same day your suspect gets injured. It's a shame really, and what are the odds?"

"Yes, it is a shame. I know Mike wants to be there."

Later that night, Garcia lies awake in bed thinking about the recent developments in the case. Furthermore, he can't get his wife's comment about the strange coincidence of Ricci getting cut the same day the suspect got cut. He knows it's just a coincidence, but it's a strange circumstance. He knows there is no way Ricci is involved, and certainly does not fit the description, other than being big and right-handed. And he doesn't walk with a limp. *We need to get that DNA match and get this over with,* thinks Garcia.

On Wednesday morning, Jackson tells Garcia that Nathan Smith, aka Snowman, has been located. He was picked up on a street corner in the North Lawndale neighborhood and transported to the station for questioning.

"We now know he doesn't fit our suspect description," states Garcia, "he's black."

"Sure, but we can't assume anything," cautions Jackson. "We only have descriptions, some vague, on a few of the cases. You never know. It's good to be thorough."

"You're right, of course," agrees Garcia.

Nathan Smith, aka Snowman, is waiting in an interview room where everything can be recorded. After introductions and a few friendly exchanges, the detectives get down to business.

"So," says Jackson, "I understand you had some dispute with Jimmy Johnson, or should I say JJ?"

"Nothing that would cause me to kill him," protests Smith.

"Just tell us what the dispute was about."

"He thought I was taking some of his customers away."

"Were you?"

"No, not at all. I don't sell anymore."

Jackson laughs, "we are well past that Nathan. We know you sell, so stop the charade. We are only interested in your involvement in JJ's death."

"There's no involvement," protests Smith.

"You were at his house the night he got killed."

"No I wasn't, and you have no proof of that."

"Then why did you run off and hide?"

"Because I heard you were after me and didn't want to be arrested for something I didn't do"

Jackson and Garcia continue to interview Smith for another 30 minutes, trying to get him to admit to some knowledge or involvement in JJ's murder. They aren't sure if Smith's DNA is in the database, so with his consent, they take several swabs of the inside of his mouth to submit to the lab. He is then free to go.

Mid-afternoon Garcia gets a call from Cindy Cross. "I have news about your DNA."

"Great," says Garcia, "who's our guy?"

"Nobody."

"What do you mean?"

"There is no match in either the state or national database," advises Cross. "Whoever our killer is, he's never been arrested on a felony charge before."

Garcia is heartbroken. "I don't believe this."

Garcia breaks the news to Jackson.

"It's not unheard of," responds Jackson. "There have been plenty of serial killers who had never been arrested prior to starting their killing spree, at least for nothing serious."

"Yeah, but we are so close, yet still so far now." Garcia has a sick feeling in his stomach. *How much more of this can our neighborhoods endure?*

On Thursday, Ricci returns to work with his left hand heavily bandaged up past his wrist. As typical, he has a large Dunkin Donuts coffee in his right hand.

"That's one big bandage," observes Garcia.

"Yeah, doc says I cut it pretty good and have to keep it immobile until Friday. Then physical therapy starts on Monday."

"Well, it's good to have you back, Mike."

"Good to be back."

The sight of Ricci's injured left hand gets Garcia thinking again of the conversation he had with Rosa about the coincidence of Mike getting injured. He also remembers previous comments made by Mike about his disdain for dealers. *Could Mike be.....no, no way. Just get that out of my mind right now. He looks nothing like our suspect description, the exception being he is over six feet. And he certainly has no trouble walking.*

"Did you hear about the DNA?" asks Garcia.

"No," Ricci responds, "did we get a match?"

"No, no database match."

"Damn," says Ricci, "we just can't catch a break, can we?"

Garcia and Ricci spend the rest of the day again reviewing reports and interviews, looking for any tidbit they may have missed. They also go through the tips received of men matching the description put out in the media. Officers are dispatched to follow-up on each tip, then contact cards are filled out and forwarded to detectives. DNA swabs have been obtained from several of those men who looked most like the description, but none of the samples have yet matched the suspect DNA.

As Ricci and Garcia are leaving for the evening, Garcia says his usual goodbye as Ricci is getting into his car. Garcia continues to his car and then it hits him. Another coincidence. Ricci drives a dark blue, Chevy Malibu four-door sedan. Ricci has always known this of course, but it never occurred to him it was similar to the description of the suspect vehicle. *If I didn't know better, I'd ask Ricci for a DNA swab, just to clear my mind,* he ponders as he drives away.

At home, Garcia shares with Rosa the other coincidence of Ricci driving a car similar to the suspect car.

"I'm sure he has nothing to do with these murders Juan, but maybe you should talk to your Commander?"

"What would I say? Hey, I think my partner might be the Candy Man Killer?"

"I don't know what you'd say, but you've always said you have to look under every rock."

"This is making me ill Rosa. I feel guilty even thinking it is possible. He's never done anything illegal, let alone murder someone. Even bringing it up could ruin my career."

"You're just stressed out Juan. Everything seems suspicious to you at this point."

"Maybe you're right," agrees Garcia.

The next morning, Friday, Ricci again calls in sick. Garcia does not know if it is related to his ulcer, being tired, or something to do with his hand. He tries to call him but there is no answer.

Garcia continues to be bothered by the coincidences with Ricci and the Candy Man Killer. He finally confides in Jackson.

"I don't know man, that sounds pretty far-fetched if you ask me," says a surprised Jackson. "You're walking on thin ice here. I agree it's a coincidence, but still."

"Yeah, I know, that's why I'm hesitant to even bring it up"

"Maybe you should talk privately to the Commander with your concern," suggests Jackson.

"Thanks Trevon, I'll think about it. Please don't say anything."

"Oh don't worry, I'm not opening up that bag of snakes," as he smiles and walks away.

By mid-afternoon, Garcia knows if he doesn't at least run it by the Commander for his opinion, it will eat at him all weekend. He doesn't want it to ruin his time with family, so he decides to talk with Commander Marshall.

"Come on in Juan, what's on your mind?" says the Commander.

"Well sir, this is probably nothing, but you know how much Mike dislikes these drug dealers, right?"

"Sure, don't we all?"

"Yes, but not to the extent Mike does. He blames them for his daughter's and wife's death."

"We all know the history, what's your point?"

"Don't you think it's quite coincidental that Mike suffered a severe cut on his left hand the same night our killer cut himself? It was the only time our suspect cut himself in eleven attacks. Also, Mike drives a car that matches the description of our suspect car."

Commander Marshall stares at Garcia for several seconds. Garcia observes Marshall's jaw tighten up.

"What are you trying to say, Juan?"

"Maybe we should check his DNA just to be absolutely sure it's all coincidental. I would even allow mine to be checked to show we are simply being thorough."

Garcia can see the Commander is not pleased.

"Detective Garcia, that is a crazy thought. Mike is one of the best, most decorated, and respected detectives in the Chicago Police Department. For you to even give the slightest hint of suspicion on Mike is insulting. Since when has Mike had a beard or walked with a limp?" he shouts.

"I just want to cover all…."

Commander Marshall cuts him off, "that's enough. I don't want to hear any more of this talk and waste of time. Go find the real killer."

"Yes sir."

"One more thing detective. If you ever bring this up again I will have you slinging parking tickets in south Chicago. Am I clear?"

"Yes sir, I understand your position."

"Now get out of here!" shouts the Commander.

Okay, that went well, Garcia thinks as he shuffles back to his desk. *The Commander is probably right, what was I thinking anyway. This case is messing with my head.*

An hour or so later, Jackson comes by Garcia's desk and can see he is depressed. "Did you speak to Marshall?"

"Oh yeah," sighs Garcia. "I may have ruined my career."

"That bad, eh?"

"He basically threw me out of his office."

Jackson starts laughing. "I knew that crazy theory wouldn't get far."

"Okay, okay stop it," pleads Garcia as he chuckles a bit himself. "Let's just focus on what we have to do. Are you still working your contacts? Someone has to know this guy!"

"We are, but I don't think he's known to people in these neighborhoods. If he was, we would have him by now. No way a guy who has a distinctive look and walks with a limp is not known if he lives in the area. We aren't going to find him through my contacts. We need someone from outside the area to recognize a friend, neighbor, anyone who fits the description and give us a call."

Meanwhile, Ricci has just completed another round of radiation treatment at the oncology center. Ricci is feeling nauseous and weaker than normal after the treatments. He is also experiencing a strange, metal-type taste in his mouth. Ricci has taken an Uber ride to and from the appointment, knowing he might not feel so good afterward. Upon returning home, he lays down and quickly falls asleep.

At home for the weekend, Garcia tells Rosa what had happened with Commander Marshall.

"So that didn't go over so well," she comments.

"That's an understatement. But unfortunately, I still can't get it out of my mind. Marshall is right, Mike's reputation is undisputed, and he does not fit the description. Although I have considered our suspect may be using a disguise. It's not hard to find a realistic-looking fake beard."

"You need to be careful Juan; I don't want you losing your career over this."

"Neither do I, but sometimes what doesn't make sense in today's light, makes more sense when you have all the facts. More crimes have been solved on hunches than you might think."

"So you think he is the Candy Man Killer?"

"Actually no, but I think it's important to cover all bases, and Mike's injury and vehicle create one base that isn't covered. A simple DNA test would satisfy my concern and I could move past this."

"What are you going to do?"

"I don't know Rosa; I just don't know yet."

Garcia wakes up Monday morning and is grateful he had not been called out over the weekend on another Candy Man Killer attack. He gets to the office early to review new leads from callers reporting men who they think fit the description. There are eight new reports.

At 8:20 am, Ricci walks in looking haggard. He looks pale and seems to be moving slower than normal. He sets down his Dunkin Donuts coffee, then takes off his jacket and hangs it on the back of his chair before sitting down. His shirt collar is unbuttoned, and he is not wearing a tie.

"How are you feeling Mike?" asks Garcia.

"In all honesty, not so well."

"Is the ulcer acting up?"

"Yeah, that and haven't been getting much sleep with this hand and all."

Garcia suspects he is not getting the entire truth from Ricci. There is something more Ricci isn't telling him about his physical health.

"Any new leads?" asks Ricci.

"Yes, here are the call-ins we got over the weekend," says Garcia as he hands the reports to Ricci. "Take a look at these and see if you see any worth following up on."

At 11:45 am, Ricci asks Garcia if he wants to go grab some lunch. Garcia refuses, telling Ricci he has a report from last week he needs to finish up.

After Ricci leaves the office, Garcia places his right hand under his desk and pulls on a latex glove. He then looks around to make sure no one is paying attention. He gets up, walks around to Ricci's desk, and again making sure no one is looking, he reaches into the wastebasket adjacent to Ricci's desk and pulls out the Dunkin Donuts paper coffee cup Ricci had discarded earlier. He then places the cup in a paper bag and seals it shut before putting it in his briefcase.

Garcia then makes a phone call to Cindy Cross. "Cindy, I have a question for you."

"Sure, what is it?" asks Cross.

"I have a cup with DNA on it that I believe may be related to our Candy Man Killer case. Can I get this cup to you and have it tested?"

"Sure, do you know who it came from?"

"Not yet," lies Garcia, "but if it matches, I'm sure I can figure out whose cup this is. There are only a few possibilities."

"Where did you find the cup?"

"I can't reveal that yet, but this is important Cindy."

Cindy pauses for a few seconds. "I can get it to our DNA analyst and have her run it as an unknown and have her compare it to our suspect DNA."

"That's great Cindy, thank you. I'll bring it over right now."

Garcia heads out the door with his briefcase containing the paper cup, hops into his detective car, and heads for the Chicago Police Forensic Laboratory. While on his drive, Garcia is thinking, *if this doesn't match and anyone finds out what I did, I'll probably get fired for this.*

During the Commander's case review meeting that afternoon, there is not much new information to share. Some reports of people matching the suspect description continue to filter in, but at a much slower pace than the previous week.

Cross looks at Garcia wondering if he is going to share that he submitted a cup for DNA analysis. Garcia notices her looking at him as she tilts her head as if saying, *are you going to mention the cup?* Garcia squints his eyes a bit and ever so slightly shakes his head no, hoping she gets the hint. Fortunately, she doesn't bring it up.

After the meeting, Cross approaches Garcia. "Why didn't you mention the coffee cup DNA test?"

"It's too early," Garcia tells her. "If it's a match, it will be self-explanatory, and if not, it won't matter. I should have told you I was not going to bring it up. Thanks for recognizing my cue."

"Commander may not be too happy if he finds out."

"Oh, believe me, I know."

Garcia is tired and stressed, so he leaves work a bit early. Upon getting home, he finds Rosa has fixed a nice dinner of steak fajitas and salad, one of Garcia's favorites. She even has a frozen margarita ready for him.

"I figured it was a stressful day for you," she says.

"Yes, now just need to wait and see what happens," says Garcia.

"Forget all that now, let's have a nice family dinner and relax tonight," Rosa tells him. "We have your favorite for dessert, chocolate chip ice cream."

It is just what Garcia needs. A good homecooked meal, margarita, family conversation, and most delicious of all, chocolate chip ice cream. For a few hours, Garcia is able to let go of his concerns.

The DNA

The next day, Garcia is anxiously awaiting the DNA results. The minutes and hours tick away with no call from Cross. *What is taking so long? I told her it was for the Candy Man Killer; it should be top priority.*

At 11:00 am, Ricci is not at his desk and Garcia can't wait any longer. He picks up the phone and calls Cross. "Cindy, what is taking so long?"

"Juan, it is a priority, but we still have lots of other cases, other homicides. Our analysts are busy and doing the best they can. We should have a result late this afternoon."

"Alright, but when you know call me on my cell phone, okay?"

"Yes, I'll call you on your cell."

The wait is excruciating for Garcia. *I hope it doesn't match. Please don't match, I don't want it to be Mike. What if it is? What if it isn't and Marshall finds out?*

Garcia finally leaves the office and goes for a walk. He stops at Marie's Café, about five blocks from the station, grabs a newspaper, and sits down. He only orders a diet Coke. Too much anxiety to eat anything right now. After another hour or so of reading and fiddling, Garcia walks back to the office. But he is too stressed to do any significant work.

Once Ricci returns to his desk, Garcia picks up his notebook and leaves, heading to the detective lounge. Garcia doesn't want to receive the phone call from Cross with Ricci within hearing distance. He doodles some sketches in his notebook to pass the time while waiting for the call from Cross.

At 3:15 pm, Garcia's cell phone finally rings. It is Cross calling.

"Hello Cindy, what have you got?"

"We have a result, Juan. The unknown DNA from the cup matches our Candy Man Killer DNA."

"Oh my god!" Garcia blurts out. He feels immediately nauseous and can feel his heart rate jump up. His face feels flush, and his breathing becomes heavy.

"Are you okay Juan?"

"Yeah, yeah….., I'm…fine," he responds between breaths. "I just…..can't believe it.

"Well, it's true, we have a match."

"Cindy, can you excuse me for a minute, I've got to go…..I'll call you right back," says Garcia just before he presses the red disconnect button on his phone.

Garcia rushes to the bathroom, trying not to be obvious to anyone who might see him. He feels the urge to vomit and can feel the heat in his forehead and cheeks. He even feels like he is shaking a bit. Garcia enters a bathroom stall and leans over the toilet. He is resisting the urge to empty his stomach and starts to take deep slow breaths to calm himself. After a few minutes, the urge to vomit starts to subside. He leaves the stall and walks to a sink where he begins to splash cold water on his face. He cups his hands, allowing them to fill with water, then drinks the cool water. It feels so refreshing and further helps calm his nerves. After about 10 minutes of deep breathing, Garcia starts to feel normal again. He still has a pit in his stomach, but at least he feels as though he can function. Garcia finds an interview room not being used and calls Cross from there.

"What happened?" asks Cross.

"I'll explain later. Can you bring the report over and meet with me and Sgt. Pennington?"

"Sure, I know this is priority one. I'll head over now. See you in about 30 minutes"

Garcia takes a few moments to further calm his emotions. His visceral reaction to the news is as a friend and colleague to Ricci. He had hoped he was wrong in his suspicion. After another twenty minutes of thinking it through, his disappointment is now turning to anger. *How can a well-respected homicide detective ever think cold-blooded murder is an answer to his misguided anger? This will blemish the entire department. We will all suffer from this.*

Garcia calls Sgt Pennington to tell her he has important critical news about the Candy Man Killer case and needs to meet with her and Cindy Cross in Pennington's office in about 10 minutes.

"Should I get the Commander in here?" she asks.

"No, I need to meet with just you and Cindy for now. You'll understand when you hear what I have to say."

"Alright, I'll be waiting."

Garcia waits in the lobby for Cross to arrive. He does not want to see Ricci, as he is not sure how he will react, and does not want to give anything away. They still need to confirm the DNA from the cup is indeed Ricci's by getting a swab of known

DNA from his mouth. Garcia is not sure how the Sergeant, or Commander, will want to approach this.

At 3:55 pm, Garcia meets Cross in the lobby. "Do you have the report?"

"Yes, it's right here in this folder. What's going on Juan?" Do you know who this DNA belongs to?"

"The cup you tested was Mike Ricci's cup from yesterday morning."

Cross looks into Garcia's eyes with her mouth hung slightly open. "Are you telling me you think this is Ricci's DNA?"

"That's exactly what I'm telling you. I felt sick about it when you told me it matched, that's why I had to get off the phone."

"Juan," Cross cautions as she speaks slowly, "You better be sure about this."

"Oh, I know Cindy, believe me, I know. Unless someone picked that cup out of his trash and licked the entire rim of the cup, it has to be his DNA."

"Technically it is still unknown DNA, so we need a known sample from Ricci himself to confirm the identification," advises Cross.

"Yes, that's what we need to talk to Sarge about."

Garcia and Cross enter Sgt. Pennington's office.

"Hello Juan, Cindy. I'm anxious to hear your critical news," says Pennington.

Garcia hands her the DNA report. The report contains the chart of the DNA sequencing, often referred to as alleles or genetic markers that are used to compare the two DNA samples. There are a total of 20 genetic markers used for comparison.

"We have two really good samples of DNA to work with," explains Cross. "One from the blood at our last scene, and one from saliva." She points to numbers on the report. "If you look at these two columns, you will see the number sequences match at each marker. That tells us the DNA from both samples are from the same person."

"This IS critical news," an excited Pennington exclaims. "Whose saliva did we test?"

Garcia hesitates, "It came from Mike Ricci's paper coffee cup from yesterday."

Pennington lifts her head from the report and leans back in her chair, eyes darting between Garcia and Cross. She takes a deep breath and then exhales. "Are you trying to tell me our Detective Ricci is the killer?"

"Yes, I believe he is," answers Garcia. "And the DNA confirms it, at least for the most recent murder. I don't know what other explanation there could be."

"This is hard to believe Juan, what drove you to test Mike's DNA?"

Garcia then proceeds to explain to Pennington the coincidences he's observed, Ricci's attitude toward dealers, and how he began to have suspicions. He also tells her how he had approached Commander Marshall with his concerns and was reprimanded. He ignored the Commander's direction and secretly obtained a sample of Ricci's DNA. Therefore, he has come to her for advice.

"We still need to get a sample from Ricci directly to confirm the results," advises Cross. "If he will not voluntarily submit to a swab, we will have to get a court order."

Pennington thinks for a few moments. "Okay, here's what we are going to do. Juan, I will go with you to tell the Commander. Let's pull Jackson in as well so he knows what's going on. Cindy, if needed, are you ready to take a sample from Ricci?"

"Yes, I have my kit with me."

"Alright, I'm not sure how the Commander will want to proceed, but several things need to be done. Get the DNA sample, and start on search warrants for Ricci's home and car. Has Ricci left yet?"

"No," says Garcia, "but it's getting late, and he may leave soon."

"I'll go tell him not to leave due to some important new developments in the case," says Pennington. "That will buy us some time to talk to Marshall. Juan, you go find Jackson and meet me at Marshall's office in fifteen minutes."

When Garcia tells Jackson the news, he is stunned. "You're screwing with me!"

"Sorry Trevon, but I'm not."

Fifteen minutes later, Pennington, Garcia, Jackson, and Cross are ready to meet with Commander Marshall. "Come on in," invites the Commander. "Must be something important. Where is Ricci?"

"He's busy right now," responds Pennington. "We have something to tell you. Our lab has matched the suspect DNA in the Candy Man Killer case to DNA taken from Detective Ricci's coffee cup. We believe he may be our serial killer."

"What the hell is going on here!?" yells Marshall. "Juan, are you behind this nonsense? What did I tell you?"

"Yes, I am sir. I'm sorry, but my suspicions never went away, so I had the lab test his paper coffee cup for DNA."

"Didn't I tell you not to do that?"

"Commander," says Pennington, "what's important now is that we have critical evidence pointing to one of our own detectives. It can't be ignored. You want us to just walk away and pretend this didn't happen?"

Marshall leans forward, puts his elbows on his desk, places his hands on both sides of his face, and runs his fingers across the sides of his head as he looks down. He holds the position for several seconds.

"No," he finally says, and then pauses again. "It's simply hard to believe Mike could be involved like this. I've known Mike for 16 years. He's been one of the finest detectives to work with."

"Commander," says Juan, "I believe the death of his daughter and then his wife filled him with rage against all drug dealers. I think it finally just consumed him."

Marshall does not respond for a few seconds. Finally, he looks at Pennington, "what do you recommend we do Gloria?"

"Some of it is up to Mike. If he agrees to voluntarily submit to a DNA swab we won't have to get a warrant. We will probably need to get search warrants for his car and home. We should first sit him down and present what we have and see how he reacts. In the meantime, I can have patrol impound his vehicle and guard his home until we can get the warrants."

"Alright then," Marshall says. "Gloria, you get officers to secure the car and home, then I want you to be lead on interviewing Mike. Juan, are you up to being in on the interview?"

"Yes, I'd like to be involved."

"Trevon, I need you to coordinate securing search warrants for both the car and home."

"Yes sir."

"Cindy, you stand by for potential DNA swabbing. I will go with Juan to bring Mike to one of the interview rooms. I need to hear what he has to say, if anything. Let's get moving."

Fifteen minutes later, Detective Mike Ricci is sitting in interview room number three with Commander Marshall, Sgt.

Pennington, and Detective Juan Garcia. The Commander has Ricci leave his service weapon and backup weapon in his desk drawer. Ricci knows something is up.

"What's this all about?" asks Ricci.

Sgt. Pennington begins, "Mike, we have reason to believe you may be involved in the homicide of Dylan Rogers last week."

"Now why would you think that?" he responds.

"Let me read you your rights first. You have the right to remain silent, anything you say…"

"Stop!" interrupts Ricci. "I know my rights. Just tell me what's going on."

"Okay Mike, we have a DNA test that has matched your DNA to that found at the crime scene last week," responds Pennington.

"And just where did you get my DNA?"

"I got it," interrupts Garcia, "off your Dunkin Donuts coffee cup from yesterday."

"You, my partner?"

"Yes Mike, just too many coincidences, especially the cut on your hand. I did it hoping to clear you of my suspicions."

Ricci stares at Garcia without saying anything more.

"Mike," continues Pennington, "we need to swab your mouth for a DNA sample to confirm or not confirm the results of the test from the coffee cup. As you well know, you can voluntarily give us a sample, or we can get a court order. Either way, we will get a swab."

Ricci stares down at the table with his head in his right hand. His injured left hand sits in his lap.

"Mike, we have also impounded your vehicle and sent officers to secure your home. We will be applying for search warrants later today."

Ricci finally speaks again, "that won't be necessary."

Commander Marshall then interjects, "why not Mike, what do you mean?"

"I'll make you a deal," says Ricci. "If you promise you will give me one hour in an interview room with my son Chris before taking me to jail, I will give you enough to make your case. I just want some time to explain to Chris why I did what I did. I will also give you consent for my DNA and to search both my car and home. That should save your detectives a lot of time"

"Deal," says Marshall, "Now tell us what you did."

"I'm not going to go through each of the murders, as I don't want to relive them," says Ricci. "However, I admit that yes, I committed all eleven homicides attributed to the Candy Man Killer. My motive was to avenge the death of my daughter and wife, as well as to save more young people from being ravaged by drugs. The knives were my calling card, a warning to all drug dealers; this could happen to you if you don't change your ways. Remember what I told you Juan? No one wants to be stopped with a bloody knife on them. The last two stabbings did not go as smoothly as previous ones. My cancer is back, and I found as I grew weaker, it was more difficult for me to quickly overcome any resistance. That's how I got cut in the last one. Had I not gotten cut, you still wouldn't know who the Candy Man is. I know you won't agree with me, but I believe by eliminating eleven dealers, I have saved dozens of young people. Is it morally wrong to save people?"

Ricci continues, "You will find what you are looking for in my garage. There is a metal cabinet along the back wall. It will have the clothing and disguise I wore. You will probably find blood spatter in the creases of the shoes in that cabinet. The clothes were always washed, but you may find something there as well. I used a beard and sometimes fake glasses to hide my identity should anyone see me. I also faked a limp if I thought I might be seen to further confuse investigators. That should give you enough to convict me on anything you want."

"Mike," asked Garcia, "how did you get into people's homes?"

"That was rather easy. I would usually spend some time learning about my target's habits and never approached a residence if someone else was in the home. I would simply knock, show them my police identification, and tell them there had been an assault or homicide, or whatever down the street and I was just checking with neighbors. Some I would tell I was there to remove them from being under suspicion. No one wants to be under suspicion."

"And what about the ones in the alleys?"

"Most of those dealers had late night jobs or did their dealing at night. I would just wait to find them on their way home. I researched my victims. I didn't just go out and cruise the streets. Much of what I got came from narcotics detectives."

"You seemed to focus on African Americans until the last two murders. What changed?"

"Nothing. This was never about race. It was only about going after predatory drug dealers. The neighborhoods we worked in simply happened to be populated by mostly black residents. I started to expand outside this area once everyone was on high alert. My last dealer happened to be white. From what I had gathered from Narcotics, he was an active dealer in the Hermosa neighborhood and someone who needed to be eliminated."

Everyone in the room is astounded at how easily Ricci can describe what he had done. He does not appear to have any remorse.

"Mike," Garcia says softly, "you do know you are going to spend the rest of your life in prison, right?"

"Well, it won't be for long Juan. My cancer has returned with a vengeance. It's in my pancreas and liver, and now that my secret is out, I will be forgoing all treatment. I should be dead in 8 months or so."

"Knowing that makes things a little clearer," says Garcia. "I'm sorry for your cancer. I'm also sorry you will only serve a short time in jail. And to think I looked up to you."

Ricci doesn't look at Garcia, he just stares at the floor.

Cindy Cross enters the room and administers the mouth swabs that will confirm Mike Ricci is the Candy Man Killer. Detective Jackson has prepared written consents to search and has Ricci sign them. Ricci's son is contacted by Commander Marshall and given the news. It will take Chris Ricci about an hour to get to the station.

Commander Marshall returns to the room. "Detective Garcia."

"Yes sir," says Garcia.

"Would you like the pleasure of placing our detective here under arrest for Eleven Counts of First Degree Murder?"

"Gladly sir." As Garcia places Ricci in handcuffs, he states, "Mike, you are under arrest for First Degree Murder."

Two officers are then assigned to sit in the interview room with Ricci until his son shows up.

Commander Marshall contacts the Chief of Police to let him know the Candy Man Killer is in custody. As expected, the Chief is pleased the case is finally solved, but clearly upset it is one of the department's own. The Chief and Commander then begin preparations for the press conference to be held later that evening.

In the meantime, Garcia receives word from Jackson that detectives have found the items Ricci described in the metal cabinet in his garage. Included with those items are two, still in the package, brand new Cardet kitchen utility knives. He also believes they have found some bloodstain evidence on the driver's floorboard of Ricci's car.

The Police Chief's live press conference takes place at 7:00 in the evening. Garcia, other detectives, and staff members gather in the detective training room to watch on TV. Employees are shocked and disappointed the killer ended up being a department member, but they are also pleased to finally have the murderer in jail.

After the press conference, Garcia completes some final paperwork, then heads home. He can hardly wait to get home to hug his wife and kids. It has been quite a stressful couple of days.

Epilogue

On Wednesday morning, Garcia is putting together the case file that will take a couple of weeks to organize when Commander Marshall calls him into his office.

"Sit down Juan," says the Commander as Garcia walks in. "That was some nice work you did."

"Thank you, sir."

"However, you did violate a direct order."

"Technically sir, you said not to bring my suspicion up again and I didn't. I waited until I had proof."

"No, you knew what I meant. You will probably receive some type of award for solving this case, but I can't let an ignored order go unpunished. As I promised, after your case file is completed, I've arranged to have you transferred to the south Chicago Traffic Unit."

Garcia doesn't know what to say and simply stares at Marshall with disbelief.

Marshall isn't able to hold it in for long before he breaks out in laughter. "I had you going there for a moment!"

Garcia exhales, "yeah, you sure did," and then begins laughing himself.

Smiling, Marshall says, "You know Juan, I think someday you might make a mighty fine detective."

"Thank you sir," says Garcia smiling.

Mark R Beckner

Wendy's Secret Admirer

Detective Don Walker is just finishing his first cup of coffee when his phone begins to ring. Kind of early for a phone call, he thinks. After all, not much happens in Rockville, Michigan, a small community of approximately 14,000, located about an hour north of Grand Rapids, Michigan. Sometimes Walker can go most of the day without a single phone call. When he is on the phone, it is usually him making the calls.

"Detective Walker," he answers. After a short pause, "You've got to be kidding me! Yeah, okay, I'll grab Steve and head right over."

"Hey Steve!" Walker yells. "We need to head over to Lincoln High School; they've just found the body of a young woman behind the school."

"What?" Replies Steve Baker, the only other detective in the Rockville Police Department.

"Yeah, you heard me," says Walker. "We have to get going, Sergeant Thomas is at the scene and needs us to respond asap. He says it looks like a homicide"

It is 7:55 am on Friday, November 13th, and a bit colder than normal for this time of year. Walker grabs his winter jacket and looks for the crime scene kit, finding it in the storage closet. Baker adjusts the 9mm Smith and Wesson handgun on the right side of his belt and grabs a 2-way handheld radio from the wall charger and attaches it to his belt on his left side. Both detectives quickly walk out of the police department to their vehicle, a white unmarked Ford Explorer. Walker drives while Baker uses the car radio to advise police dispatch they are en route to Lincoln High School.

Neither detective says much on the way, but they are both thinking the same thing. A homicide in Rockville? The last homicide in Rockville was eight years ago as the result of a domestic dispute between an estranged husband and his wife. Walker was on the force at the time, but was working patrol and had little to do with the investigation. The husband was eventually charged and convicted of 2nd Degree Murder. Baker came to the department just six years ago, but did have some limited experience with homicides during his time with the Grand Rapids Police Department. Baker had been with Grand Rapids PD for eleven years, advancing to the Detective Bureau for his last three years there. During that time, he assisted with several homicide investigations. He left Grand Rapids to enjoy the quieter small-town life with his wife and two children, a son and daughter.

The drive to the high school is only about 3 miles. Officer Andy Garrison meets the detectives out front and directs them to the backside of the school, where Sergeant Ed Thomas is waiting and protecting the crime scene.

Lincoln High School, home of the Lincoln Wildcats, is in a residential section of the city on the corner of Pinewood and Locust street. The building was originally built in an L shape, with one side facing Pinewood to the west and the front side facing Locust to the north. The football and baseball fields are on the east side of the school with a long parking area bordering both the baseball and football fields along Locust Street. This lot is used primarily for teachers and school employees during the day. A second smaller parking lot is located on the northeast corner of Pinewood and Locust, across from the school. This lot is used primarily by students. Both lots are available for use during the evening for school events, meetings, football, and other sporting events. Further to the west and behind the school, tucked into the L-shaped corner, is a small courtyard and open, grassy park-like area with some picnic tables. Students often gather here during breaks or to just meet and hang out with friends. The baseball field borders this grassy open area.

Just to the south of the school grounds runs a wooded creek. This creek runs east to west behind the football and baseball diamond, and then along the backside of the open space adjacent to the school grounds. The trees and brush along the creek are normally lush and dense. Now that it is fall, none of the trees or bushes have leaves, but it is still difficult to see the creek through the dense brown branches of the now dormant foliage. A concrete walking/bike trail runs east and west along the creek and is often used by students who walk to school. A sidewalk runs north to south, connecting the back-courtyard area to this walking trail. Since smoking is not allowed on campus, some students go to this wooded area to hide while having a smoke, while others just go to sit along the creek bank and visit with friends. There are several benches in the grassy area, just north of the walking/bike trail.

Walker drives through the parking lot and gets as close to the open space as possible. The sun is just now rising and shadows from surrounding trees make it difficult to see. The detectives finally spot Sergeant Thomas standing along a bank of trees near the creek, and he is waving them over. Walker grabs the crime scene kit and they quickly start walking in the direction of the Sergeant. It takes them several minutes to walk the length of the baseball field and open area to get to where the Sergeant is.

"Don, the body is over here," says Sergeant Thomas, as he points to a spot beyond a row of several trees and some bushes.

Being late fall, the sound of crunching leaves fills the air as they make their way through the trees and bushes to the bank of the creek. Frost is still on the grass from the cold evening. Other than their own, no footprints are visible in the frost. Upon arriving at the creek, Walker and Baker see the body of a young teenage female lying behind some bushes. She is lying on her back with her head toward the creek, about 5 feet from the edge of the bank, and her legs pointing toward the bushes. Her left leg is bent at the knee. It is obvious to both detectives that she has been dead for some time, as lividity has already set in. Her face is ashen, and she has long blond hair. She is wearing a white winter coat with a fur-lined hood, some type of yellow top, and jeans. She has one light blue New Balance tennis shoe on her left foot and white socks on both feet.

"Where is the other shoe?" asks Baker.

"I don't know, haven't found it," says Sergeant Thomas.

"Okay then, do we know who she is?" Baker asks.

"We believe she is Wendy Spire, a junior student who was reported missing late last night by her parents," responds Thomas. "She never came home Thursday night and certainly fits the description."

Baker squats down to get a closer look at the body. He notes that her hair is tussled with pieces of dried grass and leaves intertwined in her hair. The top of her jacket zipper has been torn and he observes redness and bruising around her neck area, as well as some vertical scratches. In his mind, it appears as though she has been strangled and may have tried to get someone's hands off her throat, resulting in the vertical scratches. Her pants appear to be undisturbed, so he doubts she has been sexually assaulted. A small brown leather purse with a long shoulder strap lies approximately six feet north of her left foot. Meanwhile, Detective Walker has gotten out his camera and begins to take crime scene pictures.

Baker tells Sergeant Thomas to cordon off the area with crime scene tape and start a search of the open space and courtyard area, looking for anything that could be evidence. Baker and Walker will handle searching the area immediately surrounding the body.

"You also need to call the coroner and get him out here to process the body," says Baker. "And don't forget to call the Chief."

"We're on it," responds Thomas.

Baker takes care not to disturb the crime scene, knowing that any tiny piece of evidence can be important. After Walker is finished taking pictures of the body and immediate area, Baker puts on his latex gloves and picks up the purse by its strap, and resets it in an upright position. He then carefully opens the purse to find a student ID card tucked into one of the inside pockets.

The name on the card is Wendy Spire and the photo looks like the girl lying at his feet. He also finds a cell phone, which he leaves in the purse.

"Steve" shouts Walker, "the Chief is here and wants to see the crime scene."

"Walk her in, but don't let her disturb anything. Bring her from the east side, as I think our victim was dragged through the brush in a southwest direction," responds Baker.

Police Chief Cindy Carson has been with the Rockville Police Department for twelve years. She worked her way up from animal control, patrol officer, detective, sergeant, and finally Police Chief. She has a bachelor's degree in criminal justice from Michigan State University. Town Council appointed her as Chief after the previous Chief retired three years ago. Both Walker and Sergeant Thomas had competed with her for the position, but Carson had displayed leadership skills throughout her time on the department and basically handled most of the previous Chief's duties during his last year in office. She was also well known and liked in the Rockville community. While both Walker and Thomas were disappointed, they have come to appreciate how Chief Carson has handled the position. She provides direction but allows her employees to do their jobs.

Chief Carson walks into the crime scene and is taken aback by what she sees. Sure, she's seen dead bodies before, but to see such a young victim dead in the woods from an obvious act of violence is disturbing. This does not happen in Rockville, she thinks. And, she knows this girl, Wendy Spire.

"What do we have Steve?" she asks.

"Best I can tell is she was strangled, probably sometime last night based on the condition of the body. It looks like she might have been dragged through this brush, probably to hide the body."

"I know this girl," says Carson. "She is Wendy Spire, the daughter of Joe and Becky Spire over on Worster Drive. Her parents were involved in the neighborhood watch program I facilitated when I was in patrol. They are such a good family; this is going to destroy them."

"Do you want me to have someone sent over to tell them?" asks Baker.

"No, not yet. Let's get the body out of here and then I will go over and tell them myself. I certainly don't want them trying to show up here."

"Okay," states Baker. "I've got the Coroner on the way. Once we process what we can here, I will have him take the body for further processing and an autopsy."

"The press already knows something is up," advises Chief Carson. "I've gotten two calls from the town paper already, and once this gets out, I'm sure we'll have reporters from Grand Rapids here in no time. This could get nasty. Would you like me to call the State Patrol and ask for some assistance?"

"Let's see what we find here and what the autopsy tells us, then decide," states Baker.

Within about 15 minutes, County Coroner Wilson Kolanski arrives on the scene. Walker meets him as he is walking toward the crime scene and fills him in on what they've got and what they currently know. He then walks Kolanski into the crime scene. Once there, Kolanski and Baker examine the body for any obvious evidentiary items, such as foreign fibers, hairs, blood, etc. Baker knows that any premature moving of the body could destroy such evidence. After not finding anything obvious, they decide to move the body, put it in a body bag, and load it on a gurney to take to the county hospital where the autopsy will be performed. Baker then collects samples of surrounding soil and plant material.

"Don!" shouts Sergeant Thomas, "I think we found something."

Walker strides over to Thomas to see that he is holding a wide band gold ring with a flattened area on top. Engraved in the top of the ring are the initials A.L.

"Not sure if this is related, but we found it in the grass along the bike path," says Thomas. "We took a photo and marked the location it was found."

"Good find," responds Walker, "let's hope this is important."

"Who reported finding the body?" asks Baker.

"A student by the name of Sarah Williams," answers Thomas. "She was walking to school this morning along the path and something white caught her eye through the trees. She looked closer and thought it was just a coat. When she walked toward the creek, she recognized it was more than a coat. It appeared to be a dead person. She immediately ran to the school and told the Principle, Mr. Jenkins. He thought she had to be mistaken, so he went out to check himself. Once he saw the body, he immediately called us. It will all be in my report"

"Anyone touch anything?" asks Baker.

"They both said no."

Prior to leaving the crime scene, Walker tells Sergeant Thomas to maintain control of the scene for now and assign a couple of officers to start asking students in the area if they know anything at all.

"Got it covered," says Thomas. "I'll see you back at the station later."

Back at the station, Detectives Walker and Baker start to go over what they have. Photos are loaded into the computer and they start to examine and document the evidence collected. Looking at the photos, Baker points out the drag marks in the brush, leaves, and soil, indicating Wendy Spire was dragged at least part way through the brush to her final resting place. He then carefully examines the contents of the purse and pulls out the cell phone. The contents of the phone will need to be downloaded by a computer forensics expert. The County Sheriff's Department has a computer specialist who can help with that.

News of the dead body has now been spread throughout the high school and the media has started to show up to ask questions. Given the police activity and disruption being caused in the school, Mr. Jenkins decides to cancel school for both Thursday and Friday.

At 11:45 am, Chief Carson arrives back at the PD to meet with Walker and Baker. She tells them she has notified the parents and as expected they are devastated by the news. Both parents are inconsolable. Wendy's dad, Joe Spire, advised Carson that Wendy was supposed to be meeting a male friend named Aaron after orchestra practice. Wendy told them it was just to talk and that he would walk her home. Given his emotional state, Carson did not push for more information. Carson had an officer pick up Wendy's 13-year-old sister, Lisa, from the middle school to bring her home. She then called for victim advocates from the county to be with and assist the family in any way possible. Prior to leaving, Carson was able to talk to Lisa.

According to Lisa, Wendy had planned on meeting someone after school, apparently, a friend who had found Wendy's lost yellow scarf. Yellow happened to be Wendy's favorite color and she was upset when it had been lost or stolen. Wendy had orchestra practice after school for an upcoming concert and was to meet this friend after she got out of practice sometime around 5:30 pm. Wendy told her parents she would be a little later than normal and would be getting a ride home from someone named Aaron. Wendy never came home last night. Her dad called the police at 10:30 pm to report that Wendy had not come home, they could not reach her by phone, and they were worried something might have happened. Lisa told Carson that she should talk to Katy Anderson, as she was Wendy's best friend and might know something more. That is all the information Lisa could provide. When asked about the discrepancy on how Wendy was going to get home, Lisa replied that Wendy had not been clear on what was happening last night.

Well ok, thinks Walker, *at least we have a name of someone who may have seen or been with Wendy last night.*

Chief Carson sighs, "this thing is starting to blow up. The press from Grand Rapids is now in town and there will be a live broadcast on the noon news. Once that hits, the whole town will be up in arms. We need to solve this quickly. Any luck with the phone?"

"I've got it ready to go to the county right now," states Baker. "I'm going to grab a quick lunch then head over there. They know it's coming."

"And we've got the autopsy scheduled for three o'clock this afternoon," says Walker. "I will be there to observe and take notes. We also have officers talking to students to see if they can dig anything up"

"Okay, sounds like we have things covered for now," says Carson. "You guys are doing a good job. I'll go deal with the press for now and then call each Council member to give them a general idea of what we know. Keep in touch with any updates."

Rockville is known as a nice family community with good schools. Much of the town is residential, but with enough commercial establishments to please most everyone. At one time it was largely a farming community and while it still serves area farmers, it has also become a distant suburb of Grand Rapids. Many residents work at Steelcase or one of its related businesses, while some are involved in the high-tech industry. The small-town feel, clean living, and mostly crime-free community is appealing enough to folks that the commute to Grand Rapids is worth it. Others work in local businesses that support the community itself.

Lincoln High School serves all of Rockville, and parts of the surrounding county. Most students either take the bus or drive to school. About 15% of the students live close enough to be able to walk. The school has approximately 1200 to 1300 students in any given year and is best known for its football team. For whatever reason, the Wildcats are usually one of the top class A football teams in the state and this year is no different. In fact, this is one of their best seasons. The team is undefeated, with the closest game being a 24-17 win over Shepard High School, another top-level team in their division.

The Wildcats football team is led by senior star running back Brad McGivens. McGivens was first-team all-county last season and placed on the second-team all-state. Some are predicting he will be first-team all-state this year. In 10 games, McGivens has rushed for 2,198 yards and caught 41 passes for another 698 yards. Combined, McGivens is averaging 290 yards of offense per game. His lowest rushing total this season is 127 yards against Shepard High. He runs the 40-yard dash in 4.4 seconds. If he can't run from you, he will run over you. McGivens currently has 23 college scholarship offers, including from the University of Michigan and Michigan State. He still has at least one more game to play, next Saturday's league championship, and most likely one or more games in the state playoffs.

McGivens also plays on the baseball team, leading last year's team in batting average (.407) and home runs (14). He is certainly considered the top athlete in the school and he knows it. He never shies away from the fact that he is the best. He also happens to be quite good-looking, standing at 6'0" and a muscular 205 pounds. His wavy brown hair is combed back and hangs a little past his ears, just off the shoulder. His eyes are sky blue in color. Some say he looks like a bigger, better-built Matthew McConaughey. He is also one of the older Senior students, having turned 18 in October.

Brad McGivens is also known as quite the ladies' man. He is known by everyone in the school and pretty much anyone in the community who follows high school sports. He has an outgoing and brash personality, sometimes being a bit of a bully. He can be your best friend or your worst enemy. Brad is not afraid to use his popularity and celebrity status to his advantage, especially when it comes to getting the girls. While he doesn't give much attention to the non-athletes in school, he generally isn't mean to them either, so long as they don't cross him. Many of the students are intimidated by him.

Brad is not a bad student, but he doesn't put much effort into his studies. With unimpressed teachers, Brad can usually do enough to get a C grade, and sometimes even a B. There are a few teachers who fall for Brad's charisma and fame (and potential fame) and generally give him a pass just for showing up to class. They provide him with enough A's and B's to keep his average in the B range, plenty high enough to get into most colleges offering him a scholarship.

Brad doesn't think much about his future, other than he plans to someday be a pro football player. Most of his attention is spent on having fun and dating girls. He never has a girlfriend for long, as the challenge of getting the date is what excites him. That, and of course "scoring" with each girl he dates. One of his goals is to score with every cheerleader, a total of 12, not counting the three male cheerleaders of course. He has managed to date seven of them, but the other five don't seem interested and have thus far turned down his efforts to date them. He is in his senior year, so he knows his time is running out, but still believes he can charm a few more of them before next spring.

Wednesday, November 4th

How Brad comes to be acquainted with a 16-year-old Junior named Aaron Livingston starts on this Wednesday. It is a strange relationship, as Aaron is the polar opposite of Brad. Aaron is about 5'8 and 145 lbs., with short, curly, light brown hair and wire-rim glasses. He is not a bad-looking kid, but does fit the look of what some would call nerdy. He is not interested at all in sports and has only attended two football games his entire time in high school. Nor is Aaron outgoing or brash about anything. He is shy, quiet, and very studious. He is especially insecure and shy with the girls. He lives with his mother, Megan Livingston, in a modest home and has no siblings. His father died from a heart attack when Aaron was 4 years old, and this had a profound impact on Aaron. His mother believes this is partially why Aaron tends to lack confidence in social situations.

Aaron is intelligent and cares about his grades, mostly earning A's. He does not have a lot of friends, but those he does have are like him, with like interests in technology, video games, and chess. Some of Aaron's favorite video games are Chess, League of Legends, and Darkest Dungeon, although he will play just about anything. Aaron also plays board Chess with some of his friends. He does not participate in school activities with the exception of one. He is a member of the school's Chess Club. The club meets once a week and allows Aaron to play other chess players that test his skill level. He is getting rather good at it. He now wins about 70% of his matches.

"Hey Aaron, what's up?"

Who's that? Aaron wonders. He turns around from his seat at one of the cafeteria tables in the corner and sees Brad McGivens walking toward him. *What does he want?* Two of Aaron's chess-playing friends at the table wonder the same thing.

"Uh, not much," Aaron says softly.

"Good, because I've got a hot opportunity for you," says Brad. "You see that girl over there?" as he points in the direction of Wendy Spire, sitting with a couple of friends at another table half-way across the room. "I'll bet she would be someone who would like to date you."

"But, I don't even know her," Aaron says.

"No, but you will if you let me help you."

Aaron is certainly not a lady's man, and he has never had a girlfriend, but it doesn't mean he hasn't fantasized about one. And if he is being honest, Wendy has attracted his attention in a couple of his classes. However, other than a quick "hi" or "hello," he has never spoken to her. He likes the fact that she seems to be kind to everyone, is studious like him, and appears to be on the shy side like he is. At least they have some things in

94

common. But Aaron is too shy and insecure to ever start up a conversation with her, let alone ask her out on a date.

"How could you help me?" asks Aaron.

"Well, you've seen me talking to Wendy from time to time, right? She's a friend of mine and I think you would be the perfect type of guy for her. And I could help you set up a date, maybe even score with her."

Aaron is confused now. "Score? What are you talking about?"

"Never mind, just let me help you get to know her."

"No, I don't think so."

"What, are you gay or something?'

"No, I'm not gay!" Aaron says in a louder voice.

"Well then, give it some thought big boy," says Brad as he walks away.

"What the heck was that about?" asks Timmy Goodman, one of Aaron's friends sitting at the table. The other friend at the table, Harold Best, simply sits with a puzzled look on his face.

"I don't know," Aaron responds.

Brad of course has not talked to Wendy about Aaron. Brad is angry that Wendy Spire has once again spurned his attentions. Wendy is different from any girl he has ever dated. Wendy is only 16 and a Junior. She is not a partier, does not particularly like sports (although she did attend some of the football games for the social side of it), and is much more interested in her studies than Brad. Wendy is also shy and reserved. She knows boys who are casual friends, but has not dated anyone. She also plays violin in the high school orchestra and has worked her way to second chair. Wendy is hoping to one day take over as first chair. Wendy only has a few close friends, her best one being Katy Anderson. Wendy and Katy share everything.

Three things make Wendy attractive to Brad. One, her demeanor is different than any other girl he has ever dated. Most of his girls have been partiers with big personalities like his. Wendy is just the opposite. She is quiet, studious, and highly intelligent. Second, while she is not stunning in the way some girls are, Wendy has a reserved beauty to her. She is well proportioned at 5'5", 120 lbs., and always well dressed. She has long flowing blond hair, nice skin, and comports herself with an air of class he is not used to. Third and finally, she is not someone who fawned over him or flirted with him like many other girls. In fact, she has brushed aside all his advances since he first laid eyes on her a year ago. This may be the one thing that is most attractive to him; the challenge to get her to date him. It is easy to get most girls to date him, but not Wendy. Brad takes offense to the fact that Wendy does not want anything to do with him. *How could she not want to date me?* he questions. *I'm maybe the best-looking, greatest athlete she will ever meet.* It doesn't make sense to Brad. The more she rejects him, the more he wants to get her to like him enough to go on a date, with the ultimate goal of course to score. What a victory that would be.

Trying to win Wendy over by talking to her directly has not worked for Brad. He comes to believe she simply does not like sports figures, and maybe if she can see him through different eyes, he will have a chance with her. Brad is too conceited to think maybe it is his personality she does not like. *Maybe if she gets to know me in some other way, she will learn to like me,* thinks Brad. This is when Brad develops his plan to try to win her over through someone else. Aaron Livingston seems like the perfect person to help him out.

Friday, November 13th, 2:15 pm

Sgt. Thomas walks into the detective's office.

"I think we have something," he announces.

Both Walker and Baker look up with expressions that say, *what is it?*

"While talking with students from the school, Officer Ivey located a close friend of Wendy's," shares Thomas. "She found a student by the name of, let me see, I've got it written down. Here it is, Katy Anderson. According to Anderson, Wendy was supposed to meet a boy by the name of Aaron Livingston after orchestra practice, around five-thirty last night. Katy last saw Wendy as they were leaving practice."

"Yeah, the Chief mentioned a student by the name of Aaron as someone we needed to talk to," says Baker.

"Aaron Livingston?" repeats Walker. "Didn't that ring we found in the grass have the initials of A.L.? Let me see that ring again."

Sure enough, the gold ring found at the scene has the initials A.L. engraved on the top.

"I think we may have our first lead," Baker says.

"I'm going back out to coordinate the neighborhood canvass to see if anyone saw anything suspicious last night," Sgt. Thomas says as he walks out of the office.

Just then, Chief Cindy Carson walks in for an update. Walker explains to her the new information they've received and shows her the plastic bag containing the gold ring.

"Okay then, let's get someone to track down this Aaron Livingston kid," says Carson.

"I'll work on that," says Baker. "Don is leaving for the autopsy at three-thirty."

Several minutes later, Officer Linda Ivey walks into the office with more detailed information. She had located and interviewed Wendy's friend, Katy Anderson. Officer Ivey tells the detectives that according to Anderson, Wendy had been texting with some secret admirer for a week or so. Initially, the texts were anonymous, but eventually, they found out it was Aaron Livingston doing the texting. The texts were mostly about how he admired Wendy. He admitted to being shy around girls and wanted to meet her privately just to talk. Wendy was intrigued and flattered. Wendy knew who Aaron was and while she had not socialized with him, she somewhat knew him from a couple of classes they had together. He was studious like her and seemed like a nice guy. She even thought he was kind of cute. After a series of exchanges, Aaron asked Wendy to meet him Thursday after school. Aaron had also texted he had found her yellow scarf, which had been Wendy's favorite scarf. Apparently, Wendy had lost the scarf on Tuesday of this week. Wendy suspected the scarf had been stolen from the cafeteria, but once Aaron said he found it, she figured it must have just been misplaced. Not only did Wendy want to get her scarf back, but she was curious to talk to Aaron in person. Maybe even a bit excited.

Wendy texted Aaron that she had orchestra practice on Thursday night, and it would probably be a long one, as they were getting ready for an upcoming concert. She could meet him around five-thirty. Aaron agreed, suggesting they meet out back beyond the courtyard near the creek and he would walk her home from there. Wendy typically took this path home anyway as it was shorter than going out the front of the school and walking back around in the direction of her home, so it seemed like a good place to meet. At that time of night, it would also give them some privacy.

Katy was a bit concerned given it would be getting dark by then, but certainly didn't consider a shy introvert like Aaron to be any danger. Katy now wishes she would have gone out back with Wendy. Katy now suspects Aaron had indeed stolen the scarf as a means to get her to meet with him.

Thursday, November 5th

Brad finds Aaron sitting at his usual spot in the cafeteria with Timmy Goodman and Harold Best. They are just finishing up their lunch.

"Been thinking about my offer, Aaron boy?" says Brad as he slaps Aaron on the back.

"Not really," replies Aaron.

"Why the hell not? You know how good I am with getting girls and I hate to see you go your whole four years of high school without ever meeting a girl, especially one who likes you."

Aaron looks up at Brad, "What do you mean, likes me?"

"Well, I was just talking to her about you; you've seen me talk to her before, right?"

"Sure, you seem to be over there a lot," says Aaron, referring to the number of times he's seen Brad stop at whatever cafeteria table Wendy is sitting at.

"Damn right!" Brad exclaims. "And she has told me she thinks you are a nice guy. So why don't you go over there and start a conversation, ask her out?" he says, knowing Aaron would do no such thing.

Aaron looks down at the table, "I'm not very comfortable around girls like you are Brad."

"I know that numb nuts, so let me help you set it up." Brad smiles. "Just get to know each other. I'll help you start a texting conversation, and then if it goes well, set up a meet. Let me see your phone."

Brad reaches over and grabs Aaron's phone off the table in front of him.

"Hey!" Aaron protests.

Brad holds up his hand, "I've got this."

Timmy and Harold watch in stunned silence. They are not sure how this is going to work, but it is somewhat interesting. Neither of them has ever dated and could use a few tips as well.

"We are going to text her a message," says Brad.

"Whaaaat?" Aaron says with a wide-eyed look of fear.

"Don't worry, she doesn't have you in her contacts list, so she won't even know who it's from," Brad assures him. "At least not right now anyway."

Early last year, Brad had exchanged phone numbers with Wendy before she knew who he was or what he was like. He has kept her number in his phone ever since. Brad types a message into Aaron's phone and sends it to Wendy.

Wendy, I've seen you around and wanted you to know I think you have a wonderful personality. I'm not good at talking to girls yet, that's why I'm texting you this.

Brad hits send and then shows Aaron the message.

Aaron starts to feel his face flush. "I can't believe you sent that," Aaron says in a quiet voice.

Based on his past conversations with Wendy, Brad suspects Wendy may ignore a text that talks about how beautiful she is. But, addressing her personality might get a response, as he knows personality is more important to Wendy than good looks.

"I'll check in with you tomorrow," Brad says as he walks away.

"Can you believe that?" Harold exclaims. "What are you going to do?"

"If she finds out this came from me, or at least thinks it did, I'll be so embarrassed," responds Aaron.

"Well," laughs Timmy, "at least you've started a conversation with a girl."

Ding-Ding. Wendy picks up her phone to check the new message that just arrived.

"Huh?" *who's this from?* she asks herself. At first, she thinks it might be from that obnoxious Brad McGivens. But then she remembers she still has his number in her contacts from last year, so his name would have popped up. Besides, it is not something he would say. Since when does he care about personality? She looks around the cafeteria trying to see if anyone is looking at her. After a few moments, she texts back.

Who is this? No one responds.

Friday, November 6th

On Friday, Wendy and Katy are still talking about the secret text Wendy had received the day before. Must have been a prank of some sort they believe, as no further messages have been received. Still, it is on Wendy's mind most of the morning. She finds it hard to concentrate in class, thinking about who might have sent the mysterious message.

At 12:15 pm, as is their normal routine, Wendy and Katy meet in the cafeteria to visit and get something to eat. Normally, they would talk about schoolwork, excitement about the upcoming concert, what to do on the weekend, or perhaps any significant news of the day. On this particular day, all they can talk about is the secret text. Why has there been no response back? Has this just been some joke?

Aaron, Harold, and Timmy are also in the cafeteria sitting at their usual table in the corner at the far north end. They find it is quieter there and most people leave them alone, allowing them to talk chess strategy or play games on their Ipads. It isn't long before Brad McGivens comes strolling through the cafeteria.

"Hi ladies, anyone ready to go out this weekend," Brad asks as he passes the table of Wendy and Katy.

Both girls just roll their eyes.

Brad gets to Aaron's table and sits down across from Aaron, next to Timmy.

"So?" asks Brad. "Did you get a response?"

Aaron hands Brad his phone.

"Well, that's good, at least she is interested," states Brad. "Let's see what we can do today."

"I'm not sure about this Brad," says Aaron with a worried look.

"Trust me," Brad quips back.

Brad types a new text message. *Thank you for responding. I'm too shy to reveal who I am right now, but wanted you to know I admire how you play the violin and how nice you seem to be to everyone. I also find you attractive and would like to get to know you better.* He then hits send.

"This is already embarrassing," Aaron protests.

"Well why don't you go over there, sit right down and ask her out then?" retorts Brad.

"That would be awkward for me," says Aaron.

"Exactly numb nuts," sighs Brad. "This is why I'm helping you. If she wasn't interested, she wouldn't have even asked who you were."

Aaron didn't like being called numb nuts, but he isn't going to challenge Brad either. Besides, he kind of likes the idea that he is communicating with a girl, even though it isn't him sending the texts.

Aaron's phone buzzes with a new text message. *Thank you for the kind words. Really would like to know who you are.*

"See, we have her interest," nods Brad. "Now, you want to stop?"

Aaron thinks about it for a minute. "No," he says. While Aaron thinks it will be embarrassing once Wendy finds out who he is and rejects him, he is feeling an excitement he hasn't experienced before. Maybe they can have a "texting" relationship?

Brad takes the phone again and types another message. *In good time. For now, let's just keep it mysterious. Your secret admirer* ☺

After receiving the text, Wendy and Katy look around the cafeteria to see if they can see anyone who might be doing the texting. Is anyone looking at her? A couple of people glance their way, but nothing seems obvious. Who knows if the person is even in the cafeteria, but strangely, all the texts have come when they happen to be there.

Wendy can feel a sense of mystery and excitement. She isn't sure what she is getting into, but it is something different from the norm. She isn't so great at conversing with boys either, so this isn't so bad. Still, she wants to know who this person is and has some concern someone is just pranking her, which could turn out to be very embarrassing.

That night, the Lincoln Wildcats complete their final regular-season football game by defeating the Westridge Panthers 38 to 7 to finish undefeated (10-0) and on top in their division.

McGivens ran the ball 24 times for 214 yards and caught 3 passes for another 63 yards, finishing with 277 total yards. Their next game will be the following Saturday, November 14th, for the Tri-county League Championship against another powerhouse, Ford High School.

Afterward, McGivens and about half his teammates go to the usual after-game party in the corn field behind the country home owned by quarterback Chance Mahoney's parents. The Mahoney family hosts the bonfire party after most games, weather permitting. So long as things do not get too much out of hand, the Mahoney's let the boys and their girlfriends have their fun. *It would sure be nice if Wendy was here with me,* thinks Brad.

Saturday, November 7th

It is about 11:00 am and Aaron is working on his home computer finishing a paper for his history class when his phone rings.

"Hello," answers Aaron.

"Hey, it's me," Brad responds. "Meet me at Johnson's Café in thirty minutes."

"Why? I'm busy," says Aaron.

"Because we have to follow-up on your text," explains Brad. "You can't go all weekend without sending a message. You must cultivate these things. You can't just leave a girl hangin'. You're bad at this stuff, aren't you?"

"I, uh.....can't we wait till Monday?" Aaron asks.

"Hey, this girl likes you, so don't blow it," Brad says in an irritated voice. "I'm going out of my way to help you, so meet me at the café. It won't take long."

Aaron has never been this close to maybe having a girlfriend, and if she does like him, he doesn't want to blow it.

"Okay," says Aaron, "see you in thirty minutes."

Johnson's Café is about three blocks from the high school. It is a well-maintained café specializing in typical burgers, sandwiches, salads, meatloaf, and other comfort foods. It also has a good selection of ice cream and desserts. A little convenience store is attached on the west side and four gas pumps are out front. It has 20 tables that can seat 80 people. The café serves the neighborhood, and a number of high school students walk the three blocks for lunch every day, while others drop by after school for a soda or ice cream. Inside, the walls are decorated with Lincoln Wildcat posters and memorabilia from the baseball, basketball, and football teams.

Aaron drives his silver 2014 Toyota RAV4 to the café, arriving around 11:35 am. Brad is already inside seated at a table with two cokes in front of him. When Aaron walks in, Brad waves him over.

"Here, this one's for you," says Brad, as he moves one of the cokes in front of Aaron.

"Thank you," replies Aaron.

"Now give me your cell phone," demands Brad.

Aaron hands it over and Brad starts typing a text message. *Hi Wendy, this is your secret admirer. I could not stop thinking about you last night. The more I know about you, the more I see what a nice person you are. If I wasn't so shy around girls, I would call you right now so we could talk. I've never even had a girlfriend. It may take me some time, but please don't give up on me. If you don't want me to text anymore, I will stop.*

"Brad," Aaron says. "Why did you ask her if she wanted me to stop?"

"Because," answers Brad, "it's kind of creepy to be texting her anonymously and you don't want to scare her. You gave her an option to stop if she wants to. This will make her more at ease."

This makes sense, Aaron thinks. *Brad does seem to know a lot about how to talk to girls. I would never know how to do this like he does. But will it work?*

Brad and Aaron sit for a bit drinking their cokes waiting for a response. Brad starts talking about the football game from the previous night and how well he did, sharing statistics on his accomplishments. This of course bores Aaron to death and he has no idea about most of what Brad is talking about. His mind starts to drift off when his phone buzzes. Wendy has responded.

Aaron and Brad read the text. *I've been thinking about you as well and trying to figure out who you are. I've never really had a boyfriend, so don't feel embarrassed. We can just text for now if that is more comfortable for you.*

"See," says Brad. "She is interested in you as well. I told you I know how to get girls. We will have to set a meetup next week."

"I'm not sure I'm ready for that," Aaron responds.

"You will be by then," Brad assures him.

Brad then sends another message from Aaron's phone. *I am busy most of this weekend, but will text you again next week.*

Okay, look forward to it, responds Wendy.

Friday, November 13th, 5:00 pm

Detective Baker is now working with Officer Linda Ivey in gathering information on Lincoln High student Aaron Livingston. Ivey has found that Livingston is known as a good student with outstanding grades. He is also known as a shy kid, and while he does not seem to have many friends, two close friends appear to be Timmy Goodman and Harold Best. Baker conducts a criminal history on Aaron Livingston and finds no record of him ever being in any legal trouble. And according to Principal Jenkins, Aaron has no disciplinary record at the high school. Baker obtains Livingston's home address and learns that he lives with his mom on West Emory Street. Two vehicles are listed to Megan Livingston at that address. One, a 2018 white Ford Explorer, and a second, a 2014 silver Toyota RAV4.

"We will need to talk to this Aaron kid soon," says Baker. "He may be the last one to see Wendy alive and is certainly a person of interest right now."

"I could go pick him up right now if you'd like?" asks Officer Ivey.

Baker gives it some thought, but believes it is still too early. He wants to get the autopsy results and maybe some information from Wendy's cell phone before contacting Aaron. He knows the more information they have, the better.

"No, let's wait until we get more information on how she died, and maybe we can get something off her phone as well," replies Baker. "Document everything you've told me in your report."

By now, the death of Wendy Spire is the top story on all the local news channels. Students and parents have been interviewed on TV expressing sorrow, anger, and disbelief in how this could happen in a community like Rockville.

Chief Carson walks into the office, "What's the latest Steve? I've got the press, parents, and school administrators calling me non-stop."

"Should have something from the autopsy any time now," Steve responds. "And we have more information about this

Aaron Livingston, who may be the last person to have seen her, and maybe the one who killed her. But, too early to know right now."

"Hey Steve!" shouts Officer Ivey. "Just got a call from Sgt. Thomas. He says the neighborhood canvass found a person who lives across the street from the school who saw several vehicles parked on the northeast end in front of the school. One of them caught his attention as it had someone in it, but he couldn't tell who it was."

"Can he describe the car?" asks the detective.

"Yeah, said it looked like a silver RAV4."

Monday, November 9th

Wendy has shared her texts from the weekend with Katy Anderson. Katy sees the interest Wendy has developed in this mysterious secret admirer and hopes this is not some cruel joke being played on her friend. As is typical, Katy meets Wendy in the cafeteria on their lunch break. Wendy has not received any texts since Saturday and is concerned that maybe the texts have stopped.

"I'm not sure what to think," ponders Wendy. "Seems like I would have gotten something by now."

"Why don't you text him?" Katy asks.

Aaron is in his usual spot in the cafeteria corner with Timmy and Harold, but he has not seen Brad today. Aaron glances in the direction of Wendy, wondering if she has any idea the texts have come from him. "Where is Brad?" Aaron wonders aloud.

"Maybe he was just pranking you," Harold says. "You could just text her yourself."

"I would have no idea what to say," Aaron sighs.

Just then, his phone buzzes. *Where have you been? Talk to me.*

Wendy has texted him. Aaron feels his face flush, as he senses excitement and anxiety at the same time. How should he respond? If he texts her back now, what if she sees him and comes over to confront him? That would be so embarrassing. He doesn't know what to say. Of course, neither Timmy nor Harold is any help in suggesting what he should say. He decides to let it go unanswered.

Later that afternoon, Brad approaches Aaron in the hallway between classes. "How's it going kid?"

"Where were you?" asks Aaron. "She texted me today at lunch and I didn't know what to say. You're just setting me up."

"Nooooo," says Brad. "I was busy, besides, you can't only text her at lunch hour. Won't take her long to figure out it is you hiding in the corner texting her. What did she say?"

Aaron hands his phone to Brad.

"Okay, this is good. She wants you to keep texting. See? You just have to trust me."

Brad starts typing a new text. *Sorry, I have been busy. Thx for the text. Hope you had a good weekend. Looking forward to your concert. Like your music. Maybe we can meet to talk sometime soon.*

"There, that should do it," says Brad.

Aaron is relieved to have Brad's help, but still not sure whether Brad's efforts are genuine or if he is being set up for disappointment and humiliation. He wishes he had the confidence of Brad.

Brad tells Aaron, "Now ask her if she likes Taylor Swift's music."

"Huh?"

"I know she likes Taylor Swift. It will give you something in common."

For the first time, Aaron types his own text to Wendy. She responds in minutes, expressing surprise he has heard her play the violin and that she does in fact like Taylor Swift.

"Now tell her you will text again tomorrow afternoon," Brad tells Aaron. "I will meet you here tomorrow at the same time to help you out."

Tuesday, November 10th

As promised, Brad meets Aaron on Tuesday afternoon and helps Aaron send additional texts to Wendy. They text back and forth about her upcoming orchestra concert, Aaron's interest in seeing her play, Wendy's favorite color (yellow), and their favorite foods.

Wendy is starting to feel an attraction to this mysterious secret admirer. She knows it is strange not to know who this person is, but there just seems to be a connection she can't explain. She still has some anxiety over being played for a fool, but it has also provided her some unexpected thrill to have this secret admirer. After all, he seems like a nice person and they have some of the same interests. Plus, he has promised to soon reveal his identity and set a meetup to talk in person. She can hardly wait.

Friday, November 13th, 5:46 pm

Detective Baker receives a call from the Sheriff's Computer Forensic Analyst. He learns that a preliminary examination of Wendy Spire's cell phone revealed a string of texts over the past week with another student. The texts were initially anonymous, only identified as a "secret admirer," but eventually revealed to be sent by Aaron Livingston. The texts talked of a meeting behind the school Thursday evening, the night of Wendy's death. According to the analyst, Livingston appears to be obsessed with Wendy. *This is not looking good for Livingston,* thinks Baker.

At 6:05 pm, Detective Walker returns to the office with the preliminary results from the autopsy. The Coroner's finding is that Wendy had been killed from strangulation. This was evidenced by redness and bruising about the neck area, vertical scratches on the neck, damaged cartilage, a broken hyoid bone (a U-shaped bone just under the tongue), and some petechial hemorrhaging (pinpoint rupturing of capillaries in the skin). The Coroner was impressed by the amount of damage to Wendy's neck. The Coroner told Walker it took a lot of force to cause this much damage to the neck. Wendy's neck was swabbed, and her nails scraped for potential DNA. There was no evidence of sexual assault. Toxicology and DNA samples were driven to the closest state crime lab in Grand Rapids by one of Rockville's patrol officers. Walker had called and asked to have someone stay at the lab after hours to accept the evidence so that they would have it to analyze first thing Monday morning. Walker requested testing as soon as possible, given the situation in Rockville. The lab administrator said he would have someone get on it first thing Monday.

Baker shares the texting information obtained from Wendy's cell phone. "It is looking like this Livingston kid is a person of interest."

"Hell," says Walker, "I'd call him a suspect at this point. We've got witnesses who have said he was meeting her last night, we find texts from him to Wendy, which from the sound of it he was obsessed with her, and we find a ring at the scene engraved with A.L."

"Yeah," Baker responds. "And his mom owns a silver Toyota RAV4. A car of that description was seen by a neighbor parked in front of the school on Locust."

"Let's put an officer outside his home to maintain surveillance," suggests Walker. "We need to keep tabs on him and that silver Toyota until we can search the car and have a chat with Mr. Livingston."

"I'll have an officer assigned," says Baker. He realizes things are quickly coming together and it will be a late night. His next task is to start working on a search warrant for the silver RAV4 and Livingston's cell phone. "We better get some coffee brewing."

Wednesday, November 11th

Brad's plan seems to be working. Based on her texts, it appears Wendy is enjoying this secret admirer relationship he has orchestrated with Aaron. *If I can get her to agree to a meetup with Aaron, I will have successfully won her over,* thinks Brad. It doesn't matter that Wendy doesn't know he is the writer of the texts. It still gives him pleasure that he can win her over with his words. At the same time, it angers him to know that if Wendy had only given him a chance, he could have used the same approach he is using through Aaron.

At noon, Brad walks through the cafeteria and spots Wendy sitting with Katy at their usual table. He approaches them from behind, "How are you fine ladies doing today?"

"Same as always Brad, just fine," responds Katy, as she rolls her eyes.

"You gals coming to the football game Saturday?" asks Brad. "You know it's for the league championship, right? It would give me more motivation if I knew you were there Wendy."

"You know I'm not interested in football," sighs Wendy. "And I'm not interested in you either, so I would appreciate it if you would just leave us alone Brad."

Brad just shakes his head. *Little do you know just how interested you are in me, you just don't know it yet, you bitch,* Brad says to himself. "Okay ladies, you don't know what you are missing."

As Brad starts to leave, he slides Wendy's yellow scarf off the back of her chair in a delicate sweep of his hand and slides it under his open jacket. Neither Wendy nor Katy notice. Brad swiftly walks away without saying another word.

When Wendy gets up to leave, she finds her scarf missing. "Where did my scarf go?"

"I'm not sure, did you have it when you came in here?" asks Katy.

"I thought for sure I did. Maybe someone took it."

"I didn't see anyone take your scarf. Maybe you left it in class or dropped it in the hall somewhere?" suggests Katy.

"I don't know, I thought for sure I carried it here with me. I hope no one took it, that is my favorite scarf!" exclaims Wendy. "Do you think Brad took it?"

"Why would he do that?" asks Katy. "I didn't see him take it."

That afternoon Brad meets Aaron in the courtyard behind the school for some additional texting to Wendy. Aaron has come to enjoy the texting sessions as much as Brad. He knows he never could have developed this secret relationship with Wendy without his help. However, he does worry about what will happen once his identity becomes known and Brad is no longer at his side. Will he be able to converse with Wendy? Will she still be attracted to him once she finds out who he is? Will he be humiliated? Is this some major prank? Yet, Aaron's desire to have a girlfriend, especially one as nice and beautiful as Wendy keeps him from backing out.

"I have something for you, here," Brad states, as he hands Aaron Wendy's yellow scarf.

"What's this?" inquires Aaron.

"It's the scarf you found outside the cafeteria today. It belongs to Wendy"

"Huh?" Aaron looks bewildered.

"I think tomorrow it will be time to see if she will meet up with you. This scarf is some insurance that she will say yes when you tell her you found it and want to return it."

"How do you know it's hers?" asks Aaron.

"Because I took it numb nuts."

"You stole her scarf?" Aaron asks in astonishment.

"Noooooo......I borrowed it so that you would be able to return it to her."

"I don't know about this," protests Aaron.

"Hey," responds Brad, "you just need to trust me, this is going to work out well. Now let's send a couple more texts."

Brad then dictates a couple of texts to Wendy to initiate the idea of a meetup on Thursday after school; *I'm interested in talking with you in person. Would you be willing to meet with me after school on Thursday?*

Wendy quickly responds, *yes, but only if I know who you are.*

Brad has Aaron text; *I'll let you know soon and then you can decide.*

OK, responds Wendy.

After school lets out for the day, Wendy has not yet heard back from her secret admirer. She is full of anticipation as she anxiously awaits receiving another text. *Who could it be?* She keeps coming up with different possibilities, but doesn't know enough about this secret admirer to have any idea. Will she like him? Is he cute? Katy Anderson is just about as excited as Wendy is.

"So, today is the big day!" exclaims Katy as they walk home from school. "I'm anxious to know who he is."

"Not nearly as anxious as I am," Wendy responds. "I keep thinking about this secret guy and had trouble sleeping last night. It's scary, yet exciting at the same time. I just hope he is not some type of creep or this is a big joke."

"I don't think so," assures Katy. "He knows too much about you and seems interested in the things you like. Hopefully, we know soon enough."

About 5 minutes later, Wendy receives the text she has been waiting for. *Hi Wendy, this is Aaron Livingston, your secret admirer. Sorry I didn't tell you who I was earlier, but as I told you, I am shy around girls and this was a way I could approach you to talk. If you don't want anything else to do with me, I understand.*

"Aaron Livingston," Wendy murmurs to herself. She knows who he is from a couple of previous classes and of course from seeing him often in the corner of the cafeteria with his friends playing video games. *Well, he IS a nice guy,* Wendy believes. *At least as much as I know about him, and he cares about his studies as I do. He's also kind of cute in his shy way.*

Wendy quickly allows Katy to read the latest text. "What do you think?" Wendy asks.

"I think this is real," says Katy. "He is not the type of guy to pull a prank like this. I think he likes you and this was his way of getting to know you. He's a bit nerdy in a cute sort of way; and has always been nice from what I've seen."

"Yeah, I was thinking the same thing," Wendy adds. "We do have some things in common and he certainly doesn't present any danger. I'm going to agree to meet with him and see how it goes."

As they are talking, Wendy receives another text from Aaron. *By the way, I found a yellow scarf outside the cafeteria today. I think it might be yours.*

"He found my scarf!" exclaims Wendy. "Yesterday outside the cafeteria."

"That's weird," responds Katy, "we looked all over for it."

"Well, I don't think he stole it. He's not the type to do that sort of thing," says Wendy. "Even if it doesn't work out, I can at least get my scarf back."

"Do you want me to go with you?" asks Katy.

"No, I think we need some time to talk alone," Wendy says. "I don't want to embarrass him."

Wendy texts Aaron, *Thank you Aaron. I would like to meetup and talk. And yes, I believe you have my scarf. When and where?*

"Okay," Brad instructs Aaron. "Tell her to meet you tomorrow after school out back near the creek. You will walk her home."

"Why back there?" asks Aaron with a puzzled look.

"Because it will be private, won't be many, if any, people around so you won't have to worry about being embarrassed around others if it doesn't work out."

Makes sense to Aaron. He follows Brad's advice and asks Wendy to meet him after school tomorrow back by the creek and he will walk her home. She responds that she has orchestra practice after school, but can meet afterward at around 5:30. Aaron agrees, but he is still apprehensive about meeting her face to face.

"I'm not sure what to say to her Brad."

Don't worry," Brad assures Aaron, "I will go with you to introduce the two of you and if it goes bad, we can leave. But it won't; she likes you or she wouldn't be meeting with you. Pick me up at Johnson's Café at five-fifteen tomorrow. We'll drive over together. And don't forget to bring the scarf."

This plan somewhat eases Aaron's fear. Brad has gotten him this far; he can't quit now. "Okay, I'll see you then," says Aaron.

Aaron will be sure to avoid running into Wendy at school tomorrow. He will skip going to the cafeteria to meet his friends. Now that Wendy knows who he is, he does not want to face her in school. He wants to wait until 5:30 tomorrow night when they can be alone.

Friday, November 13th

At 6:30 pm, Chief Carson walks into the office to get the latest update. She has just returned after an interview for the 6:00 news and realizes there is a frenzy in the community over Wendy's death. Rumors are spreading throughout the community. The most common rumor is that Wendy Spire has been raped and beaten to death behind the school. The police have not officially released Wendy's name, but it has gotten out from school and family friends.

"Where are we at?" asks Chief Carson.

"We have a good suspect, Aaron Livingston," says Detective Walker. "We know the death was from strangulation, but no sexual assault. We've found text messages on the victim's phone from a secret admirer who eventually identified himself as Aaron Livingston. They had developed a texting relationship of some sort. He claimed to have a scarf belonging to her, but nothing like that was found at the scene. He may still have possession of it. Based on the text and statements from a couple of witnesses, Livingston and the victim agreed to meet last night after school. We also found a ring near the scene with the initials A.L., and a vehicle matching one owned by Mrs. Livingston was observed parked in the area around the time of the planned meeting. We have an officer watching the house. Lights are on, but no activity has been reported. We are currently working on a search warrant for the car. If we see him attempt to leave, or return home, our officer will stop him."

"Okay, it sounds like things are progressing well," Chief Carson responds with a pleased tone. "That's good, as the rumors are flying out there and the press is all over this. I'm sure this Livingston kid is well aware of what is going on. When will we be contacting this kid?"

"Probably tomorrow morning," chimes in Baker. "Unless we see him outside the house before then. We need to finish up this search warrant and get it before a judge sometime tonight. In the meantime, Patrol has been told not to let anyone in the car. We will get some rest tonight, then contact him and his mom first thing in the morning."

"And forensics?" asks the Chief.

"We have asked the lab to put a rush on testing what we've collected. They know this is a big deal for us here," says Walker. "Probably Monday at the earliest."

The Chief nods her approval as she starts to leave. "We need to make an arrest on this soon."

At 7:00 pm, Sgt. Thomas returns to the office with additional witness statements. He and his officers have been working all day talking with students and school teachers. Thomas describes for detectives the personality and demeanor of Aaron Livingston as a shy, introverted personality, and known as a good student who has never been in trouble. Two of Aaron's friends, Timmy Goodman and Harold Best confirmed that Aaron had been texting Wendy for several days with the help of Brad McGivens and that Aaron was going to finally meet Wendy on Thursday evening after school. He was nervous about being embarrassed or humiliated, but was excited about meeting her.

"Brad McGivens, is that the football player?" asks Walker.

"That's him," says Thomas.

"Did we talk to him yet?"

"No, by the time his name came up, he was nowhere around. After the school grounds were closed, football practice was moved to Whalen High School. The team has a big game tomorrow."

"No problem," says Walker. "We can contact him later. He probably has no idea he was helping set that girl up to be killed."

By 10:30 pm, the affidavit for the search warrant is completed. The on-call judge agrees to meet the detectives first thing Saturday morning to review the paperwork and issue the warrant. Walker and Baker agree to be back in the office by 7:00 am Saturday.

"It's been one hell of a Friday the thirteenth, that's for sure," states Walker as they walk out of the building.

Friday, November 13th

8:05 am

Aaron Livingston does not know school has been canceled because he does not get up for school. After what happened last night, there is no way he can go. He tossed and turned all night long worrying about what happened. How could he have been so stupid? When asked about going to school, Aaron tells his mother he is feeling ill and cannot go. Aaron does not want to talk to anyone, so he shuts off his phone. He just wants to be left alone. During the remainder of the morning, Aaron falls into and out of sleep several times.

12:10 pm

Shortly after noon, Aaron's mother, Megan Livingston, comes rushing into Aaron's bedroom. "Aaron! Get up! Do you know what happened last night at the school?" she shouts.

"Huh?" says Aaron. *How could she know?* he thinks.

"A girl was found dead behind the school! It's all over the news."

Aaron quickly sits up in bed, "WHAT!?" he exclaims.

"Yes, a girl has been found dead, apparently killed by someone. The school has been closed and police have cordoned everything off."

Oh my god, thinks Aaron.

"They aren't saying who it is right now," says his mom.

Aaron is stunned and does not know what to say. He can feel his body start to shake and it feels like his face is burning up.

"I'm going to keep watching the news and will let you know what they say."

Aaron just stares at his mom as wild thoughts start to swirl through his head.

"How are you feeling Aaron?"

"Not well, mom."

"Well, you keep resting and I'll get you something to eat. I'll also keep you updated on the news."

Aaron isn't very hungry, but he needs something to drink, as his mouth is very dry. Aaron's mom brings him some chicken noodle soup and hot tea. Aaron eats what he can, which isn't much.

Meanwhile, Brad McGivens is preparing for an afternoon practice at Whalen High School. The team is in final preparations for the league championship game on Saturday. No decision has yet been made on whether to play the game, given the circumstances, but the team has to prepare until they hear otherwise. McGivens isn't very much in the mood to practice, as he cannot get the death of Wendy Spire out of his mind. He keeps going over what happened in his mind and cannot help but think, *what went so wrong? How could this have happened?*

4:05 pm

By now, the news has identified the dead girl as Wendy Spire, a 16-year-old junior at Lincoln High School. The cause of death has not yet been reported. Aaron's mom, who has been following the news all day, rushes into Aaron's bedroom to tell him the latest news.

"Aaron, that girl who was killed was a Wendy Spire. Do you know her?"

Suddenly Aaron starts hyper-ventilating and can't find a way to respond.

"Aaron, are you okay? Aaron, what's wrong?"

Finally, Aaron is able to catch his breath. "I know that girl," says Aaron in a subdued voice.

"Oh, I'm so sorry Aaron, was she a good friend?" says his mom in a sympathetic voice.

Aaron's shoulders start to tremble as he sobs, "in a way, yes."

Megan Livingston continues to console her only son as she holds him in her arms. "We'll get through this together Aaron."

4:25 pm

Timmy Goodman and Harold Best have been trying to phone Aaron most of the day to no avail. Neither has heard from Aaron since school let out on Thursday, and neither has any idea what happened during the meetup with Wendy. After they hear Wendy has been killed, they become genuinely concerned. They can't believe Aaron killed Wendy, but since they haven't heard from him, they are both worried. Finally, Timmy decides to call Mrs. Livingston.

"Hello," answers Mrs. Livingston. "Oh, hi Timmy, how are you doing?"

"Fine," says Timmy. "But we are worried about Aaron. Is he okay?"

"He will be, but he is pretty upset right now. The girl who got killed last night was a friend and it has greatly bothered him. That, and he woke up not feeling well this morning."

"Yeah, we kind of knew her as well. It's really sad," responds Timmy. "Can I talk to Aaron?"

"He's upset right now and is resting. Why don't you call back later."

"Alright, did Aaron say anything more about her?"

"No, not really, just that she was a friend."

Timmy isn't comfortable telling Mrs. Livingston about Aaron's texting relationship with Wendy, as he doesn't know what Aaron wants to keep from his mom.

"Okay," says Timmy, "just tell him we are thinking about him and if he needs anything to give us a call."

"Yeah, I will Timmy. Thank you for calling."

Timmy turns to Harold and says, "It doesn't sound like Aaron's mom knows anything about all the texting or the meetup with Wendy."

"This doesn't sound good," Harold sighs.

"No, it doesn't," agrees Timmy.

Saturday, November 14th

Both detectives arrive at the office around 7:00 am to ramp up the second day of the investigation. Detective Baker checks with the night shift officers assigned to watch the Livingston home and it's reported that no one attempted to leave the residence. The house went dark at 10:42 pm Friday. Detective Baker grabs the search warrant affidavit and leaves to meet with the on-call judge.

"I will call when I have the warrant and will meet you at the Livingston home," says Baker.

"Sounds good," Walker shouts back, "I'll get the recorder and paperwork ready."

At 7:35 am, Baker calls Walker with the news that the judge has approved the warrant to search the suspect's vehicle and cell phone. Both detectives arrive at the West Emory Street address at about 7:50 am. It now appears as though several lights are on in the home.

At 7:52 am, the detectives are knocking on the front door. A woman's voice asks, "who is it?" through a Ring doorbell.

"Detectives Baker and Walker with the Rockville Police Department," announces Walker. A woman in her mid-40's with light brown short hair, wearing an oversized gray Michigan State t-shirt and mint green pajama pants answers the door. "What is the problem?" she asks.

"Are you Mrs. Livingston?" Walker asks.

"Yes."

"And do you have a son living here by the name of Aaron?"

"Why, yes I do."

"Ma'am, we're here investigating a homicide and would like to talk to you and your son," Walker advises.

"Oh my!" exclaims Mrs. Livingston, "Is this about Wendy Spire?"

"Yes Ma'am."

Mrs. Livingston invites them in and summons Aaron from his bedroom. Aaron comes into the living room looking disheveled in blue pajama pants and a wrinkled black t-shirt. His eyes are bloodshot, and it appears as though he has not had much sleep. Detective Baker explains the reason for being there and tells Aaron they know about the meeting with Wendy Thursday night. Mrs. Livingston is shocked to hear this news.

"Aaron, were you with that girl last night!" she asks.

"Kind of," Aaron says.

"Mrs. Livingston, please let us ask the questions," advises Walker. "What do you mean by "kind of?"

"I didn't kill her!" exclaims Aaron, "really, I didn't"

"Please answer the question, Aaron."

"I went there, but it was Brad who met her. I didn't see anything. He set a meetup with her and he went while I waited in the car. He came back and said she didn't want to see me, and then we left."

"Brad who?" asks Baker.

"Brad McGivens."

"So, Brad drove you to the school?" responds Baker.

"No, I drove. I picked him up at Johnson's"

"Johnson's Café?"

"Yes."

"What time did you pick him up?"

"About five-fifteen."

"What car were you driving?"

"I drive the RAV4."

"And wasn't it you who sent all these texts? Telling her how much you liked her and wanted to meet with her?" challenges Baker.

"Yes, I mean no, not really."

"Explain," says Baker.

"Well," Aaron explains, "Brad helped me with the texting. He started the texting, then later he started to dictate the texts to send her. He tried to set me up with Wendy, but in the end, she didn't want to see me. I was nervous about doing this and then she made me feel humiliated." Aaron starts to gently cry.

"So, this really upset you?" asks Walker.

"Of course, I was afraid that might happen. That's why I didn't go to school yesterday. I was too embarrassed and didn't want to see her or my friends," explains Aaron.

"Is that why you grabbed her around the neck?" Walker asks as he leans in closer to Aaron.

"No! I told you I wasn't there! I would never hurt Wendy or anyone else."

"But you just told us you went there with Brad," reminds Baker.

"Yes, but not to the meetup. I waited in the car."

"Aaron would never hurt anyone," interrupts Mrs. Livingston. "You need to talk to whoever Brad is."

"Oh, we will, and his story better match," advises Walker. He then holds up a small plastic bag containing a gold ring. "Is this your ring Aaron?"

"Yes."

"We found this near Wendy's body. Can you explain that?"

"Brad said I should give it to her as a show of sincerity or something like that."

"So, you gave her the ring Thursday night near the creek, right?" asks Walker.

"No, no, Brad must have given it to her," says Aaron in frustration.

"How could he have given her your ring Aaron?"

"I don't, I don't know…..maybe….maybe he took it with him," stutters Aaron.

"And how could he have done that?"

"I told you I don't know; it was in my car, maybe he took it." Aaron guesses.

"Your story is sounding pretty far-fetched Aaron," says Walker.

"Okay," interrupts Baker, "You are telling us you sent all these texts to Wendy and set up a meeting with the help of Brad McGivens. There were a lot of texts Aaron. Then you drove to the school to meet Wendy Thursday night and Brad was with you, and it was him, not you, who went to meet Wendy while you waited in the car. This was after you spent over a week trying to get her to meet with you. You don't know what happened to Wendy, but your ring was at the scene. How does this make sense Aaron?"

"I'm telling the truth!" exclaims Aaron. "It was Brad who met her, not me."

"Did you ask Brad what happened?" inquires Baker.

"He just came back, got in the car, and said she decided not to see me. It was embarrassing, and I just wanted to go home."

"Tell us what happened to Wendy's shoe."

"I don't know what you are talking about."

"She was missing a shoe, Aaron. I doubt she went to school with one shoe on."

"Will we find the shoe in your car Aaron?" asks Walker.

"No, of course not," replies Aaron.

"And the yellow scarf, you texted that you had her yellow scarf, is that true?"

"I did," answers Aaron, "Brad gave it to me to give to Wendy."

"Wait a minute," says Walker, "I thought you texted that you found it?"

"Yeah, but Brad told me to say that."

"Where is the scarf now?"

"I'm not sure, I think Brad may still have it."

"This is a wild story you're telling us, Aaron. I hope Brad can confirm all this," warns Baker.

"Alright detectives," Mrs. Livingston interrupts, "I think Aaron has told you all he knows, and he is obviously terribly upset over all this. He didn't kill that girl. I know my son and he would never do anything like that! You need to talk to this Brad fellow."

"We will," Walker again assures her, "and thank you for answering our questions Aaron. Now, we have search warrants for Aaron's cell phone and the Toyota RAV4 parked out front. Here are the warrants. Aaron, you need to give us your cell phone now and Mrs. Livingston, we are going to tow your vehicle to the police department for a search and processing."

The detectives collect and bag Aaron's cell phone and a tow truck takes the silver Toyota RAV4 to the police department. The detectives give both Aaron and his mother their business cards and tell them to call if they have or remember anything else.

As they are walking back to their cars, Baker asks Walker, "what do you think Don?"

"His story sounds too incredible to be true. And did you see how nervous he was? I think he was so embarrassed and humiliated by Wendy's rejection he just lost it."

By 9:20 am, both detectives are back at the station searching the suspect vehicle. On the floorboard of the back seat, the detectives find a pair of black leather gloves and a female's yellow scarf.

"Well look at this Don," says Baker as he holds up a light blue, New Balance right foot tennis shoe he finds wrapped in the yellow scarf.

"That could be the smoking gun right there," responds Walker. "I'll bet he took it as a trophy to remember her by."

A cursory search of Aaron's cell phone confirms that the messages to Wendy Spire had come from his phone. There is no question Aaron had suggested and agreed to a meeting with Wendy Thursday night behind the school.

"Okay," says Baker, "let's get these items to the lab today for processing early next week. I'll bet we find the victim's DNA on these black gloves."

By the time the detectives finish processing the vehicle and getting evidence labeled and bagged, it is almost noon. Walker gives the Chief a call to update her on the case.

"The Chief is pleased with our progress on the case," says Walker. "I get the impression she would like to see Livingston arrested as soon as possible to bring some calm to the community. But she also agrees we need to first talk to McGivens."

"Yeah, let's wrap it up here and go find McGivens," replies Baker.

The administrations of both Lincoln and Ford high schools decide to proceed with the championship game on Saturday night. The Michigan High School Athletic Association allowed the school administrators to make the decision, but did advise them that logistically, the high school playoffs cannot be postponed the following week. Both schools have hopes of making the state playoffs with a win this Saturday, thus it is important to play the game. The game will be played at 6:00 this evening. Brad is resting at home in preparation for the game when someone rings the doorbell at 1:10 pm.

Brad lives with his two parents, Mike and Brenda McGivens, in a two-story Tudor-style brick home located in the older part of Rockville. The neighborhood is considered a wealthier, attractive area of town after the gentrification process over the last 15 years. The inside of the home is nicely decorated in a contemporary style with a large kitchen, dining room, and large open living room. The upstairs has been remodeled, combining three bedrooms into a huge master suite with a large master bath and walk-in closet, an office for Mr. McGivens, and a large library/reading/TV room. Brad's bedroom is located on the main floor next to one of two downstairs bathrooms. The backyard has a large, covered patio bordering a kidney-shaped swimming pool.

Brenda McGivens is a nurse at the local hospital and Mike McGivens owns and operates the popular McGivens Farm Equipment and Supply on the north side of town. This store provides farming goods and supplies for most of the farmers within a three-county area, as well as a healthy income for the McGivens family. Brad is the only child for Mike and Brenda, and they provide all they can for him. They are also immensely proud of Brad's athletic skills and attend every game they can. They serve as athletic boosters for both the baseball and football teams. Brad probably gets his athletic skills from both parents, as they were both involved in athletics in high school. However, his mom Brenda has the most ability, as she played women's basketball at Ferris State College and was the team's leading scorer her last two seasons. Both parents are looking forward to Saturday's playoff game. Brenda is home with Brad, while Mike is traveling back from a farming equipment conference in Des Moines, Iowa. He will be back in time for the game.

Mrs. McGivens answers the door and is surprised when Baker and Walker introduce themselves as detectives and wish to talk to Brad.

"What is this about?" she asks.

"We would like to talk to Brad to find out what he knows about Wendy Spire and her death," replies Baker.

"He knows nothing about her death. How would he know anything about that? And this is a bad time, he has an important game to get ready for, or haven't you heard?"

"We know, Mrs. McGivens," answers Baker. "However, this is important as well, and we have information that Brad is a friend of the person who may have killed Wendy, and Brad may have even helped set them up for a meeting."

"I'm sure he had nothing to do with that," Mrs. McGivens states. "Okay, ask your silly questions and make it quick, he needs to mentally prepare for tonight."

Baker gives a quick glance toward Walker as if to say, *can you believe this?* "We'll be as fast as we can, thank you."

When asked about his relationship with Aaron and Wendy, Brad admits that yes, he was helping Aaron text Wendy. He explains that Aaron was too shy to approach girls himself and had wanted to get to know Wendy, but didn't know how to go about it. Brad agreed to help Aaron with his texting. The idea of a meeting after school was Aaron's idea. Brad denies any knowledge of Wendy's death until he heard about it on Friday. He never thought Aaron would harm Wendy.

"Brad," says Baker, "Aaron told us you went with him to meet Wendy and to make the introduction."

"No, that's not true," Brad answers. "I only helped with some texting and ideas on how to talk to Wendy. I knew he was meeting with her, but I wasn't there."

"Not only were you there, but you left Aaron in the car and went to see Wendy yourself," Baker retorts.

"Not at all, I came home after practice and was here the rest of the night."

"That's true," chimes in Mrs. McGivens. "He came home from practice at about four-thirty, ate some dinner, then stayed in his room doing some schoolwork and listening to music."

"What do you know about a yellow scarf?" asks Walker.

"I don't know anything about a yellow scarf, why?"

"Did you ever talk to Wendy yourself?" Walker continues.

"Sure, I would see her from time to time and talk a bit."

"Some of her friends say you were harassing her."

"No," then Brad pauses for a bit, "in a teasing way, sometimes I would ask her to go out with me, but I never harassed her about it. It was all friendly."

"Do you know anything about a gold ring Aaron had?" asks Walker.

"He showed me a ring with his initials and said he wanted to give it to Wendy Thursday night," says Brad. "Look, if I had known he was going to harm Wendy in any way, I would not have helped him with the texts. I feel awful about this. She was my friend too."

"Did you go to Johnson's Café Thursday night?" Walker continues.

"Detectives!" interrupts Mrs. McGivens, "he has already told you he was not involved, and I've told you he was home all night, so he could not have had anything to do with Wendy's death. Now, is that all?"

Walker looks back at Brad, "I notice a fairly good scratch on your left cheek Brad. Mind telling me how you got that?"

"Uh, yeah, that was from practice on Thursday. Someone got his hand in my mask and scratched my face. No big deal," answers Brad.

"One more thing," Baker states, "we need to examine your cell phone Brad. We need to know what, if any, texts you sent to Wendy or Aaron. You can give us permission, or we can get a search warrant if needed."

Mrs. McGivens begins to object, but Brad interrupts, "It's okay mom, they can look at it. There's nothing on it." Brad then hands Baker his cell phone.

"We'll get this back to you as soon as possible," assures Baker.

On the way back to the station, Walker states, "his story is a lot different than Aaron's."

"I agree," sighs Baker. "And he does have a pretty good alibi, unless his mom is lying through her teeth."

Back at the station, Baker goes through Brad's cell phone messages and phone calls. He confirms Brad was truthful about not sending any texts or making any calls to Wendy's phone, but does find a couple of calls between Brad and Aaron. This does not seem unusual, given that both Brad and Aaron admit to working together on the texting to Wendy.

After about 30 minutes of reviewing notes, Walker gets a call from Officer Ivey. She had been sent to the Spire home with a photo of the yellow scarf found in Livingston's car. She advises Walker that all three family members identified the scarf as the one belonging to Wendy.

Baker and Walker review what they have and believe they now have probable cause to arrest Livingston for the murder of Wendy Spire. With nothing tying Brad to the crime, and with his mother providing a solid alibi, there is no reason to believe Aaron's story pointing the finger at Brad. They meet with Chief Carson to review the case.

"It sure looks like probable cause to me," agrees Carson. "And with the media frenzy and fear in this town right now, it would be nice if we could put people at ease with an arrest. Do we have any other theories?"

"Only the story Aaron told about McGivens, but that didn't pan out," says Walker. "We have no evidence that Brad was there other than Aaron saying he was, and Mrs. McGivens swears he was home all evening. He may have inadvertently helped set that poor girl up for her death."

Baker chimes in, "not only that, but we found Wendy's yellow scarf and tennis shoe in Livingston's car. Aaron lied to us about both items, telling us he didn't know anything about the shoe or where the scarf was. Yet, we found both in his car."

"Okay, I think we need to get him in custody before anything else happens. It won't be long before his name leaks out and then all hell will break loose," advises the Chief.

Saturday, November 14th 5:30 pm

Detectives Baker and Walker are at the door of the Livingston home. Mrs. Livingston answers the door.

"Mrs. Livingston, I'm sorry to tell you we have a warrant to place Aaron under arrest for the murder of Wendy Spire," announces Baker.

"Why?" she asks, "he told you what happened. He did not kill that girl."

"We have evidence that ties him to the crime ma'am. We need to see Aaron now."

Aaron can overhear the conversation and walks to the door. He is crying and quietly says, "I didn't kill Wendy, please believe me."

"Aaron, you're under arrest for the murder of Wendy Spire," advises Baker. He then places Aaron in handcuffs and leads him out the door to a waiting patrol car. Aaron is first taken to the police station where he is fingerprinted, and his mouth swabbed for DNA. He is then taken to the juvenile detention center.

Thirty minutes after Aaron's arrest, Brad McGivens is with the football team getting ready for the kickoff of the championship game against Ford High School. A win will send them to the state playoffs. However, Brad is having trouble focusing on the game. He has been a nervous wreck since talking with the detectives earlier in the day. Now, he can't seem to get Wendy's murder off his mind. He worries the detectives still think he was somehow involved. He is not the only one having trouble focusing on the game. Wendy's death created a pall among the students that has carried over to the team. They do not perform well.

Brad has the worst game of his junior and senior years, rushing for only 68 yards and catching 2 passes for another 22 yards. He drops the 4 other passes thrown his way. The Lincoln Wildcats end up losing the championship game by a score of 28-14. They will not be going to the state playoffs.

Thursday, November 12th

At 5:00 pm, Aaron leaves his home to go pick up Brad at Johnson's Café. He is both nervous and excited over finally meeting and talking to Wendy. His fear is probably greater than excitement at this point. *Will she even show up,?* he wonders. *Is Brad actually going to help introduce me?* Aaron arrives at Johnson's Café at about 5:10 pm and parks on the south side of the building. He waits for Brad.

At about the same time, Brad is at home having just finished some dinner. He tells his mom he is tired and has some schoolwork to do, game plans to review, and that he's going to his bedroom to listen to music while getting his work done. "Okay, if I don't see you, have a good night," she tells him.

Brad retreats to his bedroom and cranks up some music, loud enough for his mom to hear. He then opens the bedroom window and climbs out, as he has done before when wanting to leave without his parents knowing. It is cold outside, so he takes his winter jacket and black leather gloves to keep himself warm for the walk. If he walks quickly, it will only take him about 15 minutes to get to Johnson's Café.

It is now 5:15 pm and Brad is not there. Aaron begins to believe Brad is not coming. Then, suddenly there is a tapping on the passenger window. "Unlock the door," says Brad. Brad then hops into the front passenger seat.

"You ready for your big night?" Brad asks.

"I guess, as ready as I will ever be."

"Good, I see you have the scarf. Let's go then!"

As Aaron drives toward the school, Brad sees Aaron's ring on the console of the car. "Is this yours?" Brad asks as he holds and admires the ring.

"Yes," says Aaron. "It used to be my Dad's, but I kept it after he died."

"A.L., was his name Aaron too?" Brad inquires.

"No, his name was Allen, so our initials are the same. I sometimes wear it to remind me of my Dad."

"This might be good to give to her, show how sincere you are." Brad then slips the ring into his coat pocket without Aaron noticing.

They arrive at the school at 5:26 pm. Aaron parks the car on Locust street on the northeast side of the school. Brad tells Aaron to wait in the car while he checks to make sure Wendy shows up.

"Shouldn't I go with you?" asks Aaron.

"No," says Brad. "Let me go and make sure she understands what is going on, then I will call you and have you come over. I will show her the scarf, so she knows this is real and that I'm only here to make the introduction. This way, if she backs out, you won't be embarrassed, as I will be the one making first contact."

"Oh, well, okay," Aaron says.

Brad gets out of the car and heads toward the back of the school. *This is working out just as I planned,* Brad thinks to himself. *I can explain to Wendy that the person she fell for was me and not Aaron. I was the one who created those texts. They were my words, not Aaron's. And I'm the one who found the yellow scarf and am now returning it to her. She will realize her feelings are for me, not Aaron. He will later tell Aaron that Wendy decided she did not want to meet him.*

As Brad approaches the path along the creek, he sees Wendy sitting at one of the benches near the bike path. When Wendy sees Brad approaching, she does not quite recognize who it is, as dusk is settling in. As he gets closer, she stands up and realizes it is not Aaron Livingston. It is Brad McGivens.

"What are you doing here?!" she blurts out.

"Wendy, let me explain," Brad replies.

"I don't want to talk to you right now, I'm waiting for someone."

"Yes, you are waiting for me. I'm the one who wrote those texts. Look, I have your scarf to prove it."

Wendy is puzzled. "Those texts came from Aaron, not you."

"No Wendy, they came from Aaron's phone, but they were from me. I have always wanted you to like me Wendy, but you never gave me a chance. Now you can see me in a different light."

"See you in a different light?" she says. "If this is your idea of a joke, then you are worse than I ever imagined!"

"Wendy, come on," says Brad, as he grabs Wendy by the shoulders, "just give me a chance. One night out with me will change your mind."

"Get your hands off me Brad!"

The rejection from Wendy, after Brad worked so hard to show her another side of him is infuriating. "Just go out with me Wendy, you will see."

"I said get your hands off me. I wouldn't date you if you were the last guy on earth! You're a terrible person Brad."

Brad is now feeling enraged. He has gotten mad before, but this is not only maddening, it is embarrassing. He will be the laughingstock if this level of rejection is ever known. After all the effort he put forth to show his sensitive side, Wendy is having none of it.

Wendy now tries to pry Brad's hands off her shoulders. It is no use. Brad is so much bigger and stronger than her.

Brad starts to raise his voice, "Wendy, just go out with me one time!"

"You're hurting me Brad, stop it. I'm going to scream."

As Wendy starts to open her mouth to let out a scream, she feels Brad release her shoulders, only to place both hands around her neck in a vice-like grip. She can feel the cold leather of his gloves as he pushes her back toward the trees and creek. Wendy quickly starts to gasp as she reaches up and tries to remove Brad's hands. It is to no avail, as he is just too powerful, and she can no longer breathe. She starts to flail her arms and hands, reaching out to anything at all. *Maybe if I gouge out his eyes,* she thinks, as she tries to reach out and scratch his eyes. She also starts to kick her feet in defense of her life.

Within seconds, Wendy's neck feels like it is being crushed. She can only make weak gurgling sounds and cannot breathe at all. It feels like her eyes might pop out of their sockets. She doesn't want to die. So much to live for and accomplish in her life. How can this be happening to her? Soon, she can't see at all, as everything goes black. She can feel herself going into an unconscious state. And then, she can feel no more.

Brad continues his vice grip around Wendy's neck as he pushes her further into the trees and out of sight. The rage inside of him burns like a roaring campfire. He has never been so angry in his life. He squeezes and lifts up so hard Wendy's feet briefly come off the ground. Her gurgles finally stop, and her body goes limp. Brad continues to hold on and stare into Wendy's face as though he is in a trance. *How can you reject me like that?* he thinks.

After a few more seconds, Brad snaps out of his trance-like state and releases his grip. Wendy falls lifelessly to the ground. Brad stares at the lifeless body of Wendy Spire while standing over her and breathing heavily. *What have I just done? This was not supposed to have happened.* Brad soon realizes he is in trouble and has to think fast. Brad grabs Wendy behind the shoulders and drags her further into the trees and leaves her lying near the edge of the creek.

He realizes no one knows he is here except Aaron, and it is Aaron who set the meetup, not Brad. Brad picks the yellow scarf off the ground and then remembers the ring he had grabbed in Aaron's car. He removes it from his coat pocket and places it on the ground near the creek path. Brad then notices one of Wendy's shoes has come off in the struggle and is lying in the tall grass. *This is perfect*, he thinks to himself as he picks it up and wraps it in the yellow scarf with his leather gloves. He then sprints back toward the car.

Meanwhile, Aaron is waiting in the car wondering, *what is taking so long? It's been about 10 minutes; shouldn't he be back by now?* Aaron thinks about getting out, but doesn't want to mess up the plan. Finally, he sees Brad approach the car.

Brad quickly opens the back door on Aaron's car and throws the scarf with shoe and gloves onto the back floorboard, shuts the door, then hops into the front passenger seat. He is slightly out of breath. Aaron knows Brad opened the back door, but didn't notice Brad throwing something onto the back floorboard. He thinks maybe Brad had opened the back door by mistake and is more concerned about what Wendy may have said.

"What happened Brad?" asks Aaron.

"Hey, I tried my best buddy," says Brad between breaths. "She just decided she didn't want to meet you after all. I tried my best."

Aaron is too shocked and disappointed to notice how upset Brad is. He feels like crying, but knows that would be weak and does all he can to hold back the tears. *How stupid was I to think a girl like Wendy would ever want to be with a boy like me?* Aaron is thinking. *How will I be able to face my friends and Wendy in school now? She is probably laughing at me. This is exactly what I was afraid of.*

"Take me back to Johnson's," Brad tells him.

"I can take you home," says Aaron.

"No, just drop me off at Johnson's"

Not much else is said on the way back to Johnson's Café. Once there, Brad just says, "see you later," and takes off on foot. Aaron, disappointed in the events of the night, drives himself home.

It takes about 12 minutes for Brad to get home. The time is 6:05 pm. He climbs back into his bedroom window and everything seems normal as his music is still playing and his bedroom door still shut. Brad can't believe he has just choked Wendy to death. However, he knows if anyone finds out, his life and career in football are over. He takes a few moments to compose himself, then exits his room, heading toward the kitchen.

"Hey mom," he says, as she sits in the living room watching TV, "just getting a soda."

"Getting your work done?" she asks.

"Oh yeah," responds Brad.

Sunday, November 15th

Aaron has spent the night in the county's juvenile detention facility. He is now wearing dull green cotton-blend pants with a drawstring for holding them up and a matching green button-up shirt, white sox, and slip-on white sneakers, the standard juvenile jail-issued clothing. He has told anyone who will listen that he is innocent. No one seems to believe him.

The media has become aware of Aaron's arrest and his name and yearbook photo have already been on the news. People are generally shocked to hear that Aaron has been arrested for killing Wendy. No one saw this coming, but they are also relieved to have the person who committed this horrible crime behind bars.

It is about 10:00 am when Aaron's mom comes to visit him. Aaron spends most of the visit crying and assuring his mom he did not commit this crime. He doesn't know for sure who killed her, but knows it was Brad who met her behind the school, not him. Brad had the opportunity and Aaron now remembers Brad did seem upset when he got back to the car.

"Try not to worry too much Aaron," his mom says. "I will get you the best lawyer I can afford. Please don't give up. I believe you Aaron."

Aaron is finding it hard not to give up. He knows he will not do well spending much of his life in prison and dreads the thought. Just ten days ago his life was fine.

Meanwhile, Detectives Baker and Walker continue to put the case together. As they organize and graph the texts, document the evidence, and create a timeline of events, the case starts to come together nicely. There will be an initial appearance in court on Monday and they must be prepared. They also know that more evidence will likely be available once forensic testing is completed. Once they finish, there is not much more to do until more test results come in. By 1:30 pm, they are able to go home to spend some time with family and relax after a long, tiring weekend.

Monday, November 16th

Aaron Livingston makes his first appearance in court at 10:00 am. One of the County Assistant District Attorneys appears on behalf of the state to present the facts detailed in the arrest warrant. Given the evidence of premeditation and intentional murder of Wendy Spire, the District Attorney has filed a First Degree Murder charge against Aaron. The judge reads Aaron the elements of the charge, advises him of his rights, and against Aaron's Public Defender's pleas, sets bond at $500,000. He cites the planning and brutality of the crime, as well as community concern as reasons for the high bond. Mrs. Livingston cries softly in the courtroom as she listens to the judge. After the judge is finished, Aaron is led out of the courtroom and back to juvenile detention.

At 1:00 pm, Detective Baker gets a call from the state forensic lab. He is told that the DNA swabs off both leather gloves found in Livingston's car had a mixture of DNA, but at least one of the samples matched the DNA of Wendy Spire. It is no surprise to Baker that the gloves had a mixture of unknown DNA, as who knows how many people or objects those gloves had touched in the days prior to the murder. But he is pleased to learn that some of the DNA belonged to the victim. *All the pieces are coming together,* he believes.

It is now mid-afternoon, and Aaron has been sitting in juvenile detention for almost a full two days. His anxiety level has never been so high. He knows he didn't kill Wendy, or did he? Does he not remember what happened? Did he black out? If he didn't do it, how did her shoe get in his car? He remembers Brad opening the back door. Could Brad have put it there in that brief moment? Regardless, Aaron does not believe he can survive in prison. Only his mom seems to believe him, and prison life is not something he is willing to adjust to. With his mild, shy manner, he believes he will be picked on unmercifully in prison. Aaron begins to contemplate ways to kill himself. He doesn't know whether he can survive another night of jail. *All I wanted was a girlfriend.*

Meanwhile, Brad is sulking and spending most of his time in his bedroom. He believes the evidence against Aaron is strong enough to protect him, but he knows Aaron will continue to claim he was the murderer. Brad doesn't believe anyone saw him with Aaron that night, so he is fairly confident his alibi will hold up. Brad did not intend to harm Wendy, all he wanted was for her to accept him and agree to go on one date. *Why couldn't she just say yes,* reflects Brad. He also knows his concern over this situation affected his performance Saturday night in the biggest game of the year and blames himself for the loss. His parents, however, only believe Brad is upset over losing the game.

Back at the police department, Walker walks into the office and Baker informs him of the DNA results on the gloves. "That's great," says Walker. "Did they find Aaron's DNA as well?"

"No, he said there was a mixture of DNA and he could only identify Wendy's," responds Baker.

Walker then says, "Strange he could not find Aaron's DNA. You'd think his DNA would be all over those gloves. Did he take any samples from the inside of the gloves?"

"I don't think so, at least he didn't say he did."

"Call him back and ask him to check the inside as well," says Walker.

"What are you thinking Don?"

"I'm not sure, but Aaron's story was so, I don't know, incredible, that you wonder why would he make up such a story? Wouldn't it have been better just to say, hey, I chickened out and never went to the school?" Walker suggests.

"It is an incredible story," Baker agrees. "I'll call the lab back and ask them to do some further testing. It's better to cover any loopholes now rather than later."

Walker continues, "Remember the part about picking Brad up at Johnson's Café?"

"Sure, but he has a pretty solid alibi, unless you think mom was lying."

"Probably not, but you never know. I'm going to go check at Johnson's to see if they have any security cameras," says Walker.

Walker responds to Johnson's Café and walks around the building. He finds two outside cameras, one on the northwest corner of the building and one on the southwest corner. He then goes inside and asks the clerk if he can get the video from last Thursday evening.

"No, only the manager has access to those files," says the clerk.

"Well call him right now and get him down here," demands Walker. "We are conducting a homicide investigation and those videos could be important."

A half-hour later, one of the managers shows up and agrees to give Walker a thumb drive copy of the video from all of last Thursday and Friday.

It is around 5:30 pm when Walker returns to the office with the video. "Did you talk to the lab tech?" asks Walker.

"Yep, he said he would get on it and have results in the morning," replies Baker. He said he would also have the results from the DNA scrapings under her nails by then as well."

"Great, I'm going to stick around for a while and review this video footage from Johnson's and see if I find anything helpful," advises Walker. "You go home, nothing else we can do tonight."

At 6:00 pm, Livingston is served his dinner of two burritos, a small salad, chocolate pudding, and water. He picks at the food but is too upset to eat. He can't stand the thought of another night in jail. *And this is the best it will be,* he believes, *actual prison will be ten times worse.* He continues to think of suicide, but doesn't know how to carry it out while in jail. Even the dinnerware they give him is plastic.

At about 7:00 pm, Walker is still reviewing the video when he spots what appears to be a light-colored Toyota RAV4 cross the screen in front of the southwest camera at 5:10 pm last Thursday. He cannot see any license plate, but it looks similar to the car Aaron was driving. Four minutes later, he sees a person cross in front of the same camera, walking toward the south side of the building. He cannot tell for sure, but the subject matches the build and look of Brad McGivens. At the 5:17 mark, he sees what appears to be the same vehicle leaving the parking lot south from the SW corner of the building.

Walker continues to study the video. At the 5:50 mark, what appears to be the same light-colored Toyota RAV4 comes into view from the south and this time pulls up more in front of the building. A male subject gets out of the passenger side and starts walking in a northwest direction until he is out of view. The lighting is better from this angle and Walker believes the subject looks a lot like Brad McGivens. *Damn,* thinks Walker, *Aaron may be telling the truth after all.* Walker re-runs the video several more times trying to get further identifying details. He notices the subject who walks past the camera initially and then gets out of the car upon its return is wearing a dark winter jacket. After the fourth time watching, he notices a significant change. In the first video, the subject walking southbound has on what appear to be black gloves. In the second video, when the subject exits the vehicle at the 5:50 mark, there are no gloves on the subject's hands. *Well, I'll be damned,* thinks Walker.

Walker calls Baker at his home. "Hey Steve, sorry to bother you, but I believe I have Aaron's vehicle and Brad McGivens on video at Johnson's from Thursday night," he excitedly tells Baker.

"You've got to be kidding me!"

"I kid you not. We need to get to Brad tomorrow morning before school to confront him and get a DNA sample. Do you think the lab will be able to test it tomorrow if we get it to them first thing?" Walker asks.

"They know how big this case is for us. I'm sure I can sweet talk them into helping us out," replies Baker. "Let's get in early tomorrow and be at the McGivens place by seven."

"I think we're going to need a warrant," says Walker. "I highly doubt mom will let us just take a DNA sample from Brad."

"You're right," says Baker, "would you like me to come back in to help?"

"No, I'm already here. I can just make the necessary changes and additions to the affidavit we already have. I'll get with the on-call judge tonight on my way home to get it signed. I'll see you tomorrow morning."

Tuesday, November 17th

Walker and Baker are in the office by 6:30 am. Walker has the warrant authorizing them to collect DNA from Brad McGivens. They arrive at the McGivens residence at 6:55 am. Brad McGivens answers the door. "What's the matter?" he says.

"We need to ask you a few more questions Brad," says Baker, "and we need to collect a DNA sample from you."

"What are you talking about!?" protests Brad. "I've already told you everything I know. I did not go to the school with Aaron, and I did not kill Wendy."

Brenda McGivens walks into the living room wearing her pink robe. "What is going on here detectives? What is so important you have to disrupt us this early?"

"Sorry Mrs. McGivens," replies Walker, "but we have new information and need to ask Brad some more questions."

"He's already told you everything he knows, and I told you he was home with me all evening. You can talk to our attorney if you have more questions."

"Brad is 18, he can make up his own mind whether he wants to answer questions or not" Walker reminds her. "We also have a warrant to take a sample of Brad's DNA. We can do it here or at the police department. You're choice, Brad."

Upon hearing this, Brad is starting to feel nauseous. *What new information are they talking about?* He is not sure what to do, but he knows he doesn't want to go with the detectives to the police department.

"Brad," says Mrs. McGivens, "don't answer any more questions. We will call your dad's attorney this morning to get this taken care of."

"Okay mom," says Brad.

"We still need to get your DNA Brad," advises Walker. "I can take swabs of your mouth here, or we can take you to the police department, but either way, you have no choice."

"Just take them now then," says Brad.

Walker then takes two cotton swabs on long thin wooden sticks and swabs the inside of Brad's mouth. They are then packaged separately, sealed, labeled, and signed by Walker. Before leaving, Walker uses his cell phone to take a picture of Brad's face.

"What's that for?" protests Brad.

"Just wanted to document your football injury."

The detectives then leave the McGivens home and start the hour drive toward Grand Rapids to drop off the new DNA samples at the state crime lab.

9:30 am

Aaron Livingston has made it through the night to see another day in jail. He did not sleep well, as his increasing anxiety and depression keep him awake. He has just returned to his cell from the common eating area where breakfast is served. He has eaten very little since being put in jail, as it only seems to upset his stomach. Aaron has reached the conclusion that the only way out of this is to commit suicide. And the only way he can figure to do that is to find something to hang himself with. Earlier this morning, Aaron used the edge of one of the wire springs under his jail cell mattress to start a small rip in his bed sheet. This gave him enough of a start that he could then pull on the sheet to rip off a strip of cloth. He did this from the side of the sheet against the wall so that no one would notice.

The door to his cell is solid metal with a 2 x 3 foot solid window running vertically on the door. The window is reinforced with half-inch metal screen squares embedded in the glass. This large window allows the detention staff to check on the juvenile inmates every hour during lockdown times. The only object Aaron sees that might be used to hang himself from is the door handle on the inside of the door. In order to hang himself, he will have to kneel, cinch the strip of sheet around his neck and tie the other end to the door handle. He will then have to allow his body to go limp, cutting off the blood supply to his brain long enough to cause him to pass out from lack of oxygen to the brain. Once he passes out, his body will remain limp, keeping the pressure of the sheet against his carotid artery and preventing blood flow to the brain. Within minutes, he will die. The trick will be timing it so that no one comes by to stop him before he dies.

Aaron plans to do this sometime after his mom visits him at 10:00 am. He wants to see his mom one more time and apologize for all the trouble he has caused. As expected, Mrs. Livingston arrives promptly at 10:00 and is led to the visiting area. Aaron soon joins her.

"How are you doing Aaron?"

"I'm okay mom, just pretty depressed about all that has happened. Thank you for coming."

"Of course. Everything will be alright. I talked to your public defender and he says once we have all the information and test results, we will know more about how to proceed," she assures him.

"Can you get me out of here?" Aaron asks as he starts to tear up.

"I'm sorry Aaron, our house is not worth enough for the collateral to post the bond."

"Mom?"

"Yes dear."

"You know I love you very much, right?"

"Of course I do!" she replies. "And I love you with all my heart Aaron."

"And you know I wouldn't do anything to intentionally hurt you, right?"

Mrs. Livingston looks at her son with a puzzled look, "yes Aaron, why are you talking this way?"

"I'm just sorry for all this trouble I've caused."

"Nonsense Aaron," she says. "But why didn't you tell me what happened?"

"I was too embarrassed."

They continue to talk for another 20 minutes or so about some happier times, including when Aaron's father was still alive. Aaron doesn't have a lot of memories of his father as he was only four when he passed away. However, Aaron enjoys hearing stories about his father, as it helps bring back some of those memories. Finally, a jail attendant comes to the door to advise Mrs. Livingston it is time to go. Aaron is at peace now that he has been able to have this conversation with his mom and while she does not know it, he is saying goodbye. The attendant leads Aaron back to his cell.

Driving back from Grand Rapids, Walker and Baker continue to evaluate the case and evidence they have collected thus far. "It's too bad McGivens wouldn't talk to us," says Walker. "I wanted to press him about the video and ask about those gloves. Did you see the look on his face when I mentioned we had new information?"

"Oh yeah," replies Baker. "He did not look comfortable after you mentioned that. Mom still believes he was home all night though. But, maybe the DNA will clear things up a bit more."

"When we get back," says Walker, "I'm going to ask Wiggins if he can work on cleaning up those videos some. If we can get a clearer picture, we might be able to positively identify McGivens."

It is about 10:50 am when Walker receives a phone call from Jerry Freeman with the state crime lab. Freeman says he has some further DNA results from items dropped off over the weekend. There is no foreign DNA found on the swabs from Wendy's neck. However, Wendy's DNA, as well as foreign male and female DNA was found on the yellow scarf. He says it is difficult to type the DNA on the scarf due to the mixtures. Freeman says this is not uncommon if other friends had touched the scarf over the last few days. However, he cannot eliminate Livingston as one of the contributors to the mixture on the scarf. Only Wendy's DNA is found both on the inside and outside of the tennis shoe.

As for the DNA from inside the black gloves, Freeman only finds one type of unknown male DNA. This DNA does not match Aaron Livingston. Only two of Wendy's nail scrapings test positive for male DNA. The first and second fingers of her right hand contain her DNA, as well as unknown male DNA. The interesting fact is that the male DNA from inside the glove and under her nails come from the same male.

So most likely, our victim was able to scratch her assailant, who was wearing the gloves found in Aaron's car, ponders Walker. "Thank you Jerry, that is indeed some good news. When do you think you can test the DNA we dropped off this morning?"

"Won't be until this afternoon," advises Freeman.

11:15 am

Aaron Livingston waits until all the 11:00 room checks have been completed. He probably has about 45 minutes until the next room check occurs. He will probably be discovered when they come to let him out for lunch. Of course, people periodically walk by his door throughout the day, so he's not certain no one will notice. However, this time frame gives him his best chance. Aaron pulls out the cotton strip of sheet he has torn from under his blanket. The first task is to tie the noose around his neck in such a fashion that it tightens further as he goes limp, putting additional weight onto the homemade noose. He rolls up the sheet to make it rope-like. The thinner the better. If he makes it too wide, it might not adequately cut off his blood supply. Aaron practices making a slip knot until he is satisfied it will work as expected.

Aaron then ties the other end of his cord to the door handle, pulling it hard to make sure it will hold. Aaron positions himself along the wall just to the right of the door. This will allow him to stretch his legs out parallel to the door and then let his body weight hang from the cord. It will also keep anyone walking by from seeing his legs. Aaron thinks about Wendy and how she died from being choked to death. *This will be a fitting way for me to die as well,* thinks Aaron. Aaron slips the noose around his neck, adjusts it so that it is sure to apply pressure to his carotid artery, says a little prayer, then lets his body go limp. It takes a few minutes longer than Aaron expects, but he eventually starts to feel lightheaded. His legs start to jerk, but he concentrates on not using them to relieve the pressure. There is a visceral urge to fight off the choking sensation. He concentrates on not relieving the pressure on his neck. He starts to have difficulty taking in air as things start to go black. Just before losing consciousness, he feels the room spinning around him. Finally, he stops breathing and his body lies motionless with his neck held tight in the noose.

12:22 pm

Baker, who had been consulting with the District Attorney, returns to the office and Walker fills him in on the latest DNA results. "If Brad's DNA matches the unknown DNA from the gloves and Wendy's nails........." Walker's voice trails off.

"I'm thinking the same thing," says Baker. "If it does, you can bet that scratch on Brad's left cheek didn't happen at football practice."

Both detectives feel some sense of remorse. They can't be sure yet, at least until more test results come in, but it is looking more and more like Aaron was telling the truth.

"We need those results," says Baker.

1:10 pm

Walker receives an email from Bruce Wiggins with the Sheriff's Department. He has been able to clean up and enhance the security video from Johnson's Café and attached it to the email. Walker opens it up to view. The clarity of the subject in the video is not perfect, but Walker is now 90% sure it is Brad McGivens he sees in the video. *I knew it,* thinks Walker. Walker shows the video to Baker.

"Well, if you ask me, that's Brad McGivens."

"I agree," responds Walker. "And I believe a jury will think so as well."

1:35 pm

Baker receives a call from Officer Ivey. She informs him that their suspect, Aaron Livingston is at the county hospital in critical condition. She tells him Aaron had tried to hang himself with a sheet. Another inmate heard strange sounds and banging against the cell door and yelled for a guard. They found Aaron hanging from the door handle, unconscious, not breathing, and with no pulse. Jail staff started CPR and were able to get his pulse started again. He was then taken to the hospital by ambulance.

"Oh my god."

"What is it?" Walker asks.

"Livingston tried to hang himself today. He's in ICU in critical condition."

Mrs. Livingston is at her son's side holding his hand. She gently cries as she softly talks to Aaron, praying he will make it. The attending doctor advises her Aaron suffered some damage to his neck tendons and possibly his larynx. It is too early to know if Aaron suffered any serious brain damage. He is on a ventilator and doctors have induced a coma. At this point, it is not clear Aaron will live. If Aaron makes it through the night and his vitals have improved, they will try to get him off the ventilator tomorrow morning. And if that goes well, they will attempt to wake him later in the day. Doctors can then start to assess the level of brain damage.

At 4:45 pm, detectives finally receive the call they have been waiting for. Freeman tells Walker the male DNA samples from inside both gloves and from underneath Wendy's nails are a match to the DNA of Brad McGivens. He also cannot be eliminated as a contributor to the mixed DNA on the yellow scarf.

"We got him," announces Walker. "Brad's DNA matches the gloves and nails"

"I'm going to update the Chief and the DA, then let's get working on another arrest warrant," responds Baker. Neither says anything else, but both detectives are regretting not giving more weight to Aaron's story.

By 7:00 pm, they have the affidavit ready and once again respond to the residence of the on-call judge. "This is getting to be a habit," says the judge as he takes the affidavit from Walker.

"Sorry judge, but we didn't want to wait until tomorrow. This was a brutal murder."

"Oh, no problem," says the judge as he starts to read the affidavit. "This Brad character sounds dangerous."

The judge signs the warrant for Brad's arrest and attaches a bond amount of $1,000,000. "Here you go, now go get him," he says as he hands Walker the warrant.

By 7:45 pm, Walker and Baker are back at the front door of the McGivens' home. This time, Mike McGivens, Brad's father, answers the door. "Brad is not going to talk to you detectives."

"We're not here to talk Mr. McGivens, we have an arrest warrant for Brad," says Baker.

"Do you have a search warrant?"

"No, just an arrest warrant. We need to see Brad now," continues Baker.

"You are not getting in here without a search warrant."

"Mr. McGivens, this warrant allows us to come here and arrest your son. We can do this the easy way or the hard way," warns Baker. "This warrant allows us to enter the home Brad lives in to make the arrest if necessary. We are not here to search your home. Do I need to call for more officers to help us make this arrest?"

Mr. McGivens stands staring at the detectives. Nothing is said for a few seconds. "Alright, you can step inside and I will get Brad. But he did not commit any crime and I will sue both of you and the city for this outrageous conduct."

Before taking Brad to the county jail for booking, they transport him to the police department. Without his parents around, they are hoping Brad will talk to them. They walk Brad to the interview room, a small room with light gray walls, a small featureless table, and three metal-framed plastic chairs. A small microphone is on the table with a camera mounted on the wall opposite the table. As they walk in and seat Brad, Walker turns the recording equipment on.

"We would like to hear your side of the story, Brad," explains Walker, "but first we need to read you your Miranda Rights." After reading Brad his rights, Walker asks if he would be willing to answer some questions. To his surprise, Brad agrees.

"Go ahead Brad, tell us your side of what happened the night Wendy was killed," Walker says while scooting his chair closer to Brad. Baker sits off to the side at a 90-degree angle.

"Like I've told you, Aaron is lying. I did not go with him that night. My only involvement was in helping him get Wendy to agree to meet him. I could never hurt Wendy."

Both Baker and Walker notice Brad has lost his confidence in his statements. He has trouble making eye contact, often looking down at the table while he talks.

"Well Brad," says Walker, "we found your gloves in the back of Aaron's car."

"Those aren't my gloves. They must be Aaron's."

"Have you ever worn those gloves?"

"No."

"How do you explain your DNA being on the inside of those gloves?"

Brad stares at the table in front of him. "I don't know."

"Brad," Walker continues, "The DNA proves beyond a doubt that you wore those gloves. Aaron's DNA was not on those gloves. And that scratch of yours? That was caused from Wendy fighting for her life. I know that because your DNA was found under fingernails of her right hand, Brad,"

"It can't be," Brad says quietly. He feels like his body is shivering, like when one is cold. His throat and mouth are dry, and his stomach feels upset.

"Here, I want you to look at this." Walker opens his laptop computer, pulls up a video, and slides the laptop in front of Brad. "Watch this Brad."

Brad looks up at the screen and watches the security footage from Johnson's Café.

"You see that Brad? That's you in the video wearing black gloves at the same time you and your mom said you were home. Now, look at this, you are returning and no longer wearing gloves"

Brad remains silent.

"Not only have you lied about everything Brad, so has your mother. She has been covering for you and we will probably have to charge her as an accessory after the fact."

"Alright," Brad says in a defeated voice. He looks up with tears in his eyes. "My mom had nothing to do with this. I snuck out my bedroom window that night. She thought I was home the whole time."

"Okay Brad, now tell us what happened to Wendy."

At this point, Brad knows the gig is up. Between sobs, he explains how he had helped with the texts to win Wendy over, thinking she would be pleased when she found out it was him behind the texting. He admits going with Aaron Thursday night to meet Wendy and that Aaron had stayed in the car. Once Wendy rejected his advances, something in him triggered a response he cannot explain. He lost his temper and the next thing he knew; he had strangled Wendy. He left Aaron's ring at the scene to remove suspicion from himself, and threw Wendy's shoe, her scarf, and his gloves in the backseat of Aaron's car. He never had any intention of hurting Wendy.

Wednesday, November 18th

It is 10:30 am and Mrs. Livingston is back in the hospital at her son's bedside. The doctors have removed Aaron from the ventilator and his vitals have stabilized. Doctors tell her Aaron has shown marked improvement. If his vitals are still stable, they will begin to wake him from his coma in 30 minutes.

At 3:00 pm, Aaron has been fully awake for several hours. Early indications are Aaron may have avoided long-term damage. Damage to his larynx still makes it difficult for Aaron to speak, but doctors expect that to come back soon. Doctors speculate Aaron was found within seconds of his heart-stopping and resuscitation efforts by medical personnel saved his life.

At 3:30 pm, Detectives Walker and Baker arrive at the hospital to see Mrs. Livingston and her son. They explain how the investigation transpired and they now know Aaron did not kill Wendy. They tell Aaron and Mrs. Livingston that Brad McGivens has been arrested and charged with 1st Degree Murder.

"Aaron," says Walker, "the DA is going to drop all charges against you today. When they release you from the hospital, you will be able to go home with your mom. We are deeply sorry you had to go through this."

Aaron gives a slight smile and nods, indicating he understands and is grateful for their work in clearing his name.

Fourteen Months Later, January 24th

This past August, Brad McGivens and his attorney reached a plea bargain agreement on a reduced charge of Second Degree Murder. The DA believed the jury might find it believable Brad only wanted to date Wendy prior to meeting with her and his killing of her was a reaction to his anger, not premeditated. Brad accepted the plea to avoid a trial and possible conviction for First Degree Murder. He was sentenced to 48 years in prison, with the possibility for parole after 24 years.

Detectives Walker and Baker have continued to stay in contact with Aaron, who is now in his senior year, throughout the last 14 months. However, it is Walker who has interacted with Aaron the most, even becoming something of a mentor and father figure to him.

Aaron is now doing well in school. His grades are still good, and he is doing much better socially. He is not sure why, but after all the details became public, the kids at school seemed to be more interested in him. This helped increase Aaron's confidence in social situations. Also, the six months of therapeutic counseling helped Aaron recover from the trauma. He even has a girlfriend now. He also knows part of his recovery is due to the attention and friendship of Detective Don Walker.

Aaron gets out of school at 3:30 and heads to Johnson's Café where he is meeting Walker for their weekly chat over sodas, or sometimes even a burger and fries. Kind of like a check-in on how things are going.

"So, Aaron, have you decided yet what you are going to do after you graduate?" asks Walker.

"I'm going to apply to Michigan State. They have a good criminal justice program there and I'd like to major in criminal forensic science. My goal is to someday work in a crime lab."

"That's great, what made you decide that?"

"Well, I like science and technology, and given the fact that forensic science helped me so much, I thought, this is what I want to do."

"Good choice Aaron, I think you will make a great criminalist."

Behind The Lies

Mark R Beckner

Deadly Liaison

Justin has checked into the Comfort Inn Suites in Castle Rock, Colorado at 3:00 pm. He has already fixed himself a scotch and water and is now just relaxing in his t-shirt and boxers, waiting for Naomi to arrive. They have used this hotel in the past, as it is convenient and somewhat hidden from the highway. It is a beautiful, sunny spring day and Justin can see the large rock butte that overlooks the city, and from which the city gets its name, Castle Rock. The rock butte was formed millions of years ago after a volcanic eruption deposited large amounts of hard rock called rhyolite. Fifty million years later, erosion has left the rock monument standing tall overlooking the plains to the east of the Rocky Mountains.

Castle Rock is a suburb city approximately 24 miles south of Denver. It is the seat of Douglas County. Castle Rock is an attractive place for professionals, many of whom commute to Denver. Most of the housing is upscale.

Justin King is 41 years old, divorced from his ex-wife Molly. He keeps himself in good physical condition and stands 6'1" at 195 lbs. He wears his brown hair in a nice professional cut, tapered at the ears, short on top, and combed to the side. King owns KC Spark Electric in Castle Rock with his partner and friend, Ryan Cooper.

At 3:20 pm, King hears a knock on the door and gets up to answer it. "Hey, about time you got here."

"Yeah, the traffic was crazy today," says Naomi. "I wish they would finish that construction. Seems like they've been working on it forever. How are you honey?"

"Just fine now that you're here," replies King. "I'm already primed with my scotch. Would you like some?"

"Sure, just let me freshen up and change my clothes into something more comfortable," she says with a sly grin.

Naomi goes into the bathroom while Justin fixes her a scotch and water. When Naomi exits, she is wearing a bright red see-thru teddy that looks like it just came off the rack at Victoria's Secret. The red highlights her long shoulder-length chocolate brown hair and well-tanned skin. Her 42-year-old body looks like it could still belong to someone in her twenties. She is 5'4", slim, well-shaped figure, and has stunning brown eyes. Justin wastes no time in inviting Naomi to join him in the queen-sized bed.

It doesn't take long for the slinky outfit to come off and the passionate lovemaking to begin. The sex is good for both, but especially for Naomi. This new relationship with Justin has revitalized her spirit and hope for the future. She likes to believe there is a future for her and Justin.

There is only one problem. Naomi is still married to her husband Ryan Cooper. It's not that her husband is bad, he has just become boring to Naomi. She no longer feels they have the same connection and interests they once had together. Naomi wants excitement and adventure, while Ryan seems perfectly content to run the business. He is usually too tired at night to go out or do anything Naomi thinks is fun. And the sex life has not been so great either.

She is considering divorce, but is too afraid of living on her own without the income she and Ryan enjoy from the business. They also own a large home in Castle Rock, and she is afraid of having to sell and split the profit with Ryan. She knows she would get a large settlement, but would it be enough to live the lifestyle she is now accustomed to? After all, if she divorces, she will lose her inheritance of half the business. She'd get some money as a buyout of course, but nothing like what the business will be worth in a couple of years. The business is steadily growing, and the outlook is very bright.

Justin and Naomi started their affair approximately six months ago. After more than a few drinks at an office party, Justin started flirting with Naomi. They ended up in Justin's silver BMW 4-door sedan. Ryan was too busy buttering up clients to even notice Naomi was missing. They've been meeting almost once a week since, sometimes two when they can get away with it.

Ryan Cooper does more of the business side of KC Spark Electric, while King handles the operations side. Thus, Cooper is usually more involved in meeting with potential clients, attending vendor meetings, conferences, and such. King manages his schedule around his time at worksites and generally works fewer hours than Cooper. For instance, Cooper has a business meeting in Colorado Springs today, giving King and Naomi another afternoon together.

Eight weeks ago, King hatched a plan to get Cooper out of the picture and allow Naomi and him to get married. This plan, if it works, will give Naomi and King full control of the business, and allow Naomi to keep the house and all their assets. It has taken some convincing, but Naomi has finally agreed. The best way to insure her happiness and financial security is to kill her husband, Ryan Cooper. King promised Naomi he has a way to kill Cooper painlessly and peacefully. They will drug him with a lethal dose of a sedative.

King had been married to Molly for 12 years before she kicked him out of the house after one too many discovered affairs. They have two kids together, Alex, who is now 16, and Ethan, now 13. The divorce did not go so well for King. He lost possession of a large 5 bedroom, 3 bath home on a two-acre lot with a swimming pool in the foothills outside Castle Rock. Savings, investments, and other possessions were split in half and King was ordered to pay Molly $3800 a month in childcare. King was able to keep his half ownership in KC Spark Electric.

Since the divorce, his standard of living has been drastically reduced. He now lives in a two-bedroom condo in nearby Lone Tree. He's been divorced for almost two years now, but still carries anger over what he believes to be an unfair settlement and the awarding of $3800 in childcare payments. Even with the success of the electric company, he can no longer afford the luxuries he had while married.

After finishing off their sexually intertwined pleasures, Justin and Naomi relax naked in bed with another scotch and water on ice. Soon, it is time for Naomi to get dressed and head for home before Ryan's arrival.

"We are set for next Tuesday, right?" asks Justin.

"Yes," replies Naomi, "Ryan is scheduled to be out of town next Tuesday, so we have the whole night."

"That's great. So you'll meet me at my place and spend the night, right?"

"Yes, just have to be home before the afternoon on Wednesday."

"Alright, we'll finalize our plans next Tuesday then," Justin tells her.

"Okay, love you sweetie."

"Love you too, honey."

The Next Day

King arrives at work and Cooper is already at his desk going over the invoices from the previous three days.

"Morning Ryan," says King as he walks in the door.

"Hey, how's it going?" replies Cooper

"Good, the project at the Streamside Condos is finally going well and I believe we will be back on schedule by next Monday."

"That's great," says Cooper, "because my meeting went well yesterday. They'd like to meet again next week to talk contract. If we get it, we'll probably have to hire some more help."

"Business just keeps getting better," a pleased King responds. *If we get that contract, this business is going to expand even faster than expected,* thinks King. *This would certainly be outstanding for my plan with Naomi.*

Cooper continues, "I'll be out of town next Tuesday and back Wednesday afternoon, so I've set the meeting for Thursday in Colorado Springs. Would you like to attend?"

"I would, but I want to be around to make sure we have no setbacks on the Streamside project. I trust you'll make the right deal for us."

"Yeah, it's probably best you stick around."

King and Cooper have known each other since working for another electrical company when they were in their mid-twenties. They became friends and would often hang out after work. King even attended the wedding between Cooper and Naomi. King was already married to Molly, and they were expecting their first child when Cooper and King decided to start their own electrical company. Cooper had inherited some money when his father passed away, and this was used as seed money to start the business. King paid Cooper back half of the initial investment over a period of seven years. They each own 50% of the company and have been in business a little over sixteen years.

King has always had more interest in the operations side of the business. He has the knowledge and skills needed to accomplish projects on time and usually under budget. Cooper enjoys both sides of the business, but knows the personnel, budgeting, accounting, and contracting side of the business is not King's strength or interest, thus he decided early on to focus on that part of the business. It has worked well for them as the business has continued to grow over the years.

Recently, however, Cooper has noticed King does not have the same energy or enthusiasm he used to have about the company. In Cooper's opinion, King started to lose focus after his divorce from Molly. In the past, it would be rare for a project under King's supervision to fall behind schedule. In the last couple of years, King has not been so great about completing projects on time. Cooper also believes King does not put in the same amount of time and energy that he does. It is starting to annoy him. He knows it will have to be addressed at some point in the near future.

Cooper and his wife Naomi live by themselves on Sandy Lane, in a quiet Castle Rock neighborhood. They decided early in their marriage not to have children. Their home sits near the end of a cul-de-sac on two acres of land full of Aspens and pine trees. The home's location provides plenty of privacy. The home itself is approximately 4800 square feet, with four bedrooms, three and a half baths, a large great room with a designer stone gas fireplace, and a large sunny kitchen. The floors in the living area are solid oak. Off the great room are two French doors leading to an executive-styled office. The finished basement includes a recreation room and an entertainment media area. The upstairs master suite has a second gas fireplace, marbled bathroom, and a walk-in closet that is bigger than some bedrooms in smaller homes. An attached three-car garage and covered back patio complete the home. The Coopers had the custom home built six years ago.

For a while, the home, her part-time job, and her outside interests kept Naomi satisfied, even though she was feeling unappreciated by her husband Ryan. Recently, it's no longer been enough. Naomi works part-time as a nurse at a local medical clinic. Once the electric business started doing well, Naomi cut back her work hours to pursue other interests, such as horseback riding. She owns a horse named Biscuit and keeps him boarded at a local ranch. She normally tries to ride at least once a week, so long as the weather cooperates. Her other interests include meeting friends regularly and chairing a reader's book club twice a month.

King and Naomi have always gotten along well. She has always found him attractive and enjoyed his flirting with her soon after his divorce. It was all just friendly banter until the office party six months ago. She is not sure what it was, but King was very charming that night and his flirting created a desire inside of her. She finally gave in by sneaking off with him to his car for some romantic kissing and caressing. After that night, it was not difficult for King to convince her to meet him at a hotel just two weeks later. The affair has continued since.

Naomi has been relentless over the years in keeping her figure and good looks. For Ryan, not so much. He is not in terrible shape, but has put on some weight, and doesn't have much of his blond hair left. He has a husky look and his belly now slightly protrudes beyond his belt line. Naomi no longer finds herself attracted to her husband like she once did. It is not all due to his increased weight and hair loss, but also because he does not give her the same attention he used to. Naomi had not seriously thought about leaving Ryan until her affair with King. Now, she is thinking about going along with King's plan to kill Ryan. She's just not sure yet.

The Following Tuesday

As planned, Cooper is out of town again on business. Naomi drives to Kings condo in Lone Tree after leaving her work at the clinic. For this occasion, Naomi has packed black, lacey lingerie. She arrives at approximately 6:00 pm.

King has ordered out Chinese food for the evening and has the table prepared. The menu consists of vegetable Chow Mein and Kung Pao chicken, and a bottle of Chateau Ste. Michelle Columbia Valley Merlot, one of Naomi's favorites.

During dinner, Naomi brings up the topic of their plan to kill Cooper. "Justin, I'm not sure I can do this."

"You won't have to do anything," King tells her. "You won't even be there until after it's over. I have access to a sedative that will quickly and painlessly put Ryan to sleep for good. And the best part, it's a drug that is hard to detect unless you are specifically looking for it, and there will be no reason for them to test for this drug."

"Yes, I know, you've told me all this, but I was married to the guy and did love him at one time. I still care about him."

"Naomi, he's a good friend of mine as well, and I don't want to do this either, but it is the only way if we want to have the type of life we both enjoy. Look at me now after my divorce. I went from a beautiful home in the foothills to this two-bit condo. I can't afford a mortgage right now, nor do some of the things I'd like to be doing. Divorce is something to avoid if you can."

"Lots of people get divorced, Justin."

"Yes, and look at how many of them are miserable. Do you want to lose your home?"

"Well, no, of course not."

"Do you want to travel like we talked about?"

"Yes."

"Do you still want nice things and nice clothes?"

"Yes."

"Then this is the only way. I will not be able to provide the things you want unless we get full control of the business. Ryan will never just give that up. And we need to be able to keep your house. Even if you no longer want to live there, we can sell it and buy our own place, or build our dream home."

It all sounds so good to Naomi, but she just isn't sure she can go through with it. She also doesn't want to end up in prison. After all, she has watched the TV drama Orange Is the New Black. That is not the life for her.

"Don't worry Naomi, I'm taking the risk. If something goes wrong, no one will even know you were involved. Besides, he's only going to work himself to death anyway. Look at him, he's out of shape, never exercises anymore, doesn't sleep. I will just be speeding up the process for him. All I need is for you to find him afterward and play your role."

"You make it sound so easy and impersonal."

"That's because it is! Look, do you want to marry me?"

"Yes, I love you Justin."

"Then this is the only way. I'm not going to live my life in a constant struggle to have the things I want. I want you and me to have a good life. This is the way to get there. If you file for divorce, it will be messy, your income will at least be cut in half, the business will suffer, and both of us will lose money. You have no kids Naomi; you're not going to get $3800 a month like my wife gets."

"I suppose you're right Justin. Are you sure he will not feel anything?"

"Positive Naomi. Now let's open another bottle of this Merlot and retire to the bedroom. I can hardly wait to see what you've brought to wear for me tonight," says Justin smiling.

The next morning, Justin fixes breakfast for the two of them. Bacon, eggs, and pancakes. *I could adjust to this type of treatment,* thinks Naomi. She hasn't been pampered like this in a long time.

Before leaving, Justin reminds Naomi not to text him with her phone. "We don't want text messages between us. It is something that could later be retrieved from our accounts. If you need to get in touch, just call me. Our phones don't record our conversations."

"No, I won't," smiles Naomi, "you tell me this all the time. When do you plan to set this up?"

"Ryan has a meeting on Thursday in the Springs to go over contract details with a large development company. We need to wait until the contract is signed before doing anything. Once that contract is signed, the company will be in a position to almost double in size over the next year."

"Okay, bye sweetie," waves Naomi as she walks out the door. *I'm going to be happy, loved, and wealthy,* she reminds herself as she drives out of the parking lot and heads home.

Thursday

Late Thursday afternoon, Cooper calls King to inform him the contract negotiation went well, and they have a new contract for a mega-sized housing project on the outskirts of Colorado Springs. The expected start date is later this summer. Cooper asks King to meet him at home later this evening and he will explain all the details and discuss the next steps. They agree to meet at 7:00 pm. *Everything is working out nicely,* thinks King.

King arrives at the Cooper home at 7:10 pm. He has never been a stickler for timeliness. When Cooper hears him at the door, he simply yells "Come on in."

King walks into the open great room carrying his black leather briefcase and sees Cooper sitting in one of his high back recliners reading some paperwork. An open Coors Light sits on the small round table next to his chair. King looks through to the kitchen and sees Naomi cleaning up the dishes from dinner. She looks at him, "Hi Justin, how are you doing?"

"Fine Naomi, thanks for asking," he responds.

"Justin," says Cooper, "would you like a beer?"

"That sounds good. A little celebration."

"Hey Naomi," shouts Cooper, "would you mind bringing Justin a Coors Light?"

Naomi pulls a beer from the fridge and carries it to King, handing it to him with a smile, but not saying anything.

"Thank you, Naomi," nods King with a wink.

"Let's go into my study to review the contract and talk," suggests Cooper. Both men then retreat through the double French doors into Cooper's large office. Cooper shows King the contract and explains some of the details. He then discusses the need to hire more people over the summer in preparation for the work ahead.

"Are you ready for another beer?" asks Cooper.

"Yes, I am."

"Okay, wait here and I'll go get us one," Cooper tells him as he leaves the office.

King quickly gets up out of his chair and goes to the bookshelf behind Cooper's desk. He knows where Cooper usually keeps his handgun, hidden behind the second row of books. King reaches behind the books sweeping his hand side to side until he finds it. A silver snub nose Smith and Wesson .38 caliber revolver. King grabs it and quickly puts it in his briefcase, then sits back down in his chair. Moments later, Cooper walks back into the room with two opened cans of Coors Light. "Here you go," he says as he hands King another beer.

The two men remain in the office for another hour discussing the next steps in fulfilling the new contract, and the future of the company. Cooper then addresses what has been bothering him.

"Justin, you do know that I'm going to need you to be at the top of your game for this project," advises Cooper.

"What do you mean?" says King with a look of surprise.

"We need to keep projects on schedule, this contractor is very cost-conscious."

"I know that," says King with indignation.

"Maybe, but your effort has not been the same the last couple of years. With this new contract, you will need to step it up."

"I've done as much for this company as you have," insists King.

"I know you have. I'm just saying we need to bring our best to this project. It will mean you will probably be working more hours and not taking so many afternoons off."

"Don't worry Ryan, I'll pull my weight," says King with a bit of an angry tone. "Believe me, getting this contract was very important to me."

"Okay then, I'll see you in the office tomorrow. Have a good night Justin."

It is after 9:00 by the time they finish. Cooper walks King to the door telling him to drive safe.

"This company has a bright future," says King as he turns and walks away. *A very bright future for me that is.*

Once King returns to his condo in Lone Tree, he removes Cooper's .38 caliber revolver from his briefcase and opens the five bullet cylinder. It is empty. *Typical Ryan, he has a gun for protection and doesn't even keep it loaded. Guess I'll have to load it myself.*

Friday

The next day at noon, Naomi meets her sister, Serena Mills, for lunch at the Creamy Spoon Bistro in downtown Castle Rock. Five weeks ago Naomi had shared with Serena tales about her affair. Serena herself is happily married and not thrilled over Naomi's cheating. However, she loves her sister, so she tries to be as supportive as possible, without approving of the affair. Naomi has not told her sister who the other man is. After talking for a short time, the topic of Naomi's affair comes up.

"Are you still seeing this other guy?" asks Serena.

"Yes, and I spent the night with him on Tuesday."

"Seriously?" a surprised Serena asks.

"Yes. Now, I know you don't approve, but I haven't felt this good about myself in several years. I feel alive again."

"Have you told Ryan how you feel?"

"No, I haven't been able to do that yet."

"Naomi, if you are so unhappy with him, you need to be honest. Sneaking around with another man can only make things worse."

"Yes, I know. I will tell him soon. But I had to be sure first. I also needed a plan for life after Ryan."

"Who is this mystery guy? I'm dying to know. Will I know him?"

"Sorry Serena, I don't want to say anything until after I tell Ryan. It's only fair to him."

"Well okay. If you need anything from me, you know I am here to support you."

"I appreciate it. Thank you Serena."

On her drive home, Naomi receives a call from King. She presses the answer button on her steering wheel to talk hands-free.

"Hey Naomi, you doing okay?"

"Yes, just had lunch with my sister."

"Great. Hey, when is your next book club meeting?"

"Uh, next Wednesday evening at seven. We are meeting at my friend Debbie's house."

"That's perfect," exclaims King. "Next Wednesday night will be the night."

"The night?"

"Yes, the night you become a free woman, and then we can get married. We'll have to wait a while of course so as not to raise any questions. You haven't told anyone have you?"

"No, I haven't told anyone."

"Good. We'll talk more on Monday, bye."

Naomi feels a pit in her stomach. *Is he going to kill Ryan next Wednesday?* Naomi pulls into a nearby Circle K to calm her nerves. She sits parked in her car for ten minutes taking deep breaths trying to compose herself. Once her breathing returns to normal, she goes into the store to purchase an ice-cold soda to quench a sudden thirst. *I hope Justin knows what he is doing,* she thinks to herself.

At home that evening, Naomi tries to be herself around Ryan to avoid arousing any suspicion. She puts extra effort into being nice and acting like everything is fine. However, she feels like her emotions and guilt are displayed like flashing red lights across her chest. At times she feels nauseous. She drinks several glasses of red wine to calm her nerves and hopefully, help her get to sleep.

All her worrying over Ryan noticing something is different or wrong is a waste of emotion. Ryan is focused on the business and what needs to be done to successfully fulfill the new contract, while also keeping all their current clients happy. He chats about the new contract at dinner and joins her wine-drinking by having a Coors Light. To Ryan, everything is great. He has no suspicion of any affair or danger he may be facing.

The Following Monday

It is now Monday when King receives a text message from Naomi. *Are you going to call me soon?*

King immediately calls Naomi, "what are you doing texting me!" he screams. "I told you never to use texting. It can later be discovered on our phones."

"I'm sorry Justin," Naomi pleads, "but I hadn't heard from you and I don't know what is going on. I'm nervous."

"I've been finalizing our plan. You need to trust me."

"I do, but I need you to talk to me."

"Meet me at the Starbucks in 15 minutes, bye"

Naomi is surprised at how abrupt King had been with her. She drives to the Starbucks, only a ten-minute drive, and waits for King. He pulls up five minutes later.

"Naomi, sorry I yelled, but we need to be careful," reasons King. "I will do it this Wednesday evening while you are at book club. You won't even have to be there."

This makes Naomi feel calmer. She does not want to have an active role in killing Ryan.

"I will meet with Ryan at your house Wednesday evening. When you get home, it will be done."

"Okay, how are you going to accomplish this? You said it would be painless."

"It will be. I'll bring over some Captain Morgan and mix us a couple of rum and cokes. He likes those. While mixing them, I'll slip the drug into his drink and he will peacefully pass away."

"Won't the police be suspicious?" asks Naomi.

"No, we will make it look like a suicide. Your role will be telling the police you told him about your affair the week before. That will be his motive to commit suicide."

"He commits suicide by putting a drug into his own drink?"

"No, once he is dead, I will need to put his gun in his hand and shoot him in the head to make it look like a suicide."

"What?! No, I don't want to do that Justin."

"Naomi, we have to. Remember, he will already be dead, but we can't have the coroner digging too deep to find a cause of death. With alcohol in his blood, his grief over the affair, gun in his hand, gunshot to the head, and a suicide note, it will be an open and shut case. Even if they do a typical drug screen, they won't find this drug."

"What kind of drug is this?"

"It's called Rohypnol. Sometimes referred to as roofies or the date rape drug. It knocks people out and they usually can't remember much afterward. Too much, and it will kill you. But it's hard to detect unless it's specifically screened for. There will be no reason to screen for Rohypnol."

"You have this drug?"

"Yes, I do."

"What do you use it for?"

"Oh, it has its purposes."

"Are you sure this is the only way Justin?"

"It is if we want to be free, married, and wealthy. Ryan won't feel a thing and he will die believing you have always loved him."

"What will I tell the police?"

"As I said, tell them you told Ryan about your affair the week before and he was devastated. On Wednesday evening, you were at book club and when you came home, you found Ryan dead with a suicide note on the table. I'll print out a suicide note from his office computer before you get home."

Naomi doesn't say anything for several minutes, then softly says, "okay Justin, I'll trust you. I just want this over and live with you the rest of my life."

"Be patient Naomi, it will happen. Love you."

"Love you too Justin."

Wednesday

On Wednesday morning, King calls Cooper to set up a meeting. He tells Cooper he has some concerns over the latest contract and would like to discuss it with him that evening.

"Why not just come in and discuss it here?" asks Cooper.

"I can't leave the job site right now. How about if I stop by your place tonight, say around seven-thirty? I'll bring some of your favorite rum and we can discuss it over a couple drinks. It's nothing serious."

"Yeah, that would okay. Naomi has book club tonight."

"Good, I'll see you tonight."

Everything seems to be falling in place for King's and Naomi's plan to eliminate Cooper from the business and her life. King knows he will have to pull this off perfectly for it to work. He has been thinking about it for some time now and believes he has all the details covered. At around 5:30 pm, King tries to eat some dinner before having to leave for Cooper's place, but doesn't seem to have much of an appetite. King can feel the tension in his stomach.

Naomi leaves home at 6:50 pm. As planned, she calls King on her cell phone to let him know she is on her way to book club.

"Are you still sure about this Justin?" she nervously asks.

"Yes, everything is planned out."

"Justin, I'm very scared. I was shaking as I drove out of our cul-de-sac."

"Just calm down Naomi, you need to act like nothing is unusual tonight. Remember to call me before coming home and I will let you know if it is okay to return. Just don't text me."

"Yes, I know," says Naomi as she exhales a deep breath.

"Now just go to your club meeting and try to relax. Talk to you later," says Cooper.

After Naomi's phone call, King knows he is clear to go to Cooper's home to take care of business. He goes to his briefcase and removes the Smith and Wesson revolver he took from Cooper's bookshelf. He opens the cylinder and is reminded he still has to load it. King goes into his bedroom and retrieves a box of .38 caliber bullets next to his own Ruger 6 shot revolver from the top drawer of his dresser. King also owns a Glock semi-auto .40 caliber handgun. This would be his preferred choice of gun, but he needs to use Cooper's gun for the mock suicide. Cooper's gun will more than do the job.

King opens the box and removes five .38 caliber hollow point bullets from the box. Hollow points are better, as they cause more damage to the body. He opens the cylinder with his left hand and carefully drops a bullet into each hole of the cylinder with his right hand. He then snaps the cylinder closed and places the gun into the right-hand pocket of his blue nylon windbreaker jacket. He then zips the pocket shut.

King then goes to his bathroom, opens the medicine cabinet, and grabs a small bottle of white tablets. This is the Rohypnol he will use on Cooper. The bottle of tablets goes into his left jacket pocket, which he also zips shut. On his way out the door, King grabs the new bottle of Captain Morgan rum and a pair of latex gloves from the small table in the foyer. He is now ready.

King leaves his home in Lone Tree at approximately 7:05 pm driving his silver BMW four-door sedan. He arrives at the entrance of Sandy Lane at 7:25 pm and parks his car on the cross street of Oak Avenue about fifty feet from the corner. King does not want any of the neighbors to see his car in Cooper's driveway or parked out front. The homes on Sandy Lane sit on spacious lots with an abundance of trees and are set back from the road a good 100 feet. He walks the eighth of a mile down Sandy Lane to Coopers' home at the end of the cul-de-sac. It is now dusk, so King is hoping none of the neighbors notice him walking.

Cooper answers the door and invites King inside. He doesn't notice King's car is not in the driveway. King holds up the bottle of rum and says he will fix them a drink.

Cooper nods in agreement, "that sounds really good right now. What is it you want to discuss?"

"Let's have a drink first and relax. I just want to go over some details of the project. That will help me determine what resources we will need."

King mixes two rum and cokes in the kitchen. He does not put any Rohypnol in Cooper's drink, but he makes Cooper's strong and his weak. King wants to get Cooper's blood alcohol level up some before he gives him the drug. He walks into the living area and hands Cooper his drink. Cooper is sitting in one of the tall back leather recliners and King sits in an adjacent recliner with a small round table between them. He then starts talking about the major project in Colorado Springs and what he believes it will entail. After about a half-hour, King grabs Cooper's empty glass and goes back into the kitchen to mix them another drink.

This time, he not only makes Cooper's drink strong, but he also puts two tablets of Rohypnol in the glass. He stalls a bit to make sure the tablets are completely dissolved. The carbonation of the coke helps with the process. He then goes back into the living area and hands Cooper his second rum and coke.

King changes the topic for a bit by asking Cooper what he thinks of the Colorado Rockies' chances this year. They talk baseball for about 15 minutes as Cooper enjoys his rum and coke. Cooper then brings the conversation back to business.

"So how many people do you think we will have to hire?" asks Cooper.

"I'm thinking probably ten more electricians with one being a supervisor," answers King.

"That's in the same ballpark I was thinking. Have you checked on the supply chain for the wire and components we will need?" Cooper asks.

"If supply remains the way it is now, we will be okay. I've given our supplier a heads up and he doesn't see an issue. Of course, if something goes haywire with copper supply or parts manufacturing, you never know for sure."

King inquires, "Is there someone here you would like to promote to supervisor, or would you rather bring someone new in."

Cooper pauses for a minute. "I think, uh....., I'm sorry, what was that again?"

"Do you want to promote someone?"

Cooper hangs his head and shakes it a bit. "Damn, I think I drank, uh, yeah, drank too fast or, eh, something."

"Let me get you a glass of water."

Cooper simply nods and grabs the sides of the recliner as if to hold himself upright. The room starts to get blurry. Soon, the room begins to spin.

King brings Cooper a glass of water, knowing it won't help.

King holds the glass as Cooper tries to drink from it. He gets some in his mouth, but about half of it dribbles out onto his shirt.

Cooper slowly drawls, "whaaaat ish hippining tos mee?."

King says nothing, but steps back to watch the final minutes as Cooper struggles to keep his eyes open. He tries to ask for help, but his speech is too impaired. His tongue feels like it has swollen to three times its size. Cooper puts up a good fight, resisting the urge to completely pass out. He slumps over in his chair twice and pulls himself back up into a slouched position. He no longer has a sense of anything around him. The room starts to fade in and out of his vision until finally, his eyes roll back, and everything is black. He slumps to his left and collapses. He lies unconscious with his left arm hanging over the left arm rest, his side against the chair, and his head hanging cocked to the left resting on his left shoulder.

King is pleased with his work, but knows there is much more to do to make this plan a success. King goes into the kitchen and pours more of the rum into the sink. He then takes a small amount of rum and sprinkles it onto the front of Cooper's shirt so he will still carry a strong odor of rum when the police arrive. King then removes the latex gloves from his back pants pocket and puts them on. He then wipes down the bottle of rum and takes it into the living area. He grabs Cooper's left hand and presses it multiple times against the bottle, then pours some rum into Cooper's glass sitting on the round table. He then places the rum bottle next to the glass. Next, he takes the glass he was using for his rum and coke, washes it, dries it, and puts it back in the cupboard.

King then takes a rag and begins to wipe down anything in the kitchen or living room he may have touched. After being satisfied he has gotten everything in the two rooms, he pulls out the small revolver and completely wipes down the outside of the gun, then puts it back in his jacket pocket. He then enters Cooper's office, sits down at his computer, and types out a letter. He then crumples the letter a bit and leaves it on Cooper's desk. *That should seal the deal,* he muses.

King goes back into the living area, keeping his latex gloves on to not leave fingerprints anywhere. He sits on a couch facing Cooper, who hasn't moved since losing consciousness. King takes in a deep breath and begins to imagine himself owning the entire business and the money he will make. As he is pondering his future, he notices the glass of water on the coffee table in front of the two recliners. *Oh my god, I forgot about that glass!* He quickly rises, grabs the glass, and takes it to the kitchen where he washes it and returns it to the cupboard. *That could have been a fatal error.* This causes King to look around more closely for anything else he may have forgotten. Satisfied he has covered his tracks, he sits back down to relax. The only thing to do now is wait for Naomi to return home.

At 8:40 pm, King receives a phone call from Naomi.

"Is it alright for me to come home now?"

"Yes Naomi, I'm waiting for you."

"Okay, I'll be there soon."

At 8:52 pm, King hears the garage door opening. Naomi is home. She enters from the garage into the laundry room and then the kitchen. King is now standing in the living area.

"It's done Naomi," announces King, "come look."

Shaking with nerves and some regret, Naomi slowly walks through the kitchen until she sees Ryan slumped over in his recliner.

"Ahh!" she screams as she puts her left hand to her mouth.

"Calm down Naomi, it's going to be okay."

"Is he dead?" she whimpers.

"If not, he's awfully close. Remember, we need to make this look like a suicide. Now, I need you to stand right here for a minute," as King points to a spot on the living area floor, about ten feet from Cooper.

"Why?"

"You'll see, just stand there for a moment."

Naomi takes a few steps to the spot King pointed to and looks at him. "Now what?"

King reaches into his right jacket pocket and removes the loaded revolver.

"No!, shouts Naomi, "you said you wouldn't do that in front of me."

"I promise Naomi, I'm not going to shoot Ryan," says King as he stares at Naomi with a steely look in his eyes.

Naomi is taken aback, as the tone of King's voice and look in his eyes scares her. She then sees King raise his right arm and point the revolver right at her chest.

"Justin, what are…"

BAM! BAM!

King fires two quick shots into the middle of Naomi's chest. Naomi gasps, steps back, then immediately falls to the floor. Naomi twitches for only a couple seconds before her body lies still. King's shots were dead on; the hollow point bullets blowing up the heart inside of Naomi's chest. Her death comes quickly.

King stands there looking at Naomi as gun smoke and the smell of burnt gun powder fills the room. His plan has worked perfectly. King feels a calmness come over him, as the tension has been relieved. The hard part is over, now all he has to do is play it out.

After several minutes of just taking in the scene, King takes his glove-covered hand and rubs it on the outside of Cooper's limp right hand, hoping to transfer gunshot residue from his glove onto Cooper's hand. He then takes the gun and presses it into Cooper's right hand and fingers several times. He then wraps Cooper's fingers around the gun and rests his right hand on the right arm rest, with the gun still in the hand.

King takes one more look around to be sure he has covered all his bases. He doesn't want to leave any trace of him being there this night. Once he is satisfied, he steps out on the front porch, locking and closing the door behind him. King then looks down the street to see if anyone is out and about. He does not want to be seen leaving the house. Not seeing anyone, King quietly, but quickly, walks to the end of the cul-de-sac to his parked car on Oak Avenue, just around the corner. He gets in and drives away. *Couldn't have gone better,* he thinks to himself.

After the Shooting

The next day, Thursday, King arrives at the office a bit late as usual. He says hi to Lisa, the administrative assistant, and continues straight to his office and closes the door. He tries to focus on what he needs to accomplish at multiple job sites, but finds it difficult to concentrate. He finds his mind drifting to what he will say when the police come to interview him. He's practiced it in his head numerous times, but wants to be sure he is consistent in his answers. He tries to anticipate what the police might ask him.

After about 45 minutes in his office, Lisa knocks on his door.

"What is it Lisa?"

"I've had a couple of phone calls for Ryan but he's not in the office yet. Was he going to be late today?" she asks.

"Not that I know of," responds King as he shrugs his shoulders.

"I tried to reach him on his cell, but it went to voice message," Lisa tells him.

"Yeah, maybe he had a meeting this morning and forgot to tell you," suggests King.

"Hmm, maybe," says Lisa as she shuts the door.

At about 9:00 am, Cooper is starting to regain consciousness. He opens his eyes, but items in the room are blurry and his head is pounding. He sits up, but closes his eyes again, and rests in a drowsy condition. He is finally able to sit up in the chair, but doesn't feel like he can stand yet. He also feels a bit nauseous, and the air has a strange smell to it. *What the hell happened to me last night,* he thinks.

Cooper's mouth is extremely dry. As he starts to further gain consciousness, he decides to try to pull himself up to walk to the kitchen for a glass of water. He puts one hand on each arm rest, carefully centers his legs, then pushes himself into a standing position. He takes a few seconds to maintain his balance. As he turns to start to walk, he sees something lying on the floor about twelve feet away. At first, he is not sure what he sees, but quickly realizes it is Naomi. He starts to move quickly toward her, but loses his balance and falls, hitting his right hip on the coffee table in the center of the room. He screams out as pain shoots into his hip. Cooper slowly gets up on his hands and knees and crawls over to Naomi.

He can't believe what he sees. Naomi's blouse is soaked in dried blood. Her mouth is open, and her eyes are shut. Her head is turned to the right and there is a small trail of dried blood that has dripped from the corner of her mouth. Cooper touches her arm and face, knowing instantly she is dead.

"WHAT HAPPENED!?" screams out Cooper. "Who killed my sweet Naomi? HELP! SOMEONE HELP ME!"

No one can hear Cooper's screams. He realizes he needs to find his cell phone to call the police. The shock of finding Naomi dead has helped clear his mind, although he is still unsteady on his feet. He sees his cell phone on the round table next to his recliner. He also sees a drink glass and bottle of rum on the table. He grabs the phone and quickly dials 911.

"911, what's your emergency?"

"I need help! I believe my wife has been shot and she is dead! Someone came in last night and killed her," he says between panting breaths.

"Okay sir, try to stay calm. I have your address here and we are sending officers out now. Can you tell me what happened?"

"I don't know. I woke up this morning and was very dizzy, then I saw my wife on the floor. When I checked on her, she was dead. It looks like she was shot."

"Alright, do you know who came into your house?"

"No, I must have been asleep, I just don't understand right now. I just don't know."

"Are there any weapons in the house right now?"

"No, no weapons. Well, I do have a gun in my office, but that's it."

"Our officers are almost there sir, can you walk out your front door for us?"

"Uh, yes I think I can walk now."

"Okay, when officers arrive, I will need you to walk out your front door with no weapons and your hands in the air. This is only for our officers' protection."

"I don't have a weapon."

"I know, it's just a precaution. Can you do that for me?"

"Yes."

The dispatcher keeps Cooper on the phone for another minute or so until officers are on the scene.

"The officers are outside now and ready for you. You can walk outside now. Remember, keep your hands in the air."

Cooper slowly makes his way to the front door. He unlocks and opens it. He steps outside and hears the command, "hands in the air sir."

Cooper puts his hands in the air and two officers approach from the side of the house. One officer pats him down for weapons, then tells him he can put his hands down. The second officer, Officer Regan, asks where Cooper's wife is.

"She is in the living room on the floor"

Just then a third officer arrives and stands with Cooper as Officer Regan and his partner go into the home. Officers find Naomi dead on the floor with what appear to be two gunshots to the chest. Officer Regan finds a Smith and Wesson five-shot revolver on the floor just to the right of the recliner Cooper had been sitting in. Officers check the entire house for any other persons, then quickly secure the scene for detectives and crime scene investigators.

Officer Regan then approaches Cooper again, "Can you tell me what happened here?"

Cooper is crying, "I don't know, I woke up and she was dead on the floor. That's all I know."

"Were you home all night?"

"Yes, as far as I know."

"What do you mean by that?"

"Well, I can't remember much of last night."

"Where were you sleeping?"

"I woke up in my recliner"

"Which one is that?"

Cooper points to his recliner, "that one."

"Is the gun on the floor yours?"

"Huh? What gun?"

"Alright, I think we better wait for homicide detectives to get here," Officer Regan says in frustration. "They will want to take you to the station to get a full interview from you. You willing to do that?"

"Of course officer, anything I can do to help."

Cooper is placed in the back of a police cruiser to keep him secure and out of the crime scene. Paramedics check his vitals and provide him an orange-flavored beverage containing electrolytes. Fifteen minutes later, two detectives arrive followed by two crime scene technicians. By now, neighbors have started to gather in their yards to see what is going on.

Detectives Bill Masters and Jane Tippen arrive and get a quick briefing from officers. Masters and Tippen are seasoned detectives who have worked a number of homicides. Masters and Tippen make a good pair, as Masters takes more of a hard-line approach, while Tippen likes to take more time to build a rapport with witnesses and suspects alike. Masters is 42 years old, about six foot two, with broad shoulders. He has brown straight hair he parts on the left side and wears a neatly trimmed mustache. He typically wears dress pants, a sports jacket, and tie. Today he is wearing a blue tweed sport coat with a matching blue striped tie. Tippen is 37 years old, about five foot six, husky build with short blond curly hair. She typically dresses in cotton-blend pants, a blouse, and a jacket. Today she is wearing beige pants, an emerald green blouse, and matching beige jacket.

Detective Masters immediately asks patrol to cover Cooper's hands with paper bags to protect any possible forensic evidence, then transport Cooper to the station and sit with him until detectives return to get his statement. Both detectives then examine the crime scene, taking notes and initial photos of what they observe. Without touching the weapon, Masters examines the gun lying on the floor. From the look of the victim, it does not appear as though she had any chance of survival. The victim, identified as Naomi Cooper, is wearing a light cream-colored blouse, and dark-colored pants. The blouse is soaked in blood and there appear to be two entrance wounds on the victim's chest. A set of car keys are lying on the floor next to her body. A small hand-held black purse is on the kitchen table.

"Maybe she came home from somewhere and surprised an intruder," suggests Tippen.

"Maybe," responds Masters, "but I'm putting my money on the husband killing her. I don't think an intruder would have left his gun behind."

"No, probably not," agrees Tippen.

"Regan said the husband was sleeping in this recliner," advises Masters. "Looks like he may have been drinking and had the gun with him. If he drank that much rum, it's no wonder he doesn't remember much"

"Any sign of forced entry?" asks Tippen.

"Patrol said no, and I haven't seen any. Regan told me he could hear Cooper unlock the door handle before opening it."

"What about the deadbolt?"

"No, just the doorknob lock."

"So, someone could have locked the doorknob and pulled the door shut as he or she was leaving," suggests Tippen.

"Yeah, I suppose so," agrees Masters.

Back at the station, Ryan Cooper's hands are processed for gunshot residue and two samples of his blood are drawn for drug and blood alcohol testing. He is also fingerprinted. He is then placed in an interview room where he is watched by an officer through the one-way window. He is given a large cup of coffee to help him become more alert and coherent. After the electrolytes and now coffee, Cooper is starting to feel better. He continues to review in his head what happened to Naomi and tries to remember the series of events from the night before. He believes he remembers King being at the house, but is not sure.

It seems to Cooper like he has been in the room for hours, but it has only been forty-five minutes when Detectives Masters and Tippen enter the room, sitting down at the table across from him

"Hello Mr. Cooper," says Masters. "We are very sorry about your wife."

Cooper is unable to fight back the tears. Tippen hands him a small box of tissues.

"May we call you Ryan?" asks Masters.

"Yes."

"Ryan, right now we don't know what happened in your home last night, other than your wife has been shot. Right now, you are the only witness we have, and we would like to ask you a series of questions. You are not under arrest at this time, and you are free to go if you wish. However, your help would be appreciated," explains Masters.

"Of course detective, I want to help find who killed my wife. Ask me anything."

"Why don't you just tell us what happened."

"Well," starts Cooper, "I am having trouble remembering last night. I remember coming home from work, and I believe Naomi had a book club meeting she went to, although everything is kind of hazy in my mind. She would have left a little before seven o'clock. I don't remember her coming home though."

Tippen speaks up, "What time would she normally have gotten home?"

"Usually sometime around nine o'clock."

Tippen continues, "But you don't remember her coming home? Were you home all night?"

"I believe so. I don't remember leaving."

"Okay, just continue with what happened throughout the evening," says Tippen.

"I have a vague memory of my partner, Justin King coming over to talk business, but I'm just not sure. He often comes over in the evenings when we have things to discuss, so I might be confused. I don't remember much more, other than waking up this morning in my recliner feeling awful. My mind was in a fog. Once I was able to get up, I saw Naomi on the floor. I crawled over to her and saw that she was dead."

Cooper starts to cry again and has to pause to compose himself. He uses a couple of tissues to wipe his eyes and blow his nose.

"Take your time," assures Tippen.

Cooper continues, "I saw blood all over her blouse and on the floor. She was cold to the touch. It was horrible. Who would want to kill sweet Naomi? I then immediately called the police. Now here I am, in a police station with my wife dead."

"Ryan," questions Masters, "how much did you have to drink last night?"

"I don't remember."

"You must remember drinking?"

"Yeah, I can remember drinking. I think Justin was there with me. But again, I'm just not clear on that. I usually don't drink more than a couple at a time."

"Ryan, you were passed out and can't remember anything," says Masters. "Don't you think you may have had too much to drink?"

"Yeah, I guess I must have."

"You think your partner was there last night; did he have any reason to kill your wife?" asks Masters.

"No, of course not, they were friends."

"Were you drinking with Justin?"

"I believe so, but again, my mind is fuzzy."

"What would you say if I told you there was no evidence, at least to this point, that anyone else was there?" continues Masters. "We will ask him of course, but there were no other drink glasses found other than yours."

"I seem to remember him being there, that's all I can say."

"Ryan," Tippen says, "Let me show you a picture I took with my phone here. Can you see that? And if so, what is it?"

"It looks like a gun," answers Cooper.

"Do you recognize the gun?"

"I can't be sure, but it looks like my small revolver I keep in my office. Where did you find it?"

"It was on the floor on the right side of the chair you say you fell asleep in," states Tippen.

"Well, I sure as hell don't know how it got there. It was hidden behind some books in my office."

"Did you handle the gun last night?"

"No, I haven't handled that gun in a long time."

"Ryan," interjects Masters, "how were you and your wife getting along?"

"Just fine, why?"

"Why?" repeats Masters, "because your wife is found shot to death in the room you are passed out in and what will probably turn out to be the murder weapon is on the floor next to your chair. And, you claim to have no memory of what happened. Now, tell me, what problems were the two of you having?"

"None, other than normal stuff. She always wanted me to be more spontaneous and thought I worked too much at times. But no, we didn't have any serious issues. I loved my wife very much."

Just then, another detective steps into the room and asks Masters and Tippen to step out for a minute. They stop the interview and exit the room.

"What's up?" asks Masters.

"The crime scene techs found something you might be interested in. A printed letter was found on Mr. Cooper's desk to him from his wife Naomi. He texted me a photo. Look at this."

Masters and Tippen look at the enlarged photo on the laptop handed to them. The letter reads as follows:

Dear Ryan,

I am so sorry I hurt you last week by telling you about my affair. I hesitated in telling you because I was afraid of what you might do. I did not intend to hurt you. It just happened.

I still love you, but not the way I used to. It is not fair to you or me to continue this way. When I get home tonight, I would like to discuss a peaceful way to end our marriage. I just don't want to fight with you anymore.

Sincerely,
Naomi

"Whoa," says Masters, "that certainly sheds some light on this case. He probably sat there drinking and stewing about this letter. He had time to plan what he was going to do."

"It doesn't look good, does it?" agrees Tippen.

Masters gets a copy of the photo printed out and takes it back into the room. He lays the copy on the table in front of Cooper.

"Want to tell us what this is about?" says Masters.

After reading it, Cooper says, "where did this come from? I've never seen this, and Naomi was not having an affair."

Tippen leans in, "Come on Ryan, don't play dumb. Tell us the truth about what happened last night."

"I've told you what I remember!"

Tippen continues, "this is starting to look like you killed your wife because you were angry over the affair and the end of your marriage. You drank a lot, got your gun, and shot her when she got home last night. It's understandable, you had to be incredibly angry."

"That is not true!" shouts Cooper. "I loved my wife and have never seen this letter. You can ask Justin. I would have told him if I knew Naomi was having an affair."

"So let me get this straight Ryan," says Masters. "You think you remember your partner being at the house, but you're not sure. You drank rum until you passed out, and then woke up this morning with your wife dead from two gunshots. Your gun was next to the chair you slept in, and your dead wife was only feet away. A letter from your wife is found in your office, but you say you knew nothing about her affair, although she says in the letter you found out a week ago. Do I have this straight?"

Cooper remains silent for several seconds. "I don't know what to say. I'm telling you the truth."

"Are the clothes you are wearing now the ones you were in all night?"

"Yes, they are the same clothes I had on when I came home from work."

"We are going to need to collect those clothes," Masters tells him. "An officer will be in with a change of clothes to collect those you are wearing. After that, you will be able to leave. You will also need to find a place to stay tonight. We won't be releasing the crime scene until sometime tomorrow."

Both detectives then leave the room. Within minutes, an officer comes into the room to collect Cooper's clothing. Once he is done changing, he is allowed to call his brother Richard to pick him up.

Back in the office, Tippen looks at Masters and asks him what he thinks.

"I think he killed his wife," says Masters.

Tippen nods her head in agreement.

"Let's complete our reports from today and make a list of people we need to interview. We can then get started first thing tomorrow," suggests Masters.

While waiting for his brother Richard, Cooper thinks, *what is going on? Am I crazy? Did I kill Naomi and don't remember it?* During the drive to Richard's house, Cooper explains to Richard all he knows about the murder.

"Was Naomi having an affair?" asks Richard.

"Not that I know of," says Cooper. "She never said anything, and I never saw that note."

Friday

On Friday at 9:00 am, Masters and Tippen are at KC Spark Electric to talk to Justin King. King invites them into his office. Detectives explain why they are there.

"Yes, it's horrible," says King. "When Ryan didn't come in yesterday I got worried and tried to call him. I later heard on the news that his wife had been murdered. He finally called me from his brother's phone in late afternoon and told me what had happened. I'm just sick about it."

"I can imagine," says Tippen. "were you at Ryan's home Wednesday night?"

"No. But you know what? He told me he thought I was there, and we were drinking. Really strange."

"Why would he say you were at his home?" Tippen presses.

"I don't know, I guess he was confused. We often meet at his house to either talk business or socialize."

"When was the last time you were there?"

"It would have been Tuesday night. We needed to go over some details on a large new contract we had recently signed. He probably has Tuesday mixed up with Wednesday. Naomi can confirm I was," King stops in mid-sentence. "Sorry, it's just so hard to believe she is gone."

"Justin, were you aware Naomi was having an affair?" asks Masters.

"Yes, I was. She told me about it a week or so ago. I told her if she didn't tell Ryan I would. He is my partner and good friend."

"Did you tell Ryan?"

"No, she promised me she would."

"Who was she having an affair with?"

"I don't know, she wouldn't tell me."

"Any ideas?" challenges Masters.

"No, I really don't. But I can tell you this, Ryan did not seem himself this past week."

"What do you mean?" asks Tippen.

"He seemed noticeably quiet and sullen, like depressed. I asked what was eating at him a couple of times, but he just said he was okay. I figured Naomi must have told him."

Masters then asks, "Do you have any idea who might have wanted to kill Naomi?"

"I hate to say this," cautions King, "but I think Ryan couldn't take the news and lost it. From what he told me, it sounds like he shot her and blacked out or something."

"Did Naomi ever express any fear of Ryan?"

"She was afraid of how he might react."

"In what way?"

"She wasn't sure, but she was afraid, I know that."

"I need to ask one more time," says Masters. "Are you sure you were not at the Cooper home anytime on Wednesday?"

"Positive, Ryan has to be confusing Tuesday night for Wednesday," King assures them.

Masters then shows King a picture of the gun. "Do you recognize this gun?"

"I'm not sure, it looks like the one Ryan owns. He went to the range with me one time and had a five-shot revolver like this one."

"Do you know where he kept it?"

"No, only that he kept it hidden somewhere."

"We would like to take your fingerprints for elimination purposes. You did say you were there Tuesday."

"Yes, that's fine," replies King.

Before leaving the police station, King has his fingerprints scanned by a crime technician.

The next interview is with Naomi's sister, Serena Mills. Mills lives in a quaint country home with her husband and daughter about five miles south of Castle Rock. Upon the detectives' arrival, Mills, while being visibly upset, invites the detectives in and offers them fresh coffee. Masters graciously accepts. He figures it's going to be a long day.

Mills tells Masters and Tippen that yes, Naomi was having an affair. Naomi had told her this several weeks ago and Mills had encouraged Naomi to tell Ryan. Mills is now upset and blaming herself for Naomi's death.

"If only I hadn't encouraged her to tell Ryan, maybe she would still be alive right now," cried Mills.

"Don't blame yourself, Mrs. Mills," says Tippen with a comforting tone. "She had to tell him sometime, or he would have eventually found out anyway. Who was she having the affair with?"

"I don't know, she wouldn't tell me," Mills replies sadly.

"Was she unhappy with Ryan?"

"Yes, she said he was inattentive to her and worked too much. She told me her affair made her feel alive again."

While driving from Mills' home, Tippen says, "I sure wish we knew who this mystery lover is."

"Sounds like Mrs. Cooper was very secretive about it," states Masters. "Maybe it's because she knew how her husband would react. King indicated she had been afraid to tell him."

"Drive to 1512 North Spencer Avenue," advises Tippen. "That's the accounting office where Debbie Davis works, the host of the book club meeting. I already called and told her we were coming."

Detectives contact Davis at her office, and she invites them in. With tears in her eyes, she says, "I can't believe Naomi is dead. It is devastating. She was a close friend."

"We are sorry for your loss Mrs. Davis," sympathizes Tippen. "Were you aware of an affair Naomi was having?"

"No, not at all. That doesn't sound like Naomi," says Davis.

"Did she mention any problems with her husband?" Tippen continues.

"No, not that I remember."

"What time did Naomi arrive on Wednesday night?"

"Around seven pm. That's when we start."

"And when did she leave?"

"Oh, I believe it was about a quarter to nine."

"Is that pretty normal for book club?"

"Close, it was a little earlier than normal. We usually go until nine o'clock."

"Do you know why she left early?"

"I think her husband called her. She received a phone call, or maybe she made a call, I'm not quite sure. She left immediately after, saying she had to go."

"Did she say why?"

"No, other than she was tired. She did seem kind of distracted during our meeting."

"How so?" asks Tippen.

"She wasn't engaged in the discussion like she normally is. She was noticeably quiet that night."

"Did she ever mention having problems with her marriage?"

"No, nothing like that."

"Okay, thank you Mrs. Davis. If you think of anything else, please give us a call," Tippen tells her.

Before going back to the station, Masters and Tippen stop at Popeye's for a quick late lunch. Masters orders the Spicy Chicken Sandwich, his favorite, and Tippen orders the chicken fingers. Both have large sodas to quench their thirst as well as for the caffeine. They get back to their office at about 3:00 pm.

On their desks are dozens of officer and crime scene technician reports to review. Soon, the autopsy report will be in and forensic results will start arriving after the weekend. Both detectives spend the rest of the day sorting through the reports.

By 3:30 pm the same day, Cooper's memory is starting to become clearer. He now believes King was visiting him on Wednesday night and having a couple of drinks. He calls King to find out what happened.

"Justin, I know you came over Wednesday night, but I must have passed out. What happened?"

"Ryan," Justin answers, "like I already told you, I was not at your place Wednesday night. I was there Tuesday night. You are confusing the days."

"No Justin, I remember because you wanted to talk business and it was the same night Naomi was at book club. Please tell me what happened."

"I'm sorry man, but I was not there. It was Tuesday night. You were very depressed, probably over Naomi's affair."

"I never knew about an affair!" insists Cooper.

"You had a lot to drink Tuesday night. Were you also drinking Wednesday night?"

"Yes, with you."

"I don't know what to tell you Ryan, I was there Tuesday night."

Cooper is now starting to doubt his own memory. *Is it actually Tuesday night I am thinking of?* After all, he had blacked out and initially couldn't remember much of anything. Is he now confused? Could he have killed Naomi and just not remember it? *No, it can't be,* he says to himself.

"Justin, did you know about an affair?"

"Yes," answers King, "she told me over a week ago and said she was going to tell you."

"Who with?"

"She never told me Ryan, sorry."

"Justin," says Cooper as he lowers his voice, "do you know what happened to Naomi?"

"I hate to say this Ryan, but I think you were overcome with emotion, had too much to drink, and shot her when she got home Wednesday night."

"No, no!" responds Cooper in a much louder voice. "I would never have done such a thing. How can you think that?"

"It's just the way I see it Ryan."

"You were there that night," Cooper says sternly, "I remember. You brought over a bottle of rum."

"You're talking crazy now, have you been drinking again?"

"No, I'm completely sober."

"Well, I've had enough of this conversation, I'll talk to you later," says King as he disconnects the call.

Cooper is a bit shocked and confused. He now remembers King being at his home, but King adamantly denies it. *Am I going insane, or is Justin hiding something from me?*

Saturday

On Saturday morning, the detectives are back at it. They have scheduled in-office interviews with Lisa Morgan, the administrative assistant for KC Spark Electric, and Richard Cooper, Ryan Cooper's brother. First up is Lisa Morgan. After introductions, Tippen starts the interview.

"Were you aware of any trouble or problems in Ryan's marriage?"

"No," responds Morgan, "as far as I knew, everything was fine."

"Did you know Naomi Cooper?"

"Oh yes, I had met her numerous times at office parties. She would also stop in the office from time to time. Very friendly."

"Were you aware of Mrs. Cooper having an affair?"

"No."

"Can you tell us what Ryan's demeanor was like in the last week or so."

"What do you mean?"

"His mood, anything unusual, any changes in personality, that type of thing."

"No, he seemed fine to me."

"How well did Justin know Naomi?"

"Very well, they were good friends."

"Could something have been going on between Justin and Naomi?"

"No, Justin and Ryan are partners and good friends. I don't believe Justin would do anything like that. And I never saw anything to give me that indication."

"Thank you for your time, Lisa," says Tippen as she ends the interview.

Next up is Richard Cooper. Tippen agrees to allow Masters to lead this interview.

"Thank you for coming in Richard," says Masters, "I'm sure this is difficult."

"Yes, it is," Richard responds, "and you can call me Rich."

"Okay Rich, tell us what you know about Naomi's affair."

"Only what Ryan has told me. He said he didn't know anything about an affair until you showed him the note found in his office. He said he had never seen that note before."

"How were they getting along otherwise?"

"Goodness, I don't know. Everything seemed fine to me. I know she sometimes complained about the hours Ryan worked, but other than that I didn't see any issues."

"I know this is hard, but it is important," Masters tells him, "what did Ryan tell you about last Wednesday night?"

"He was shaken up, and it was hard for him to talk about. He said he kept having visions of Naomi lying dead on the floor covered in blood. He could not remember much until Friday morning when his memory started coming back. He said his partner, Justin King, had come over Wednesday evening while Naomi was at a book thing. Justin wanted to talk business and have a few drinks. He said Justin brought some rum with him and they were drinking rum and cokes. That is pretty much all he remembers until waking up the next morning and finding Naomi dead."

"Did he say how Naomi was shot?"

"He doesn't know. He said maybe someone came in after he passed out and Justin had left. Now that he knows about an affair, he thinks maybe it was the guy she was screwing around with."

"Isn't it more likely Ryan shot Naomi out of anger?"

"Hell no, he would never do anything like that. He is devastated by her death."

"Is there any reason to believe Justin may have shot Naomi?"

"Why would he do that?" Rich responds with a surprised look. "Justin is Ryan's friend and partner, has been for a long time. He had no beef with Naomi."

"Just have to ask," says Masters. "Did you know Ryan owned a handgun?"

"Yes, he has a small revolver."

"Does this look like his handgun?" asks Masters as he shows Rich a photo of the gun.

"Yes, it looks like the one he owns,"

"Okay Rich, thank you for your time today."

"You don't think Ryan shot Naomi do you?" asks Rich.

"At this point, we don't know", answers Masters.

"He would never hurt Naomi like that."

"You'd be surprised what people will do when it involves relationships."

"No, not Ryan."

"Okay Mr. Cooper, thank you for your time today."

After Richard Cooper had left, Tippen says to Masters, "Sounds like Ryan may really believe Justin was there the night of the murder."

"He might," responds Masters, "but it may just be a rouse. The evidence thus far points to Cooper. I'm anxious to get some results from forensics. If King was there drinking with Cooper, where is the extra glass? We should also expect to find his prints somewhere in that living room or kitchen."

There is not much else for the detectives to do except wait until they receive some forensic results from the crime scene. The evidence may help answer some questions, and be useful in the re-interviewing of Ryan Cooper.

Both Masters and Tippen agree to take Sunday off to relax and recharge their bodies for what will likely be a long week.

"See you first thing Monday," says Tippen as she walks out the door.

"Yep, have a good one," replies Masters.

Following Week

On Monday morning, Masters fires up his computer and among his multiple emails is one from the Douglas County Coroner. He opens it up and attached is the autopsy report for Naomi Cooper. He scans to the summary.

Manner of death: Homicide.

Cause of death: Extreme penetrating trauma to the upper chest caused by two .38 caliber hollow-point bullets. Extensive damage was observed to the heart, right lung, aorta, and sternum.

Toxicology Report: No alcohol or drugs detected.

Justin King is back in the office at KC Spark Electric when he is advised by Lisa that Cooper has taken some time off to recover and plan Naomi's funeral. She also informs him of numerous voice messages on the business voice mail system. Many are friends and associates expressing sorrow for Naomi's death. Others are from clients wondering if the business will be able to complete current projects.

"Call them back Lisa and thank them, then assure them there will be no delays on their projects," instructs King. "I'm going to need you to step up and do some of the accounting Ryan was doing. Can you do that?"

"Yes of course," Lisa answers. "Justin, did you know about Naomi having an affair?"

"Huh? oh yeah, she told me almost two weeks ago."

"Really? Did you tell Ryan?"

"No, Naomi said she was going to tell him. Why are you asking me these questions?"

"Just curious why she would tell you?"

Ignoring the question, King says, "I also need you to pull a copy of the partnership agreement for me, specifically the morals clause and dissolution of the partnership."

"What are you thinking?" says Lisa.

"Nothing, just want to be prepared should Ryan be arrested and sent to prison."

"You think he killed her?"

"Isn't it kind of obvious?" retorts King.

As soon as they arrest Ryan, I'll have grounds to start proceedings to dissolve the partnership and become sole owner, thinks King. *So thankful Ryan insisted on adding that clause to the agreement.*

Detective Tippen walks into the detective bureau with some good news. "I just got the gunshot residue results back from the lab. They found residue on Cooper's right hand."

"That's a big piece right there," says an excited Masters. "I'd call that probable cause to arrest."

"Would you like me to get started on an arrest warrant affidavit?" asks Tippen.

"Yes, let's get the body of the affidavit completed with what we know now, and then add as we get more information from forensics. No rush. Cooper may have killed his wife out of anger, but I don't think he is a threat to anyone else. Oh, I forgot to ask, did the gun come back registered to Cooper?"

"Yes," replies Tippen, "he is the registered owner."

"That pretty much eliminates an intruder theory, don't you think?" asks Masters. "Didn't Cooper tell us his gun was hidden in his office?"

"Yes he did," responds Tippen. "What do you make of his amnesia story?"

Masters laughs, "That's bullshit. I'm sure he passed out from drinking after he shot his wife, but not having any memory of it? Nah, he just doesn't have any other defense."

Both detectives are growing more confident that as the evidence grows they will soon have this case solved.

Meanwhile, Ryan Cooper has become increasingly concerned over the police believing he killed his wife. Cooper has contacted an attorney, Chris Inglesby. Inglesby is a former Assistant DA in El Paso County, which includes Colorado Springs. He quit the DA's office two years ago to open a private practice in Castle Rock. He had risen to the level of being one of their best homicide prosecutors. He did this for three years prior to leaving.

Cooper meets with Inglesby and tells him the story of Naomi's death, still claiming not to remember much of anything, other than he believes his business partner and friend, Justin King, was at his house prior to him passing out.

"You say that Justin denies being at your house?" asks Inglesby.

"Yes, he claims I have the day mixed up, that it was Tuesday night when he was there."

"And why are you so sure it was Wednesday night?"

"Because it was the night Naomi had her book club. That's where she was when Justin came over," insists Cooper.

"What is the last thing you remember before passing out?"

"As I can recall, Justin made us some drinks of rum and coke. We were chatting and drinking, and then, I don't really know what happened, but apparently I passed out. The next thing I knew, it was morning, and I woke up feeling awful. It took me a few moments to not feel faint. That's when I found Naomi on the floor."

"Do you often drink and pass out?"

"No, I can't remember the last time I got drunk."

"The police theory will probably be that you shot Naomi, then continued to drink until you passed out."

"No, I did not shoot Naomi."

"Okay, let's wait until we hear what evidence the police actually have. I'm sure they are processing evidence as we speak. In the meantime, do not answer any more questions from the police without my presence. Not on the phone or in person, you got that?"

"Yeah, I got it. Thank you."

Late that afternoon, Tippen obtains additional testing results back from the lab while Masters and another detective are out interviewing the neighbors on Sandy Lane. She is anxious to share them with Masters. Based on the testing results:

Ryan Cooper's fingerprints were found on the drink glass retrieved from the round table next to the recliner. A small unidentified print was found on the bottom of the same glass. The liquid in the glass was determined to be rum.

Ryan Cooper's fingerprints were found all over the half-empty bottle of rum, also retrieved from the round table.

The letter to Ryan from Naomi had no fingerprints or smudges on it.

Ryan Cooper's fingerprints were found on the revolver.

Ryan Cooper's blood test showed a small amount of alcohol and no drugs.

No fingerprints were found on the round table or coffee table.

A small amount of Naomi Cooper's blood was found on the left sleeve of Ryan Cooper's shirt.

No gunshot residue was found on Cooper's clothing.

About an hour later, Masters returns to the office. He tells Tippen they were unable to get any information from any of the neighbors. No one saw or heard anything that night. No one saw any cars parked in the driveway or in front of Cooper's home.

"Well," says Tippen, "I've got some good news. Take a look at these results."

Masters quickly reads over the findings. "This is fantastic. If the ballistics tell us the bullets came from Cooper's gun, we have a pretty solid case."

"Yes we do," says an excited Tippen.

Tuesday

By mid-morning the next day, Tippen had completed the affidavit for an arrest warrant and is with Assistant County DA Jean Simmons. Simmons has just finished reading the affidavit.

"What do you think?" asks Tippen.

"Oh, this is plenty of probable cause for an arrest," replies Simmons. "This looks like a solid case for first-degree murder. No sign of a fight before she was shot?"

"No," advises Tippen, "it looked as though she had just gotten home. Her purse was on the kitchen table, she was dressed in the same clothes she had on at book club, and the time of death was estimated to be between eight and eleven the night before. However, we know she couldn't have arrived home much before nine, so that narrows it down even more. It's all in the affidavit."

"Yeah, but he may try to claim heat of the moment type thing, or that she attacked him first," says Simmons."

"He may," responds Tippen, "but as of right now we have no evidence of that. He has already claimed to not remember anything."

Simmons signs off on the affidavit. Tippen takes the affidavit to one of the District Judges. After reading the affidavit, the Judge agrees there is probable cause to arrest for First Degree Homicide and signs the warrant for the arrest of Ryan Cooper.

That afternoon, Masters and Tippen, accompanied by two patrol officers, arrive at the home of Ryan Cooper. Masters knocks on the front door. Initially, there is no answer. Masters knocks again, louder this time. Five seconds later, Cooper opens the door. He is wearing blue jeans and a Bronco's t-shirt. It appears as though he hasn't shaved in a couple of days.

"Yes detectives, what is it?" he asks.

"Mr. Cooper," announces Masters, "we have a warrant for your arrest on charges of First Degree Murder and Felony Domestic Violence. We are placing you under arrest. Please turn around and place your hands on top of your head."

"What?!" exclaims Cooper, "I did not kill my wife!"

"Just turn around Mr. Cooper, right now we have a warrant. Let's make this easy."

In frustration, Cooper turns around and places his hands on top of his head. "Someone came in my house and killed Naomi while I was passed out," says Cooper in a loud voice.

"Right now is not the time to debate it," says Masters, as one of the patrol officers pats Cooper down for any weapons, then handcuffs his hands behind his back. "We can talk about it some more at the station."

At the station, Cooper is escorted to the detective bureau and placed in one of the sparsely furnished interview rooms. Masters sits down across from Cooper while Tippen walks behind him and uncuffs his hands. She then joins Masters in sitting across from Cooper.

"We have some more questions to ask you," says Masters.

"I'm not going to talk without my attorney," insists Cooper.

"So, the man who didn't shoot his wife wants an attorney now, eh?" retorts Masters. "Who is your attorney?"

"Chris Inglesby."

"We'll go contact your attorney. You sit here and wait."

Masters and Tippen leave the room. Tippen watches Cooper in the interview room from the monitor in the media room while

Masters calls Inglesby. Masters returns in a few minutes and tells Tippen the attorney is on his way.

After waiting twenty minutes, Inglesby arrives and briefly meets with Tippen and Masters. They advise Inglesby of the new evidence and the charge for first-degree murder. They tell Inglesby they would like to ask Cooper some more questions.

"It depends on what you ask as to whether I will let him answer," warns Inglesby.

"We understand," replies Tippen.

All three enter the interview room. Inglesby tells Cooper they will listen to the questions, but he only wants Cooper to answer when he tells him it is okay to answer. Cooper agrees.

"Ryan," starts Masters, "why did you have your gun with you last Wednesday night."

"He's not going to answer that," says Inglesby. "I can tell you he has no memory of handling any gun that night."

"Then why can't he say that himself?"

"I'm not going to let him answer any accusatory questions," explains Inglesby.

"We found his fingerprints all over the gun."

"Of course you did," answered Inglesby, "it was his gun."

"What questions will you let him answer then?" asks Masters.

"Ask him about his partner Justin King being there that night. His memory is much clearer now."

"I'll bet it is. Okay, Ryan, what do you now remember about Justin King?"

"I'm sure he was there that night," answers Cooper. "He came over to discuss business and we had a couple of drinks of rum and coke. At some point, I passed out and that is all I remember."

"He denies being there at all," challenges Masters. "He says he was there Tuesday night, not Wednesday. We have no evidence or witnesses that put him at your house that night. How do you explain that?"

Inglesby nods indicating it is okay for Cooper to answer.

"No one else was there except me and Justin. I know it was Wednesday night because it was the night Naomi had book club. That's why we were the only two in the house."

"Why would he lie about being there?"

"I have no idea, other than maybe he's scared he will be blamed for Naomi's death."

"Did he have reason to kill Naomi?"

"No, not that I know of."

Masters presses harder, "So if he was there and had no reason to kill Naomi, that leaves you and you certainly had a reason."

"Okay," interrupts Inglesby, "that's enough. You need to find out why Mr. King is lying about not being there. There are things about this case that are not adding up. I need copies of your reports and lab findings."

"You will get copies once the DA has all of them," Masters tells him. "And just so you know, we also have gunshot residue from Ryan's hands and his prints on the glass and rum bottle. We have not found any circumstantial or forensic evidence that Mr. King was there."

Masters and Tippen conclude the interview. Tippen escorts Cooper out of the interview room to a waiting patrol car that will take him to the Douglas County Jail. Masters escorts Inglesby out of the police station. Before parting, Masters assures Inglesby they will confront King again about his whereabouts last Wednesday. Inglesby thanks him.

At the jail, Cooper is taken to an intake room where he is again fingerprinted, and swabs of his DNA are taken. This is a routine procedure for homicide arrestees. After the intake paperwork is completed, Cooper is taken to another smaller concrete block room with a cement floor. There is one bench seat along the back wall. Cooper is made to take off all his clothing, including underwear. Cooper is stressed and the room feels chilly, causing Cooper to shiver. A corrections officer then conducts a strip search of Cooper's body.

This is humiliating. Why is this happening to me? thinks Cooper.

After the strip search, Cooper is given an orange jumpsuit to wear. Once he is redressed in the jumpsuit, he is escorted by two corrections officers through a large steel door that clangs shut behind them. He is walked down a long hall past numerous jail cells containing prisoners. Some of the prisoners get up to the bars of their cells to see who the new resident is.

Cooper is taken to a vacant eight by ten-foot block walled cell and placed inside. As the officers leave, they close the heavy steel barred door behind them. It makes a large clanging sound as it is closed, sending a shiver down Cooper's back. A week after Naomi's death, Cooper is now sitting in jail for her murder. Cooper's eyes well up with tears as he thinks, *how am I going to prove my innocence? I know I didn't kill Naomi. Why can't I remember what happened?*

Two Days Later

On Thursday, Tippen and Masters have called King back to the police station for another interview. He arrives at approximately 10:30 am.

"Justin," starts Tippen, "we have a few more questions to ask you."

"Sure," says King, "anything I can do to help."

"Ryan's memory has cleared up since last week, and he is now sure you were at his home on the night of the murder," advises Tippen.

"Well, simply not true. I was there on Tuesday night, not Wednesday night."

"He's pretty clear it was Wednesday night Justin. He knows because that was the night Naomi was gone for book club. You were the only two there."

"I don't know what he's saying, but I wasn't there."

"Then where were you that night?"

"I had worked a long day and was home. Had a beer to relax, then went to bed at about nine o'clock."

"Did you call anyone that night?"

"No, at least I don't remember calling anyone."

Masters interrupts, "Justin, we found your fingerprints at the scene, we know you were there."

"Where did you find them?"

"What does it matter? Why would your prints be there if you say you weren't there?"

"I have no idea, unless they were there from the night before. Where did you find them?"

"We found one of your prints on the gun Justin."

Now Justin knows the detective is bluffing. He had made sure to thoroughly wipe the gun down.

"Impossible," says a defiant King, "I never touched any gun. I don't even know where he kept that damn gun."

"We also know you were having an affair with Naomi," continues Masters.

This shocks King a bit, as now he is not sure if the detective is bluffing, or if he actually knows. Whichever it is, he cannot admit to an affair. For the first time, he feels a bit nervous.

"I was not having an affair with Naomi or anyone else. That's insulting you would even say that. Who told you that nonsense?"

"We have our sources."

"I think you are lying," says King. "Naomi wouldn't even tell me who she was having an affair with. All I know is she was having one and told Ryan about it."

Masters leans in toward King and challenges him, "I think Naomi was going to tell Ryan it was you and you had to kill her to save your partnership."

"We were not having an affair and I had nothing to do with Naomi's death," says King in a raised voice. "You've already arrested Ryan for the murder, and now you're telling me you think I did it? Arrest me then and I will sue the both of you and the city, because I know you have no evidence against me."

"Justin, if you were there, we will find out," warns Masters. "I hope you are telling us the truth."

"I certainly am."

"One more thing," says Tippen, "are you sure you didn't make or receive any calls from anyone that night?"

"Not that I recall. That was over a week ago now."

"Okay, thank you."

The interview concludes and King is allowed to leave.

Tippen turns to Masters, "you pushed him real hard, and he stuck to his story."

"Yeah, I wanted to see what kind of reaction we got or whether he would admit to being there. Except for the now revived memory of our drunk suspect, we have nothing to indicate anyone else was there."

Back at the office that afternoon, Lisa provides King the language from the partnership agreement he was looking for. The partnership agreement includes a morals clause to protect both partners in the event one of them does something so egregious as to harm the reputation or profitability of the company. The clause states:

Partners will not engage in activities or conduct which is harmful to the reputation or business activities of the partnership. These activities include immoral acts which become public, misappropriation of company funds, or the commission of any serious felony. If a partner engages in such activities and causes harm to the company, the other partner(s) may terminate the partnership with said offender. The partner removed from the partnership will be entitled to compensation for his/her share of the company. If a settlement amount is not agreed upon through negotiation, all partners agree to settle the dispute through arbitration.

"What do you need this for Justin?" asks Lisa.

"Ryan has been arrested for first-degree murder, Lisa. This case is now getting lots of media attention. Headlines scream KC Spark Electric Owner Arrested for Murdering Wife. You've gotten some of the calls, customers are concerned. I've gotten three calls this week of clients wanting to back out of contracts."

"Yes," says Lisa, "but he has not been convicted of anything. I still don't believe he did it."

"You are one of the only ones Lisa. The evidence against him keeps mounting. I need to protect this business."

This disturbs Lisa, as she believes King is acting too quickly in planning to take over the business. *It's only been a little over a week,* thinks Lisa. *Shouldn't he be more supportive of Ryan right now?*

Late Thursday afternoon, Tippen receives the ballistics report from their firearms expert. The report confirms both bullets were fired from the five-shot Smith and Wesson revolver found at the scene and belonging to Ryan Cooper. Tippen shares the report with Masters.

"That's more icing on the cake," exclaims Masters. "Did our CSIs find any other bullets in the house to match those in the gun?"

"Not according to the search inventory," responds Tippen.

Friday

On Friday morning, nine days after Naomi's murder, Cooper appears in court with his attorney, Chris Inglesby, for his arraignment. Representing the state is Assistant DA Jean Simmons. The judge explains the charge of First Degree Murder to Cooper and explains to him his rights. He is then asked how he pleads, guilty or not guilty to the charge. Cooper pleads not guilty. A trial date is set for November 14th, approximately six months from Naomi's death. The judge must now set bail for Cooper.

Cooper's attorney, Inglesby, argues that Cooper is local, has ties to the community, is a respected business owner, has never been in any legal trouble, and is not a flight risk. Inglesby argues for a reasonable bail amount.

Assistant DA Simmons argues against bail, citing the violence of the crime and the seriousness of the charge. She also argues that an unknown person may be in danger should Cooper be released. Simmons talks of the unknown identity of the person Naomi was having an affair with and that the evidence strongly supports the motive for killing Naomi was the affair. Releasing Cooper would put this person in danger.

After listening to both arguments, the judge refuses to set a bail amount, however, he agrees to reconsider after a preliminary hearing. After the hearing concludes, Cooper is taken back to the county jail in handcuffs.

The Next Week

On Monday, Tippen and Masters have received the phone records from the phones of both Naomi and Ryan Cooper. Masters begins to review the phone records while Tippen works on reviewing all the forensic reports.

While reviewing the reports, Tippen receives a phone call from Cooper's attorney, Chris Inglesby.

"What can I do for you?" asks Tippen.

"I've gotten all the reports from the DA's office and have been pouring over them," says Inglesby. "I see where there were no boxes of bullets found in the home, is that correct?"

"That's correct."

"And no loose bullets other than those in the gun?"

"No other bullets were located," assures Tippen.

"Well, just so you are aware, Ryan says he didn't have any bullets for that gun. He had used what he had last summer while target shooting and just never got around to buying anymore."

"Doesn't mean he didn't have five left in the gun," counters Tippen.

"No, but he says he didn't. And the fact that there were no other bullets in the house should at least raise some questions, don't you think?"

"That's something to argue in court," counters Tippen. "We have plenty of evidence to believe your client is guilty."

"Ryan is still adamant that King was there that night. I don't see a report here. Did you ever re-interview King?"

"Yes," answers Tippen, "and Bill pushed him real hard, even bluffed him with evidence and he didn't waver. Says he was only there on the night before."

"One more question, is it accurate that no fingerprints of any kind were found on the alleged note from Naomi?"

"That's correct."

"Yet the note was somewhat crinkled, indicating someone had handled it, right?"

"Yes."

"Okay, thank you detective."

We do have some loose ends in this case, thinks Tippen, *but that is not so unusual. No case is perfect.*

Later the same day, Tippen receives a phone call from Lisa Morgan, the assistant at KC Spark Electric.

"What can I do for you Ms. Morgan?", asks Tippen.

"It may be nothing," Morgan starts, "but Justin has been acting strange."

"How so?"

"Well, he just doesn't seem to be upset over the arrest of his friend and longtime partner. And now, he's starting a process to remove Mr. Cooper from the partnership. He doesn't even call Ryan to check up on him or anything. He just seems so focused on taking over ownership."

"How is he planning to remove him from the partnership?"

"There is some clause about committing a crime that allows someone to be removed."

"Can you fax me a copy of the clause?" asks Tippen.

"Yes, I will do that."

"Okay, thank you for the information Ms. Morgan."

At 3:00 pm, Tippen and Masters meet to review the case file. Masters starts it off with a review of the phone records.

"This is interesting. Naomi did not receive a call at the book club meeting. She made the call to 555-334-5670."

"Who's number is that?" asks Tippen.

"Justin King."

"Seriously? He's definitely hiding something"

"In fact," continues Masters, "she made an earlier call to King at approximately six-fifty pm, about the time she left for book club. There are numerous phone calls between Naomi and the same phone number over the last six months"

"Oh my god," replies a shocked Tippen. "I'll bet that son of a bitch was the one she was having an affair with."

"Yeah, and that's not all I found. On the Monday before her murder, Naomi sent a text to the same number. It said, *"Are you going to call me soon?"*

"Should we drag him back in here for another go around?"

"Yes, but not yet. Let's go over everything again. We might be missing something."

"What do you think about there not being any other bullets in the house?" asks Tippen.

"Somewhat unusual, but not proof of anything. The gun was certainly Coopers."

"What is the likelihood of getting prints off the casings?"

"Not likely on the fired ones, but possible on the ones that have not been fired. We can ask the lab to use the fuming process to try and bring up any prints. And something else I want to ask them. How likely would it be not to have any prints or smudges on that note from Naomi? It had obviously been handled by someone."

"I agree," says Tippen. "I was wondering that myself. Inglesby called me and asked about it as well."

"The attorney?"

"Yeah, and something else. Lisa Morgan called and told me she thought King was not showing the appropriate level of concern for his partner, and in fact was taking steps to remove him from the partnership."

"Hmmm, it does seem a bit early for that."

"I also questioned Brent, our fingerprint tech, about that unidentifiable partial print from the bottom of the drink glass," continues Tippen. "He said the print was a partial print from the side of a finger. He said it probably was left there by a person holding the glass with one finger on the bottom supporting it."

Tippen then picks up a Coke can off the desk and holds it in her right hand, fingers and thumb wrapped around the can and her pinky finger underneath the can to support it, making it easier to hold.

"Like this," she says

"Can he identify it?"

"For him to declare a match to anyone, he needs at least twelve points of comparison. This print only has seven. But it can be used to eliminate people."

"So, is Cooper eliminated as a possible source?"

"He's working on that right now," assures Tippen.

"Okay, the next time you talk to Brent, ask him about the typed note from Naomi and the lack of any prints, even smudges."

"Yeah, I will."

"Alright," says Masters, "you work on the forensics and I will work on these phone records. I need to get a copy of King's records and if possible, location data. With this new information on these phone calls, I'm starting to believe maybe King was there after all."

Tuesday

In the morning, Lisa goes into King's office to let him know customers are calling to express concern over work not getting done.

"Justin, I'm trying to keep our customers happy, but things are starting to fall behind. You need to get out of the office and pay more attention to our contractors. I can handle things here in the office."

"Okay Lisa, I know. It's been a hard week. The police have been on my back harassing me, I'm trying to get the partnership straightened out, and we have this Colorado Springs contract I need to get started on. Give me a break."

"You don't need to do anything with the partnership right now, just focus on the business at hand Justin."

"I'm trying, just give me some peace right now, okay?"

"Alright Justin, let me know if I can do anything more to help."

Lisa walks out and shuts the door behind her. *This is not going to end well if Justin doesn't get his act together,* Lisa says to herself.

At 2:30 pm, Masters and Tippen meet to share what they've learned since yesterday.

"As for the partial fingerprint from the glass," Tippen says, "Brent can eliminate Ryan Cooper as a contributor."

Masters looks at Tippen with raised eyebrows, "really."

"And get this, he cannot eliminate Justin King."

"Interesting," replies Masters.

"As for the note, Brent said it would be highly unusual to not have any prints or smudges on a handled piece of paper unless it was handled in a cold, dry climate or the person handling the paper wore gloves. Since the note was found inside the house, he would expect it to show some signs of being touched. He's still working on the bullet casings."

"Nothing solid, but it does raise more questions, doesn't it?" asks Masters.

"Sure does," agrees Tippen.

"As do the phone records," states Masters. "There are plenty of phone calls back and forth between Naomi and King. There is also a day about two weeks before her death when, according to the cell site location data, both phones made outgoing calls from the same area."

"What area would that be?"

"Lone Tree."

"Isn't that…"

"Yep," Masters interrupts, "where King lives. I've been thinking, if King was actually at the Cooper residence on the night Naomi was killed, he had to have driven there. I'm wondering with all the ring doorbells and security cameras these days, whether we might be able to find some footage from around Cooper's home."

"It's worth a shot. But even if we can prove King lied about being there, we still have Cooper's prints on the gun, gunshot residue on his hands, and the affair as a motive."

"Yeah, I still think Cooper probably killed his wife out of anger, but King is hiding something. Maybe he just doesn't want us to know he was the one having the affair. Either way, we need more answers. I'll go out this afternoon and see if I can't dig up some security footage."

"Great," responds Tippen. "Oh, I almost forgot. I got a call from DA Simmons late yesterday. Inglesby has requested to have Cooper's blood sample re-tested for Rohypnol, GHB, and Ketamine. Apparently, Inglesby had Cooper interviewed by a doctor, and based on Cooper's description of his conditions, the doctor suggested he may have been drugged by one of those three."

"All three are considered date rape drugs," says Masters. "They do knock you out pretty well. Given the half-empty bottle of rum, I hadn't thought of that. It's a good idea, especially with all this new information."

"Yeah, the DA has already requested the new testing."

Later that afternoon, Masters responds to Sandy Lane to check for security cameras in the neighborhood. He finds one neighbor, Robert Saunders, has an advanced security system. Saunders used to be in the security business, and lives in the first house on Sandy Lane off of Oak Avenue,

"Yes, my system keeps data for thirty days," informs Saunders. "I would still have footage for that Wednesday."

"What type of coverage does it have?" asks Masters.

"I've got one camera focused on the drive looking out into the street. You can see out to the corner of Sandy Lane and Oak."

"Would I be able to get a copy of that? It might help us with the investigation of Naomi Cooper's murder."

"Absolutely. I can email you a digital copy this afternoon. What time frame are you looking for?"

"How about from five pm to ten pm?"

"No problem. Give me some time to find it and make a copy for you. You should have it in the next hour."

"Thank you very much, Mr. Saunders."

"Happy to help. Have a good day detective."

Masters is feeling excited about the potential to see who came and left that Wednesday evening on Sandy Lane, but also weary knowing he has a long night ahead of him. It isn't long after arriving back at his desk that he sees the file in his email. He gets himself a sandwich out of the cafeteria vending machine, grabs a cup of coffee, and settles in to watch some video.

This same night, at about 7:00 pm, King receives a phone call from Cooper's next-door neighbor, Frank Parker. Parker is an outgoing gregarious man who knows King from his many visits to Cooper's home and summer bar-b-ques.

"Hey Justin, just thought you might want to know that the police keep coming out here asking if we saw anyone or anything suspicious on the night of Naomi's murder. They even asked me about you."

"They did?" asks King. "What did they want?"

"The first time they were asking if we saw anyone. This time they were asking specifically about you and wanted to know if I had any security cameras. The detective wanted to know if I'd ever seen you and Naomi together. What's going on? I thought they had solved the case already."

"I don't know Frank," says King. They've already charged Ryan with the murder."

"Yeah, that's why I thought it was strange they were asking about you."

"Do you have any cameras?"

"No, I don't, but Bob Saunders on the corner does."

"You don't say. Do you know where the cameras are?"

"No, but he was in security and has a good system, I know that. He tried talking me into one."

"Well I don't know why they are asking Frank, but thanks for telling me. I gotta go."

"Alright, good night Justin."

Why are they looking for security footage? ponders King. *And why are they still asking about me and Naomi? They've already arrested and charged Ryan. Did I make a mistake somewhere? Do they know about my affair with Naomi?*

For the first time since putting his plan in place six months ago by starting his affair with Naomi, King is worried it may not be working as well as he thought. He is starting to get nervous. King goes to his dresser drawer and pulls out his Glock Model 22 semi-auto .40 caliber handgun. He ejects the magazine to be sure it is fully loaded, then snaps the magazine back into the gun and chambers one round. He decides he needs to start keeping his gun with him for protection. *I'm not going to prison,* he says to himself.

Meanwhile, Masters is at his desk watching and re-watching security video. At the 6:51 pm mark, he observes Naomi driving past the Saunders residence in her white Ford Escape, then turning left onto Oak Avenue. *That has to be her going to book club,* thinks Masters. Then, at the 7:25 mark, Masters sees a vehicle headed east on Oak Avenue. It slows down and appears to be parking along the south curb, just past Sandy Lane. The car appears to be a light-colored BMW. The car eventually leaves the frame before stopping. Masters is unable to read the plate. A few minutes later, he views a male walking southbound on the sidewalk across the street from Saunders' home. The male fits the size and physique of King and is wearing a dark-colored windbreaker-type jacket. Masters believes it could be King.

Masters continues studying the video until he sees Naomi turning south onto Sandy Lane at the 8:52 mark and continuing south toward her home. *That is Naomi returning from book club. King is still at the house.*

At the 9:34 mark, Masters observes the same male figure walking northbound toward Oak Avenue. The male cuts across the front lawn of the far corner property toward the location where Masters believes the BMW is parked. He believes the car is King's and it is King he sees walking, but others may not see it the same way. Masters hopes getting the digital file enhanced will make the license plate and walking male more identifiable.

At 8:45 pm, Tippen snuggles into bed with a James Patterson novel, hoping to get some reading in before falling asleep. At 9:15, she is sound asleep with the book lying open across her stomach when she is awakened by her phone ringing on the bedside table. She sees the call is from Masters.

"What is it Bill?"

"He was there!" exclaims Masters.

"What are you talking about Bill?"

"King! He was at the house with Cooper the night of the murder. And get this, he was there when Naomi returned home."

"How do you know?"

"He's on the Saunders security video."

Tippen is still processing what Masters has just told her when he blurts out, "he and Naomi may have been arguing with Cooper over the affair when she was shot."

"This just keeps getting stranger all the time," replies Tippen.

"Yes, it does. I just wanted to share the news. I have to go and get this ready for our tech people to work on tomorrow. See you then," says Masters as he hangs up the phone.

Wednesday

In the morning, Tippen arrives at work at eight o'clock and finds Masters is already there working.

"Did you go home last night?"

"Yes, about ten-thirty. Just wanted to get an early start today. I didn't sleep well anyway."

"No, I didn't either, not after your phone call anyway. I started going through different possible scenarios in my mind."

"No kidding," says Masters, "we need to somehow figure out what happened between Cooper and King, and then what happened when Naomi returned home. If Cooper shot Naomi over the affair, why not also shoot King?"

"Yeah, I was thinking the same thing."

By early afternoon, none of the forensic results they are waiting on have been completed. Finally, Tippen receives a phone call from Brent Butler, the fingerprint analyst.

"I've got some news I think might impact your case," announces Butler.

"Well? What is it?"

"We were able to get three comparable prints off those unfired bullet casings using cyanoacrylate fuming, what you detectives call superglue fuming. We found no prints belonging to Ryan Cooper. All three prints are positively identified as belonging to Justin King."

"Holy crap," says Tippen.

"That's not all. Remember the partial off the bottom of the drink glass?"

"Yeah."

"As I said, we only have seven points for comparison, so I can't make a positive ID, but all seven points match the side of King's right-hand pinky finger, making it highly probable he is the contributor of that print as well."

"Thank you so much Brent, this is great information."

Tippen wastes no time in telling Masters the news.

Masters summarizes, "So now we have King at the scene, and have him as the one who loaded the bullets in the gun that killed

Naomi. And we now believe he was having an affair with Naomi. This case is getting turned upside down."

"This new information has me thinking," says Tippen. "The fingerprints found on the gun were from Cooper's right hand, correct?"

"Yes."

"Do you remember him signing the property receipt when we gathered his clothing and cell phone?"

"No, didn't an officer handle that?"

"Yes, but I saw him signing before he left. If I remember correctly, I believe he signed with his left hand."

"Call the assistant at the electric company," suggests Masters, "she will be able to tell you if Cooper is left-handed."

Ten minutes later, Tippen returns to Masters' desk and tells him Lisa Morgan confirmed what she remembers, Cooper is left-handed. She also tells him that according to Morgan, King is acting stranger every day. He is letting work slide, wants to remove Cooper as a partner, and is complaining about how the investigation is going.

"You know Jane, I'm starting to think we may have gotten suckered into some grand scheme of King's."

"It's certainly looking like it," she agrees.

"And the more I think about it," continues Masters, "I would not be surprised if this second blood test shows Cooper was indeed drugged."

Later that afternoon, the results continue to come in. Masters receives an enhanced copy of the security footage. Masters is now able to make out the plate on the BMW. It is Colorado plate KCS173. He is also able to see more clearly the person walking in the direction of Cooper's home, and later away from his home.

He can now see it is indeed Justin King. Masters shows the video to Tippen.

"Amazing how well they were able to enhance this video," she says.

Just then, Tippen receives a phone call on her cell. It is the forensic lab calling.

"Hello. Yes, this is Jane," she answers, then listens for several seconds.

"Really? Yes, if you send me a copy that will be great."

"More good news?" asks Masters.

"I'll say, the blood work came back positive for Rohypnol. Cooper was drugged."

"Better get yourself a large coffee," says Masters. "This is going to be another long night. We need to get into King's condo tonight. If we find Rohypnol and the box of bullets, we will have enough for an arrest warrant on King. I'll start on a search warrant affidavit if you call DA Simmons and let her know what's going on. Then you work on organizing and listing our evidence for me to include in the affidavit. Is that okay with you?"

"Absolutely, I'll go call Simmons now."

Two hours later, Masters has completed the affidavit and included a detailed list of the evidence supporting a search warrant of King's condo.

"This looks real good Bill," says Tippen.

"Great, I just sent a copy over to Simmons for her review. Once we get the okay, we'll take it to a judge."

Thirty minutes later, Simmons calls Masters and gives him her approval to get the warrant signed. It is after 5:00 pm, so Masters and Tippen head over to the on-call judge's home for issuance of the search warrant. They arrive at 5:35 pm. The judge reads the affidavit.

"This is a strange twist of events," says the judge.

"Yes sir," replies Masters, "it took a while to figure it all out."

"Nicely done," says the judge as he signs the search warrant and hands it back to Masters.

"Thank you sir, have a good night."

Masters had already requested assistance from the Lone Tree Police Department in executing the search of King's condo. They agree to have two uniformed officers meet them in the parking lot of the condo complex. Masters and Tippen arrive at 6:30 pm. Introductions are made, and Masters briefly explains the case and who they are dealing with. The officers will assist with entry into the condo, then stand by for security as the detectives conduct their search.

The officers approach the door and knock loudly on the door several times. There is no answer. With the use of a crowbar, the officers are able to get the door open. With guns drawn, the Lone Tree officers search the condo and find it empty. They then turn it over to Masters and Tippen.

As they walk into the condo, they notice it is not well kept. A pizza box and some fast food wrappers are still on the coffee table in the living room. Dirty dishes are in the sink and on the kitchen table. A pile of dirty clothes sits at the foot of the bed in the master bedroom and the bed looks like it hasn't been made in several days. The second bedroom looks as though it is used for storage only. The bathroom has a towel on the floor and various toiletries scattered on the sink counter.

"Where should we start?" asks Tippen.

"Let's start in the most obvious places first. I'll take the master bedroom if you take the bathroom."

"Okay."

Masters is searching the bedroom closet and shelves when he hears Tippen yell out.

"I think I found something."

Masters goes to the bathroom and finds Tippen holding a small tinted pill bottle, unlabeled, with 7 small white tablets inside.

"Do you think this is the Rohypnol?"

"I've seen Rohypnol that looks like that, so it could very well be. Where was it?"

"Right here in his medicine cabinet."

"I wonder how many women he's used that on," comments Masters.

Masters returns to the bedroom and finishes searching the closet. Finding nothing, he goes to the dresser and opens the top drawer. To his delight, he sees a box of Smith and Wesson 38 caliber hollow point bullets. He also finds a Ruger six-shot revolver. Using latex gloves, Masters opens the box and sees eleven bullets missing. He then closes the box and picks up the revolver. He opens the cylinder and sees the gun is loaded with six bullets. *That makes eleven. Six in this gun and five in Cooper's gun,* he says to himself.

"I think I found the bullets used to kill Naomi," shouts Masters. Tippen enters the bedroom and Masters shows her the box of bullets with eleven bullets missing. Masters then collects the box and revolver, carefully packing them in paper bags.

While they are searching, King arrives home from work. He drives into the parking lot when he notices two Lone Tree police cars parked near his condo. He glances around and sees two uniformed officers talking outside his condo door and the door is partially opened. *Are they searching my condo?*

King feels his face turn flush and his body starts to tingle with anxiety. Trying not to be noticed, King makes a K turn in the parking lot and drives back onto the street. He doesn't know where he is going, but he is not going home right now.

In searching the living room, Masters finds a dark blue windbreaker jacket hanging over the arm of the beige cloth couch. He asks Tippen if she thinks it looks like the same jacket he was wearing in the video.

"Yes, it looks the same to me."

Masters carefully folds it and seals it in a paper bag. Tippen finds a pile of old receipts on an oak desk in the dining area. She quickly looks through them and finds several for local hotel charges. One is for the Comfort Inn Suites in Castle Rock from approximately three weeks earlier. She shows the receipts to Masters.

"Good find," he says. "I'll bet we can match some of those up to the phone records."

Tippen carefully packages them up in individual envelopes. Once completed, both agree there is nothing left to search. They complete the inventory of items seized, then leave a copy on the kitchen counter. They leave the condo at 7:45 pm.

"If these pills turn out to be Rohypnol, I think we have enough to arrest King," states Tippen.

"Oh, I agree," responds Masters. "It shouldn't take long to identify these pills. And if that box of bullets turns out to be the exact same as those in the gun, we even have a stronger case against King. How would he explain having his bullets with his prints on them in Cooper's gun? A gun he said he didn't know where Cooper kept it"

"Good question Bill."

King is afraid to return to his condo. Afraid the police are watching it and will arrest him if he shows up. He checks into a local Best Western for the night. *What could they possibly have to tie me to the murder? How could they know about our affair?*

Thursday

King does not show up for work on Thursday. He is too afraid the police are looking for him. He is not sure what to do. He calls Lisa, his assistant.

"Hey Lisa, I'm not going to make it in today. I'm not feeling well."

"What's wrong Justin?"

"Nothing, just haven't gotten much sleep and need some time off. It's been stressful. Hey, if the police call or stop by looking for me, let me know and I will call them right back."

"Okay Justin,"

Just before noon, detectives get a quick answer from the lab. The pills recovered from King's bathroom are in fact Rohypnol. The bullets found in King's top dresser drawer are the same make and type as those found in the murder weapon. Whether they are from the same manufacturer's batch will take longer to determine. Tippen shares this information with DA Simmons. Simmons agrees they have enough to obtain an arrest warrant on King. They still are not sure who shot Naomi, but there is enough evidence now to at least charge King as a co-conspirator in the death of Naomi Cooper.

By 3:30 pm, detectives have their warrant for the arrest of Justin King on charges of First Degree Murder and Conspiracy to Commit Murder.

"King is probably still at work," says Masters. "Why don't we try to pick him up there before he leaves."

"Thinking the same thing," responds Tippen.

Masters and Tippen arrive at KC Spark Electric at 4:10 pm, accompanied by four Castle Rock patrol officers. Two officers station themselves at the rear door in the alley. Masters, Tippen, and the other two officers enter the front door.

"Hi Lisa," says Tippen.

A startled Lisa responds, "Hello, what's going on?"

"We need to speak with Justin. Is he in?"

"No, he called in today. Said he wasn't feeling well."

"Do you mind if we look around?"

"Of course not. Am I in any danger here?"

"No, Lisa, we just need to talk to Justin."

A quick search of the office area confirms King is not in the office.

"Lisa," says Tippen, "if Justin shows up, please give us a call, but don't tell him you called. We need to talk to him."

"Okay," says a frightened Lisa.

Once the police have left, Lisa calls King.

"What's up Lisa?"

"The police were just here looking for you. You told me to call."

"Yeah, what did they want?"

"They said they needed to talk to you."

"Did they say why?"

"No, they seemed kind of secretive about it. When will you be back in the office?"

"I'm not sure Lisa, I'll call you later," says King as he disconnects.

Masters and Tippen plan their next move. They both agree King was probably spooked after finding out his condo had been searched. The question now is, where can they find him?

"Let's have Lone Tree PD check out his condo," suggests Masters. "If he is there, they can hold him until we get there."

After contacting the Lone Tree police, Masters and Tippen head back to the station to wait. It is not long before they receive word that King is not at his condo. They now believe King may be on the run. They decide to put out a BOLO (be on the lookout) for King and his white BMW four-door, license number KCS173

"Nothing to do now but wait," says Masters. "Why don't we go home and get some rest and dinner. It's been a long week and who knows when someone will find King. We'll tell dispatch to notify us if anyone finds him."

"That's the best idea you've had in a long time," jokes Tippen.

Friday

Since seeing officers at his condo, King tries to keep off the main streets. He is afraid to return home or go to his office for fear of being arrested. He so wants to know what the officers have against him, but is afraid to be confronted. He is adamant he will not go to prison for this. He has managed to stay out of sight by only leaving his hotel for walks to get food or visit a nearby bar. By mid-afternoon, he decides he needs to leave but is not sure where to go.

He gets in his car and starts driving through the foothills a while to clear his mind. King eventually finds himself in the village of Castle Pines, a small community of approximately 10,000 just a bit north of Castle Rock. Having only eaten junk food for the last two days, King is hungry for some good food. He drives around town until he finds a small quaint café in Castle Pines with animal heads decorating the walls. He hasn't seen or heard anything on the news, so he doesn't believe anyone will recognize him or even know the police are looking for him. He orders the meatloaf, mashed potatoes, and green beans with a Coors Light to quench his thirst. Comfort food is what he needs right now.

After dinner, King knows he has to get out of the area to give himself some time to think without being worried about being arrested. He has a friend who has a cabin up in Red Feather Lakes, a mountain community about an hour northwest of Ft. Collins. He's stayed with this friend before and has been told he is always welcome. King figures he can go up there and chill out for a while.

King has no clothes or possessions with him, so first, he will have to get to his condo to get some warm clothing and other essentials. He also wants to get his passport and some business files. He hopes he will be able to conduct some business by phone while Lisa runs the office. King believes the police must not have gotten all the forensic evidence analyzed yet. Because once they do, they will realize only Cooper could have been the shooter.

It is now dark as King drives from Castle Pines to Lone Tree. As he gets closer to his condo complex, he carefully scans the area looking for the police or anyone who might look like an undercover officer. Seeing no one as he approaches, he pulls into the parking lot adjacent to his building and parks his car. He sits in the car for a few moments looking around. Seeing nothing suspicious, King decides it is safe to enter his condo to pack his things. He figures he will only need ten or fifteen minutes at the most to pack what he wants to take.

King carefully exits his car and briskly walks to his front door. He sees pry marks on the door and frame. The lock is no longer secure, and anyone could enter if they wanted to. King still uses his key to not cause any further damage. King quickly grabs a duffle bag and starts to pack his clothing.

The Lone Tree Police Department has been tasked with regularly checking on King's condo in the event he might return, and to also provide some security due to the damaged door. They are aware he is now wanted on a murder charge. As King is packing, a Lone Tree officer slowly drives into the parking lot looking for evidence of King's return. He immediately notices a light is on in King's condo. The officer then scans the parking lot and spots the white BMW with license plate KCS173. He immediately gets on his radio to report the suspect has returned and requests immediate backup. He also asks dispatch to notify the Castle Rock Police Department.

King continues to pack his belongings for several more minutes. He notices his Ruger revolver is missing. *Damn cops,* he says to himself. He grabs his toiletries from the bathroom and haphazardly throws the items in his bag. *Okay, I think I've got everything I need.* Once satisfied, King secures the front door as best he can, then starts walking toward his car. He looks up and is shocked to see two Lone Tree police cars blocking the exit from his parking lot. King stops for a moment. He's not sure what to do.

"Freeze!" King hears.

"Police! Don't move! Drop the bag and put your hands up!"

King now realizes there are two officers crouched behind parked vehicles about fifty feet away with guns pointed at him. King immediately leaps and spins, dropping his bag and running for his front door.

"Stop! Police!" he hears again as he runs for the door. *I'm not going to jail,* he keeps telling himself. King reaches the front door and does not bother trying to unlock or open the door. King simply runs toward the door, lowers his left shoulder, and crashes into it as hard as he can. The already damaged frame splinters at the deadbolt and the door goes flying open as King tumbles into his condo. King rolls until he hits the edge of the wall separating his kitchen from the living room. King feels a sharp pain shoot through his left shoulder like an arrow. He thinks he may have broken his collar bone against the door.

King gets up as quickly as possible and shuts the door. He then slides a heavy chair over and pushes it against the door to keep it shut. King falls back against the wall, taking several deep breaths and holding his shoulder. He is not sure what to do next, but he knows he's not going to jail. After a few moments, King realizes the shouting has stopped and it is quiet. He peeks out the front window and now sees two Lone Tree police cars and one Douglas County Sheriff's car. *The calvary is coming.*

It is 7:12 pm when Masters gets a phone call from dispatch. He is told that King has been located at his condo and is currently barricaded inside. Once off the phone, Masters immediately calls Tippen.

"Jane, they've found King."

"Where at?"

"He's holed up in his condo. Police found him there and tried to arrest him, but he ran back inside. I'll be over in 10 minutes to pick you up."

"Alright, I'll be ready."

Masters quickly straps on his holster and Smith and Wesson .45 semi-auto pistol, grabs a couple extra magazines of ammunition, throws on a jacket, and heads out the door. He drives lights and siren over to Tippen's. She is standing outside when he arrives.

Tippen quickly gets in the car and Masters accelerates and heads for the interstate that will take them to Lone Tree. Masters runs with emergency lights and siren the entire way. It takes Masters and Tippen only twelve minutes to get to King's condo complex sixteen miles away. By the time Masters and Tippen arrive, numerous police officers and Douglas County SWAT team members are on the scene. Evacuations of nearby neighbors have already occurred.

The SWAT Commander approaches Masters and Tippen and fills them in on what has happened thus far. They have been unable to get King to exit his condo. They've tried bullhorn and calling him, but he is not responding. Masters asks if he can give it a try.

"Sure, he may respond to you."

Masters takes the bullhorn and walks closer to the condo, keeping behind cover as best he can.

"Justin," announces Masters, "this is Detective Bill Masters. Detective Jane Tippen is also with me. We need to talk. I'm going to call you on my cell phone. Please answer the phone."

Masters then takes his cell phone and calls King's number. It rings four times with no answer. On the fifth ring, King answers the phone.

"Hello, Detective."

"Justin, thank you for answering. Tell me, what is going on here?" asks Masters.

"You tell me. Why am I surrounded by the police, treating me like a wanted criminal? You have the person who killed Naomi. Stop harassing me."

"Justin, we just need to talk. We know you have more information than what you've told us. We need to clarify exactly what happened."

"I've told you everything I know."

"Justin, please come out and talk to me. No one is going to hurt you."

"No, you need to leave me alone now."

"You know I can't do that Justin. We need to talk."

"Talk about what?"

"The fact that you were with Naomi and Ryan on the night she was killed."

"That's not true and you have no evidence of that!"

"We already know you were Justin, that's why I need you to explain to me what happened while you were there."

"You're just making crap up now. I wasn't there and you can't prove I was."

"Justin, listen to me carefully. You did a great job of wiping your prints off Ryan's gun, but you forgot about the bullets." Masters pauses and there is no response.

"You see Justin, we were able to process the prints you left on those bullets. They are your fingerprints Justin and nobody else's. But you would know that, right?"

"You're talking crazy now."

At this point, Masters knows he has him. King did not deny loading the gun or that his fingerprints were on the bullets. He's trying to divert the conversation by attacking Masters.

"And if that weren't enough Justin, we obtained your phone records, as well as Naomi's. She called you the night of her murder from her book club meeting."

Again, no response.

"Oh, another thing, we have you and your car arriving on the evening of the murder. We even have you leaving after she was shot."

"You're bluffing."

Again, Masters makes a mental note that King did not deny it.

"This is why we need to talk Justin. Let's clear this all up, and if you can do that, you will be free to go."

King is sitting on the floor in his condo contemplating his predicament, wondering how he is ever going to get out of this now. He feels like a trapped animal. He doesn't want to admit it to himself, but he knows the ruse is over.

"I'm not going to jail detective."

"Maybe not, at least not if we can talk and figure all this out. But if you won't talk with us, we have no choice but to take you to jail. We need you to explain this evidence and why you lied to us. It's time to come out now Justin. No one will hurt you."

"Can you promise me I won't go to jail?"

"You know I can't promise you that Justin. Unless of course, you can explain all this evidence pointing to your involvement."

"I'm not going to jail."

"So what are you going to do, sit in your condo for the rest of your life? Think about your kids Justin."

"You're going to have to come in and get me."

"Justin, we have an entire SWAT team out here. Don't be stupid. Stop this nonsense and come out. Detective Tippen and I will take you with us back to the station where we can talk. We need your version of what happened."

There is a long pause.

"Justin," continues Masters, "your friend Ryan is sitting in jail charged with First Degree Murder. He was drugged with Rohypnol on the night of Naomi's murder. Did you drug your friend and partner to frame him for murder? How is this fair to Ryan?"

King of course knows Masters is right. He starts to feel shame for what he has done to Cooper. His dissatisfaction with his own life led him to do things he never thought possible. King knows the truth may be the only thing to keep Cooper out of jail. Of course, the truth will put him in jail, and that is not an option for King.

"Detective," says King, "I need you to record what I'm going to tell you."

Masters had already set his phone on speaker so that the SWAT Commander could listen and Tippen has been recording the entire conversation.

"We are Justin, go ahead and say what you need to say."

King takes a deep breath, "Ryan had nothing to do with Naomi's murder. I planned it and shot Naomi with Ryan's gun to make it look like he shot her. I drugged Ryan with Rohypnol prior to Naomi coming home. Ryan never knew what happened. I was having an affair with Naomi, but Ryan didn't know it. The letter was a fake, written by me. After I shot Naomi, I wiped down the gun, then placed it in Ryan's hand. I take full responsibility."

"Why Justin?"

"I was drowning in debt and saw the only way out was to get full control of the business. I know that was selfish, but I was not thinking clearly. Please tell Naomi's family I am sorry."

"But why kill Naomi?"

"I had to. She was in line to inherit Ryan's half of the business and I needed full control. She wanted to marry me, and I wanted no part of that. After the divorce I went through, no way I was ever getting married again. With her death and Ryan taking the blame, I would be able to remove him as partner and have it all to myself. It sounds so stupid now. Tell Ryan I'm sorry as well, will you?" says Ryan as his voice gets softer.

"You can tell him yourself, Justin. It's time to come out now."

"I'll be coming out in a few minutes."

The SWAT Commander radios to his team to be ready, the suspect will be exiting soon. SWAT officers have surrounded the condo with snipers and an arrest team. Officers have .223 caliber rifles and twelve-gauge shotguns aimed at King's front door. They are ready to take him into custody. They are also ready to shoot if need be.

"Okay Justin, tell me when you are coming out and an officer will give you directions. Be sure to come out without any weapons and with your hands high in the air. We don't want anyone to get hurt."

"Okay," is all King says. He then disconnects his phone.

"He's offline," Masters shouts to the Commander. The Commander communicates this to his team.

SWAT officers now wait for King to exit, ready to give him commands for a safe conclusion.

King remains sitting on the floor of his condo and is now crying. He can't believe it has all come down to this. King uses his cell phone to call his mother who now lives in a retirement community in Scottsdale, Arizona. She is 76 years old.

"Hey mom, it's Justin."

"Oh hi Justin, so nice of you to call. Is something wrong?"

"No, why mom?"

"You usually don't call this late, but so glad to hear from you. How are you doing?"

"I'm doing well mom," says King as he tries to hold back his tears.

"And how are those grandkids of mine?"

"Oh, they're still growing. They're fine mom. I was just thinking of you and wanted to call to let you know how much I love you."

"That is so sweet of you. I love you too Justin. You sound sad, are you sure you are okay?"

"Yep, I feel better having called you to hear your voice. How is your arthritis?"

"I'm managing. The pain is not so bad right now. When are you bringing the kids down to see me?"

"Probably later this summer mom, but hey, I've got to go. Again, I love you, please remember that."

"Well thank you Justin, and remember that I love you too."

"Okay, goodbye mom."

"Goodbye Justin."

King puts down his phone and stands up. It's time to go outside and take his punishment. King moves the chair away from the front door and lets the door swing in, giving him a view outside. He sees bright spotlights pointed at the front of his condo, making it look like a bright sunny day. An officer on a megaphone starts giving King commands to come out with his hands in the air.

King reaches behind his back with his right hand and grabs the semi-auto handgun tucked into the back of his pants and pulls it out. It is now in his right hand hanging at his side. He hears more shouts to come out with his hands up. King takes one more deep breath, then bolts out the door, running straight toward the bright lights. As he gets a couple of steps outside, he quickly raises his right arm, points it at the lights, and starts to pull the trigger.

KABOOM! KABOOM! BAM! BAM! KABOOM!

Shots ring out across the complex shaking windows. King first gets hit in the right shoulder with a .223 rifle round, ripping flesh and bone from his body. He then simultaneously gets hit in the abdomen with a twelve-gauge shotgun blast and another .223 round into the left upper chest. Both shots are fatal as King crumples toward the ground. As he is falling, another shotgun blast hits him in the chin and neck, seriously disfiguring his lower jaw. King is only able to get off one round into the ground before being pelted with police fire. There is no need for medical help. King is clearly dead.

The Following Monday

Detectives Masters and Tippen are back in the office on Monday morning finishing up reports from last Friday's events when the Police Chief stops by to congratulate them on their investigation.

"You two did one hell of a job in getting to the bottom of this one," praised the Chief. "I don't believe I've ever heard of a case quite like it."

"No sir," says Tippen, "it had us stumped for a while. Had King not made a few mistakes, I think Mr. Cooper would have been convicted of killing his wife."

"It wasn't just his mistakes," replied the Chief, "it was also the tenacity and work you two put into this. I just wanted to personally congratulate you. Really great work."

"Well, thank you, sir," says Tippen.

"Yes, thank you, Chief," chimes in Masters.

Shortly after the Chief leaves, Tippen receives a call from DA Simmons.

"Just wanted to let you know we filed to dismiss all charges against Ryan Cooper this morning. He will be out of jail before noon today."

"Thank you for letting us know," replies Tippen.

Tippen turns to Masters, "Cooper is getting out this morning."

Masters sighs, "This was one hell of a case Jane, and I hope we never get another one like it."

Tippen laughs, "Me either Bill."

ABOUT THE AUTHOR

Mark Beckner is known in Colorado from his time with the Boulder Police Department from 1978 to 2014. He rose through the ranks to become Boulder's Police Chief in 1998 and remained in that position until his retirement in 2014. Chief Beckner took the reins of a department that was in turmoil and suffering from widespread criticism in the wake of the 1996 JonBenet Ramsey murder. Given the propensity of strange and unusual happenings in Boulder, the Department and Chief Beckner often found themselves in the news.

However, it wasn't until he took over command of the JonBenet Ramsey investigation in late 1997 that he became known across the country by those interested in the bizarre nature of JonBenet's death. While the case has never been solved, Chief Beckner was able to bring order to the investigation and played a role in getting the case to a grand jury. Most within the local media respected Chief Beckner for his honesty and straightforward approach.

Mark Beckner still lives in Colorado and is now using his law enforcement experience and writing skills to create dramatic, suspenseful, and realistic murder-mystery thrillers.